Grantley Berkeley

Anecdotes of the upper Ten Thousand - Their Legends and their Lives

Vol. II

Grantley Berkeley

Anecdotes of the upper Ten Thousand - Their Legends and their Lives
Vol. II

ISBN/EAN: 9783337150310

Printed in Europe, USA, Canada, Australia, Japan

Cover: Foto ©Andreas Hilbeck / pixelio.de

More available books at **www.hansebooks.com**

ANECDOTES

OF THE

UPPER TEN THOUSAND:

THEIR LEGENDS AND THEIR LIVES.

BY

THE HON. GRANTLEY F. BERKELEY,

AUTHOR OF "MY LIFE AND RECOLLECTIONS," ETC.

IN TWO VOLUMES.

VOL. II.

LONDON:

RICHARD BENTLEY,

Publisher in Ordinary to Her Majesty.

1867.

LONDON:
STRANGEWAYS AND WALDEN, PRINTERS,
28 Castle St. Leicester Sq.

CONTENTS.

CHAPTER I.

Part I.

CHAPTER II.

CHAPTER III.

Part I.

CONTENTS.

CHAPTER IV.

PAGE

Anecdotes of Netley—Lord King—Mr. Lomax—Mr. R. Berkeley of Spetchley—George Fitzgerald—The Duke de Grammont—Billy Duff—Augustus Berkeley and the Umbrella-Mender—Boxing, Swimming, and Muscular Accomplishments 59

CHAPTER V.

CHAPTER VI.

CHAPTER VII.

PART II.

CHAPTER VIII.

CHAPTER IX.

PART I.

CHAPTER X.

PART II.

CHAPTER XI.

PART III.

CHAPTER XII.

CHAPTER XIII.

Part II.

CHAPTER XIV.

Part IV.

CHAPTER XV.

CHAPTER XVI.

Part V.

Anecdotes

OF THE

UPPER TEN THOUSAND:

THEIR LEGENDS AND THEIR LIVES.

CHAPTER I.

DEAN SWIFT, BIDDY FLOYD, HER LOVER, AND THE JESTER.

Part I.

To me there is something peculiarly beautiful, rich, and sweet in the Vale of Gloucester and Berkeley, stretching along the banks of the Severn as it does; the river near Berkeley being an arm of the sea, and bringing up with it on the breast of its returning tide, from its foster-mother the mighty Ocean, the fresh aroma of the salt sea-weed.

That health-invigorating sigh, that essence from the boundless realms of air and water, storm-worn rock, and salt-impregnated sand, then comes over the primrose and cowslip banks and violet-perfumed dells, touched by the breath of kine; and all so sweetly mingled, mild and beautiful, that man may well for the moment pause in his worldly aspirations, were it but to turn to his God in thankfulness for mere existence. I know that I have done so, and hard as the lines are that have been driven o'er my brow, there are still left records in the heart that can bear the wear and tear of time, the throes of grim misfortune, and set at nought the efforts of mankind to mar their just perfections. But to scenes of other days.

It was the spring of the year 1708, at that sweet time when the weather is fine, and everything so charming and so ever new—so much resembling childhood's time of mortal life. The banks of the hedges throughout the Vale, from Aust to Ilimbridge, or, in a wider sense, from the vicinity of Bristol to Gloucester, were golden with the clustering primrose; and the face of nature beamed to the sun with hues as bright as those his beams sent down. Blackbird, thrush, and cushat, and all the lesser songsters of the woods and fields, poured forth their melody; and it was a glorious time in the olden merry month of May!

At the time of which I speak there was a small

but goodly house, in the hamlet or town of Berkeley, whose well-kept little garden ran from its front windows to the road; and the ground in the garden had been raised to enable its possessors to stand, and leaning their arms on the wall, thus to take a comfortable view of the passing events in the vicinity of their little world. On the afternoon to which I refer, Biddy Floyd, a very pretty girl, her bonnet flung carelessly on her head, and her rich auburn tresses doing as they liked, which, I suppose, must have been to fall luxuriously and lovingly down to kiss and sport with her cheeks, her neck, and shoulders, stood at the foot of that garden, and looked on the passers-by. While thus employed, her inferiors—old and young, male and female, as they wended on their way—each greeted her with a token of admiration and respect : and, in return, she had a smile, and such a sweet one! for everybody.

In short, as she was known to be in the habit, at certain times, of looking over that wall, the smartest young men in the vicinity used, somehow or other, always to pass about the right time; and some of them even dared to stop, and admiringly approaching the wall, surmounted as it was by her sweet face, to exchange compliments and remarks upon the weather (of course), and then pass on, more engrossed with that wall than ever.

Biddy in all her beauty, surrounded by the attributes of a lovely spring day, and as a youthful agriculturist, supposed to be the poet of the place, once said, "outshining the beams of the luminary that came to do her homage," was at the wonted time taking a view of passing humanity from her accustomed position in the garden, when a tall, dark man, came strolling by from the direction of the Castle; clerically dressed, certainly, as a Dean should be; but with so sly, and intelligent, and caustic a glance, that there could be no doubt but that things other than sacerdotal very frequently engaged his attention.

Biddy, smiling, kissed her hand to him; while he, with scarce a sign to his hat, came immediately beneath the wall and commenced talking.

"Oh, what a day, Miss Biddy! the young world is budding forth; and on my life, you really look as if all the bloom around us sought your full breast to give it sweetness for the longing air."

"Oh, don't, sir! Your Reverence is always so complimentary, that I feel before you as if I must ever blush. I hope your Reverence is well?"

"Pretty well, my darling: but not so well as I should be were I on the other side the wall. I can only see your face and arms. Humph! if those stones were mine, they should be otherwise employed than in concealing you: we can't afford, even in our eyes, to lose the lower part of anything half as bewitching as you are. How are all the lovers? And how is—is—ahem!—the lover loved of all?"

"Oh!" replied Biddy, "I don't know; lovers never come to any harm, or much good either; they're certain to take care of themselves, whatever they may do by their poor sweethearts. If I had all the lovers tied up in a sack, I'd put them into the sea!"

"No! Would you, Biddy?" replied the Dean. "And the best place for 'em, too! Well, you *do* look so lovely this morning, that the poetry of my soul's on fire; and I don't know but that instead of a sermon on sin, I shall devote myself to a love-ditty, a dissertation on devotion; and you shall be the theme of it."

"Oh, don't, sir! your Reverence is too bad!" exclaimed Biddy.

"Oh, don't!" was a favourite expression of hers.

"Well, my darling," resumed the Dean, "good day to you; don't join

> ' All the maids in Wanswell,
> And dance in an egg-shell,'

for I should be sorry to lose the prettiest bird in the Berkeley bowers!"

So saying, the Dean waved his hand and passed along the road, greeting others whom he met, and one farmer in particular.

"Well, Farmer King, it's a fine day."

"Hum," replied the double-cheesemaker. "Can't, zir, zaye so much anent thick, zir; the day's well enough, but we do want rain."

"Want rain!" muttered the Dean to himself as he strode on his way; "farmers are never satisfied, there is ever something wanted. Too much rain or too little, everything burnt up, or all too damp for making hay. The weather is never what it should be; but, somehow or other, God Almighty arranges that it all comes right in the end."

Then there met the Dean a tall, good-looking man, with whom he exchanged greeting; and after the youth had passed by, the Dean turned more than once to gaze after him, and with a sly look and shake of the head he said to himself— "There's no Nathan nor David in this case, but, Master George Malpus, 'Thou art the man!'"

George Malpus, after his greeting with Dean Swift, passed on. But before I proceed with this narrative, my readers — and certainly the readeresses — will perhaps like to know what manner of young man he was. But three-and-twenty summers had he seen, and he was a tall, graceful youth, of what would now be termed the middle-class, or, in the days of chivalry, an esquire, who had yet to win the spurs that should put him on an equality with knight and noble. Poor George Malpus! If aspirations, and a will to distinguish himself, could have gained him gentility, or, in other words, a lift into the castles and halls of " the Upper Ten Thousand," he would very soon have been there; but at the moment of which I am writing there was no open path to honours prone to his acceptance, for money was wanting to purchase him a commission; and then, as now, gold was the grist that made the mare to go: so, having no gold, George Malpus was at a dead-lock, or stand-still, and really had little else to do than to fish for eels and flounders and to fall in love. Now George had *fancied himself* in love from a very early age, had gone to sleep each night with the Christian name of his ideal love on his lips, and rose the next morning, having slept from ten on Monday night till eight on Tuesday morning, with the same syllables on his lips that had clung to them all night through many a happy dream, and gathered strength to keep there with the waking beam of day. Still, out of all the imaginary loves, there was no love like that which the presence of Biddy Floyd inspired. He had supposed himself stricken by other rural beauties, and had walked and talked with them throughout whole seasons of nutting in the woods and hedgerows, and many succeeding days of gathering cowslips in the quiet meadows; but now a power seemed to be seated in his soul, a name glued to his lips, and an image graven on his heart, that ejected every other earthly consideration from his hitherto wayward and very active mind. In short, my dear reader, he *was in love*—as I have been, and very likely as you have been, or may be so now; and in love so truly and so fervently, that he felt his very existence depended on the smiling approbation of Biddy Floyd.

George Malpus passed down the street, and, of course, stopped under the wall where grew the sweetest wall-flower in the world. Biddy saw him coming, and looked more dearly kind and brightly beautiful than ever, greeting him in all that unaffected yet telling way that is not to be artificially put on, or thoroughly learned in art among the brilliant fêtes of "the Upper Ten Thousand." As the crow and the hawk, the kite

and magpie, fly from the stricken deer when the
eagle descends to claim the quarry as his own,
so did several young men pass from under that
wall and away, who had been in conversation with
the local beauty.   They had tacit discernment
enough to know that George, as the Dean had
said, " was the man :" so they cleared the ground,
and left it free to his better pretensions ; and thus
the two lovers, *if* the affection *was* mutual, at
least for a space, could unburden their hearts
and say what they pleased.

Common-place greetings over — common-place
so long as a lingering footstep was near — George
exclaimed, " Well, my sweetest Biddy, when are we
to have our walk in the meadows? when do you go
to pay a passing visit to your relations at Thornbury? Remember, then we are to have a few
happy hours together."   A form of the most perfect loveliness and symmetry had been by nature
bestowed on Biddy; but now, as she leant this
way or that way on the wall, or picked a dragon
flower, or portion of moss, playfully to fling down
on the admiring George, each motion was fraught
with grace, and the lover felt that such homage
on his part amounted to idolatry — idolatry, but
with a real deity to accept the worship and make
the madness sane.

" Well," she replied, with coquettish play-fulness, " and suppose I don't go to Thornbury; what then? Suppose they won't let me go" (tossing her sweetly-rounded little head over the corner of her shoulder towards the house), " what then, O most doughty champion! will you do? Die, of course; or fling yourself from the rock at Sharpness Point.

" Oh, my sweetest love," replied George, " pray don't suppose anything of the kind. We are now for a few moments together—that is, we have free speech of each other: there are no real difficulties in the way; if the day is fine, *let it be to-morrow.* Tell me it shall be so, and at what hour. Believe me, *there is ever danger in delay:* let no golden opportunity be lost; never postpone anything till to-morrow which can be done to-day: tell me the time you will be at Thornbury, and the hour—the moment—you will be in the field at the back of Thornbury Castle, and leave the rest to me."

Biddy, still delaying and still coquetting, paused to devise a little more torture for her lover, when the side of the wall next to the churchyard from a little by-lane was scaled, and a curious-looking object, whom she well knew, cast himself on the greensward at her feet, making at the same time signs to her not to notice his presence. The abruptness of his appearance, however, had so startled her, that George Malpus had seen it from the street; and deeming it to be the advent of some of her family, none of whom favoured his views, he took the hint and immediately passed on, with nothing settled as regarded the meeting on the following day.

Then, and too late, the rustic beauty repented of the wanton delay in her reply to her lover, and turning round sharply, and with a flush on her beautiful cheek, she exclaimed to the strange and comical form that had fallen from the wall, rather than jumped from it,—"Oh, you fool! on what errand are you bent now?"

"Fool, quotha!" replied the half-idiot-looking thing to which she had addressed herself. "Which is the bigger fool, the lover outside the wall or the lover within it? Fool, sweet mistress! Well, I'd rather be the fool at the wedding than the wise man at the feast; I'd rather be with the bride than without her: it's always cold on t'other side the wall—now an't it, dear? So let me kiss your hand!"

"Indeed, Master Dicky Pierce, I shall do no such thing: so hence, with your foolery and nonsense! I know your folly gains you a license

you don't deserve, and makes you tolerated anywhere, but I am in no mood to be amused with
such vagaries: so up, tomfool, and away! I wish
to be alone."

These last words were uttered in a tone of
anger; for then, or at that moment, she felt the
force of George Malpus's remark, that " nothing
should be postponed which could be done to-day,"
and now she wished that she had, when the opportunity offered, settled the time and place for
a meeting on the morrow.

" Humph," said the jester; " yes, I see—
Wisdom is ever angry with Folly, if Folly gets the
start, and gains the wished-for place, which Wisdom
desired to be otherwise occupied. If George was
Dick, why George would be but as Dick is—
at your feet. If Dick was George he'd be upon
his guard, and, like old Dame Podger with her
single pippin from the dying tree, he would put
the forbidden fruit into a bag, lest the wasps and
hornets from the biggest hive of all should be
down on the treasure and clutch it clean away.
By-by, sweet one; remember your poor fool: but
whether that fool is George or Dick no matter
now, I go to attend my lord."

Thus saying, the jester swung himself lightly
over the wall, and, lighting on his motley-coloured

legs, ran away as fast as they could carry him to the Castle.

Biddy stood a little withdrawn from her place by the wall, and deeply mused over the sayings of the jester; for in all that that strange jumble of conceits did or said, amidst the fogs or mists of folly, there was ever a gleam of wisdom, or timely caution of some impending danger, in the matter of his discourse. Was she the apple on whom the hornets of the higher hive had a design? and what need was there of her being " put into a bag?" and who were the " wasps and hornets " to whom the jester had so pointedly alluded? Were they her friends at the Castle, those friends who had ever treated her with kindness and distinction, who had asked her to their halls, and allowed her to come and go at her own immediate pleasure? Impossible! they could have no design upon her: so, with a wave of her small and snowy hand, she dismissed Master Dicky Pierce and his vagaries from all further consideration, and with a spirit repentant at the delay she herself had made in the appointment with George for to-morrow, she set about devising some immediate communication with him, that all things might be arranged to their mutual satisfaction. And in this generous endeavour we must leave the rural beauty, and wish her every possible success.

The morning following the occurrences I have just related was a lovely one, and as the morn in its modest mists began, screening as these early veils had done the glowing beauties of the really naked sky—for there was not a cloud to stint the heaven of its pellucid blue—so the day broke forth, and seemed to pour down streams of fresh vitality into herb and flower. Bird, beast and insect, felt the seasonable joy; bud, bloom, and flower, the youngest primrose and the crimson-lipped daisy, opened their calixes to the lord of light, and in his beams became the full-grown beauty of the lawn and bank: all Nature teemed with love. But who are those that share the sweetened hour, seated by yon rippling little brook, beneath the oaks beside the tangled wood? They are the handsomest girl and youth from out the town of Berkeley, for Biddy Floyd had found some way of fixing this meeting with her lover, despite the warnings of the jester: and there they were, George and Biddy, seated side-by-side and hand-in-hand, and no living thing near them but the sweet-breathing kine.

" Well, Biddy, my darling Biddy!" exclaimed

George, tossing back the long and glossy deeply-shaded brown hair that had fallen over his forehead, and hidden his darkly-pencilled eyebrows, " is this not a happy hour? Here, my own, my sweetest love, I hear, I see nothing but you; and seem, indeed, to exist, now that I am near you, unwatched by jealous eyes, and heard alone by you or that little willow wren, who sits chiding us on yonder alder spray. Nay, love! darling love! I deserve a kiss for the pain you chose to give me yesterday." The kiss was given; and as he lay, bending over the lovely form now reclining on the grass, the bonnet cast away, and the rich luxuriant tresses of her hair mingling with the long grassy herbage that served her as a downy couch, —" Tell me," he cried, " tell me more of the jester, and what the fool said that has made you be so kind to me."

Biddy told him every word, when, as they thought of all the jester had uttered or hinted at, they both agreed that there was, or might be, more in it than appeared on the surface of his discourse; and despite themselves, and despite the happiness of *their* hour, each felt, impalpable at first, but eventually a shade of gloom sink upon their hearts, and though they knew not why, each on a sudden became similarly sad.

The hour *was* approaching when they *must* sever; they had met before; and then, previously to this meeting, they knew a time would come when, *for* the time, they must say " good-bye:" why, therefore, should greater gloom attach to this meeting than to others ? why were both their spirits so suddenly cast down ? why did each heart feel a latent dread of some impalpable danger? and why did they fear to tear themselves away? And yet it was so; and now a dusky, lurid gloom veiled the hitherto clear and gently encrimsoned horizon, for the sun had begun to descend behind the Welsh hills, and the Sugarloaf Mountain loomed deeper in the blue distance, over Severn.

" Biddy," exclaimed George, " promise me one thing—that whatever happens, or however or whenever we should be severed, as we may be for a time, you will never forget me, nor the sincere and overwhelming affection I feel for you. Say—promise me, my own love—and I will live on the remembrance of this hour, and love you more and more till we meet again !"

" Oh, George !" replied Biddy, " you know I love no one else. Who can I love but you ? Who is there in the hamlet, or in our rural circle, fitting to be loved but you ? You need not doubt me, George.   When there are none to win, you need not fear to lose ; so let not this needless gloom at parting dwell upon your mind. We have met and parted before, and but to meet again."

As she said this the mists in the West had deepened to the hue of thunder, and a long, low, muttering, suppressed rattle, caused by the electric fluid struggling to leap to life, reached their ears ; and Biddy sprang to her feet, in haste to reach the home of her friends in Thornbury ere the apprehended storm should burst. Soon they reached a stile near the wall of Thornbury Castle, and there, it being the spot on which they must part, each paused to bid a sad adieu. Biddy either really felt no fear as to their future happiness, or she put on a gaiety which did not at the moment belong to her, in an abortive attempt to reassure her still desponding lover.

" Adieu, then, George ; adieu till the day after to-morrow. To-morrow I must be at the Castle, for I have promised my lady there to spend the day : but after that, then seek me at the wall."

While she said this George held her hand.

" One word yet," he impassionately exclaimed. " Biddy, dear Biddy ! you have said that ' when there are none to win I need not fear to lose ;'

and in so saying you alluded to our immediate vicinity, the society around our homes. What if you should be taken to where there are those who might win; what, then, may I expect? Say, tell me, assure me of your unalterable love before we part?"

"George," replied the beauty, her lovely eyes and arch and arched eyebrows once more assuming an air or semblance of coquettishness,—"George," she said, "I make no promises : adieu, adieu." And in a moment she had turned a corner, and was screened from his ardent, loving, but still desponding gaze. "I make no promises!" They are but a few words, but a brief assertion; and yet no sentence on a doomed criminal ever fell from the lips of a legal judge with such cruel and harsh intensity, as those four words struck on the ear of George Malpus,—"I make no promises!"

George was young in the world's ways, and unhackneyed in the paths of love. His ardent soul was susceptible of deep impression, for as yet he knew not that one deeply engraven image could be effaced by another; and love was life, and life was love to him. "I make no promises!"

There were a million winters in those last words, that now seemed to hang over the summer of his life, and to freeze every hope left to him in the icy chains of winter. What, too, did the crafty idiot, the jester, mean, by what he had said to Biddy, " that she had better be put in a bag to prevent the larger wasps and hornets from possessing themselves of the treasured fruit ?" Did that mean the higher class of society, Biddy's patrons and friends at the Castle ? or was there nothing really in it ? Was it the saying of a gibing fool, and were Biddy's last words the mere offspring of a coquettish wish to teaze her adoring lover ? To this last idea poor George Malpus clung, as a drowning man to a straw ; but whether he was a drowning man, Biddy a beautiful coquette, and the " fool" an ass, or a wise man, must remain for the pages of another chapter.

CHAPTER II.

To the north of the village of Glammis, in bonny Scotland, and in its own majestic forest of mighty trees, stands Glammis Castle, the ancient site of the anecdote I am about to relate. It is, perhaps, one of the finest specimens of Scotch castellated architecture that remain to the present day; and it would be unaccountable indeed if, with the superstitions still entertained in the North, and throughout the Highlands particularly, some such strange stories as the one under narration did not still " come to the fore." Earl Patie (*Scoticè* for Patrick), Earl of Strathmore, whose portrait still decks the great hall of the Castle, in the dress of a belted Knight, was—so the legend runs—so addicted to gambling, that he could not refrain from cards—

rightly named, perhaps, by the Forfarshire people, as the " deevil's bricks"—even on Sunday. With sorrow be it said, a similar passion exists, and has existed in my day, among sundry lords, baronets, and esquires, all friends of mine, and honourable men ; therefore the noble descendants of Earl Patie need take no offence at this portion of my chronicle.

There are all sorts of bloody deeds said to have been done within these walls, and so there have been attributed to many another ancient castle, both in England, Ireland, and Scotland. The owners of old edifices, therefore, need not feel hurt that their possessions have followed suit, and come within the category of deeds of death to be dwelt upon in modern days.

At Glammis Castle Malcolm II. is said to have been murdered ; and tradition still assumes to point out a passage in the Castle where that horrid deed of the year 1030 was perpetrated.

There are many other rumours afloat, but for the present I must content myself with that which has to do with the sin of cards when in " untenty" hands.

The bell, if there was one, in this the finest specimen of Scotch castellated architecture, could outsing the one in the song I have so often heard the brilliant voice of the present Lady Hopetoun give, when in her teens; for, instead of chiming,—

> "For full five hundred years I've swung
>   In my breezy turret high,
> And many a different tale I've sung
>   As the time went stealing by,"

the clock at Glammis Castle could say, "For full nine hundred years I've swung;" for the edifice claims a frowning castellated front erected before the year 1030; and it, the village and the property, give the name as the title of the eldest son.

It was, then, on a dark and stormy night in the end of the dreary month of November, when the same harsh, frosty hurricane that had roared all day, was still tearing at the coping-stones of the battlements and shaking every casement in the building, that the Earl found himself bored with his forced inactivity from horse, hawk, and hound all day, and consequent inability to drink himself to sleep by his huge fire in the early night: so, having footballed his page and cursed his esquires, he called for a pack of cards.

Now if any of my readers will pay a visit to

this fine old place, they will see in one of the great halls of Glammis, and dressed as a belted knight, the alleged portrait of Patrick, Earl of Strathmore, and that the noble Lord is therein depicted with a rather rubicund nose and a dissipated appearance. Far be it from me to say that such were his features or the condition of his figure, for it must not be forgotten that artists, as well as the unprofessional nobility, at times disguise their pencils as well as their better perfections in liquor; when a man in the last stage of upright intoxication will stare in the face of some perfectly sober friend, who wishes to prevent his making a further fool of himself, and assure him that he (his friend) is " very drunk indeed:" So an inebriated painter may transfer to the canvas under his hand, and to the attempted likeness of the sitter, the besetting sin under which he himself is at the moment labouring. In this instance, however, Lord Patrick decidedly is made to look as if he loved wine, whisky, and late hours, better than water and an early bed.

Perhaps it will be no offence to the descendants of this noble lord to admit, at least, that he was like a good many more of his countrymen whom I have known in my time—Maxwell among others, who used in my younger days to visit the Lord

Stair at. Stranraer, and cause the Lowland Lord after dinner to be carried senseless to his bedroom, while the guest was lifted speechless into his carriage, the two having lost their wits in passing what they termed " a comfortable evening." There was one thing, however, which the Lord of Glammis loved above all. others, and that was a game at cards: no matter whether it was the Lord's day or a week day, the " deevil's bricks,"· as the Forfarshire people call the cards, were in his hands; a game he must have ; and if no partner were to be obtained he would sit, drink, and play dummy, till the little hours of the morn.

Now we all know that the term " gude man " is very frequently applied to Scotchmen, and that they have a horror of transgression or desecration on the Lord's day; so the failing of their master being known, as sure as the Sabbath came so sure was every soul in the Castle prone to seek excuses to escape the card-table and to save their consciences. Some lied, some pretended to be ill, and all, on the Lord's day to which I now more immediately allude, were not forthcoming; so Lord Patie, in a furious rage, found that his entire castle could not give him a partner for a game at cards. Even the chaplain, fenced in the armour of holy words

and reeking from the confines of the pulpit, refused to play, on the score of wickedness ; and
there was, owing probably to the secret exhortations of the holy man, a general strike in the
Castle, from the factor to the foot-boy and scullion,
and a resolution to die rather than fly in the face
of Heaven.

Those who are moderately acquainted with the
way in which the thwarted will of a feudal lord
vents itself in execrations, and the length of the
distance he is apt to send every offending soul
around him, may have a faint idea of what fell
from the lips of the owner of Glammis Castle on
this memorable occasion. It would be wrong in me
to attempt to hand down his pithy expressions, as
well as vain to try to link them together in the
curious way in which he did when assigning to the
living offenders strangely unhappy localities in
after life: suffice it to say, that closing his terrible
tirade with the assertion that, " 'fore God he was
ready to play with the de'il himsel' rather than be
done out of his favourite game by having no
partner;" he took up a couple of packs of cards,
and, swearing all the way he went up the old
oak stairs, he sought his chamber, forced into a
solitary game of dummy.

Now history has not told me what the domestic

state of our Scottish lord's affections were. Whether the so-called partner of his bosom was dead, or whether she was nearly as good as dead by satisfactory severance, or whether he had kept himself assuredly master of his castle by continuing single or unattached to any "incumbrance," as the domestics of the present day call a wife and family: so on this point I know not what to say; all I am assured of is, that on the November night I treat of, and in what is still called "the walled chamber," in a very gruff and peevish mood Lord Strathmore sat with two packs of cards before him, the sole occupant of a table end, listening to the roaring of the old majestic forest trees that surrounded his castle.

"Wae's me!" sighed his lordship to himself; "it's d——d hard out of all my halls have nursed, that I can't get a friend, nor a dependant, nor a priest, though they'll do a'maist anything on the Lord's day, to tak' a hand at cards with me!—' the de'il's bricks,' as the untenty loons of Forfarshire call 'em; as if Old Gooseberry would ever try to raise a foundation for anything out o' such puir, innocent, flimsy material! Nae, nae! he would rather clutch on something more substantial. However, be that as it may, the de'il himsel' would be acceptable just noo, if he'd cool his claws and tak' a friendly game at cards . . . . There's a knock at the door! If it's one of my people, priest or layman, I'll nail him to a hand . . . . Come in! Eh, Gude guide us! it's nane o' my folks, but just Old Boreas: he knocks at everything."

"He does *not!*" said a deep voice in the corridor. "*I* knocked, and should have entered on your invitation, if you hadn't asked for other guidance. If you need a partner for a game of cards say so, without ornament of any kind."

"Then, in the foul fiend's name," replied Lord Patie, "enter, whoever you are! Here are cards, whisky, and a seat," was the instantaneous reply. The door then opened, and a total stranger appeared, wrapped up in a cloak; who, advancing into the room, took a chair opposite the noble lord, without removing bonnet or cloak, and sat him down in the place of dummy.

The Earl stared at the strange guest, and had some misgivings as to who and what he was; he remembered who it was he said he would play with in default of any other, and for a moment felt a kind of repentance for his rashness. However, Patie was not the man to flinch from his word, nor to be scared from any resolution he had once taken, however bad appearances might be:

so, staring at his guest fixedly but without fear, he bade him welcome to Glammis Castle.

"Thanks, my lord," replied the strange guest; "you're muckle kind. It's not the first time I have had a welcome here! nor the last, I hope; for it's a comfortable and a roomy place in which to transact business. You'll excuse my bonnet and cloak, but I am deformed, and it might shock a decent body to see my ailments."

"Not a bit of it, friend," replied the Earl; "make yourself at home, and do just as you like—it's Liberty Hall, and a cosey game of cards."

"Aweel, then, I'm a little chilly—perhaps unusually so. I'll even keep on my bonnet and cloak till the game's made!"

"Agreed, my hearty!" said the Earl; "here goes—*the deal's mine!*"

"Humph!" retorted his guest with a leer; "if so, exchange is no robbery. *I'll have you!*"

"Done!" said his lordship.

"Stay yet a moment," replied the guest; "let's name the stakes we play for?"

"Anything you like," was the rejoinder, "from baubees to bright gold pieces: so name the wager and let's at once begin."

"So be it, then! I hate your paltry stakes.

We'll play high; and as I know that with you Scottish lords 'short's' the word sometimes," replied the stranger, "if you have not the ready rhino, I'll take your bond for anything that is due to me."

"Due to you!" rejoined the dauntless lord. "You make pretty sure of winning; but I'd rather play here till the day of judgment, if you'll stick to 'the bricks,' than strike my colours."

"Bravo, my lord! it's just what I should like: so now mind your aces."

Fast and furious then became the game; and, according to legendary intelligence, it seemed as if the stout Earl had strong suspicions that the stranger, like some mortals, had not long thumb-nails for nothing, for there were exclamations of unfair play, marked cards, and, on the part of the stout Earl, calls for a fresh pack. The night wore late, and the wild and violent altercations were heard by the retainers in the Castle to continue, so much so that the curiosity of the old butler was aroused, and he crept to what has since been called the "walled chamber" door, out of timid curiosity to learn which of the household it was that his lord had got for a partner, thus profaning the Lord's day, for it was not a week day, and who of them it was who dared to bandy words, oaths, and curses, with a master who would never submit to contradiction.

The old white-haired man, who in his time had been the death of untold oceans of wine and whisky, could make nothing of what reached his ear, save as to his master's and a strange voice in loud, profane, and perpetual altercation; but when he heard his master call for fresh cards—perplexed, in great timidity, but still with accustomed obedi-, ence, his trembling hand essayed the door in vain, for it was fastened on the inner side.

Well did that old man know that his lord never locked a door: so, astonished at this unusual occurrence, he put his eye to the keyhole, when, at the same instant, the table within the room received an emphatic thump from a heavy and angry hand, and the strange voice simultaneously and bitterly exclaimed, " Smite that eye!"

From his cards the Earl, in astonishment at those loud and apparently unmeaning words, looked up full into the face of his gambling antagonist; and, to the day of his death, he affirmed that he saw a sharp, vivid, bluish flame, like forked lightning in miniature, dart from the lighted lamp by which they were playing, direct to the keyhole of the door; when, from the other side the door, a frantic yell of agony rang through the vaulted hall and chambers of the Castle, followed by a heavy fall; and at one and the same moment the Earl from within, and the retainers *en masse* from without, rushed to the spot, and found the poor old faithful butler insensible on the oaken floor, with a blue, not a black, halo round his eye—a mark, it was subsequently affirmed, of the devil's vengeance for attempting an intrusion on the impious game at cards, and which altered the visage of the faithful servant to the day of his death.

Lord Strathmore stood over the body of his old servant for a length of time, and the old man regained not his senses till the Chaplain of the Castle came, and then only did he slowly recover.

"I'll see to this!" cried the Earl; "this is some devilish cantrip or other. Has any one left the chamber save myself?"

"No, my lord!" exclaimed a dozen voices at the same time; "we'll swear that no one passed this way."

"Then tarry all of you here; seize, strike, slay, any soul who attempts to force an exit, while I go into the chamber to reckon up with my guest, who, at least, shall be safe in regard to violent molestation while under my sacred roof: he owes me money, since I gave and signed the bond for what I had previously lost, though I *know not exactly how much that was.*"

Thus saying, and, curiously enough, drawing his claymore after what he had said as to his guest's personal safety while under the protection of his roof, the Earl retired into the chamber amidst the wondering, listening silence of his people, who no doubt expected to hear some resumption of the high words and altercation. But no: they heard the Earl's footsteps alone, all over the chamber, as if he was looking beneath every bench and chair for some object; when, at last, the well-known step approached the door again, and as it approached they heard the equally well-known voice mutter, "It is not here! then *the de'il has got the bond for all I lost, and taken it with him!*"

Well, even this lesson, though for a short time it had its effect, did not lessen Lord Patie's love of cards. True, for a time he did not by gambling desecrate the Lord's day; but before the year was out he was heard testily to exclaim, "That as it must be more wicked and unseemly to hunt and hawk on a Sunday in public, than to play at cards in his private chamber, he would be d——d if he did not so amuse himself, whether the foul fiend played with him or not."

The fiend *never came again:* it was likely, so the elders in the village said, that he had got all he wanted; and in due time Patrick, Earl of Strathmore, died, and was in all pomp and funereal devices buried with his fathers.

" Aweel, sir," said a newly-established retainer to the seneschal of the household in Glammis Castle, under the successor to Lord Patie, " I canna remain in his lairdship's service; it 's just nae that cannie what I hear gaeing on o' nichts o' the Lord's day. There's a muckle din atween they twa up in the old chamber, as the eve comes round, still at their games of cards—still at the deevil's bricks; and it is more than ony decent folks should do to bide within earshot of it. May the de'il weasand me—and that 's braid Scotch — if he and the old Earl an't at their cantrips all night long of the Lord's day, till the church clock strikes twal!"

It is impossible for me, as a true historian, to vouch for the fact of the continuance of these unearthly noises; but it is certain that the stoutest retainers of Glammis Castle would rather have died than set their eyes to, or attempt " to skeek " through, the keyhole of this haunted chamber. Perhaps it would be as well if more modern domestics had the same prudent sensibility. So established was the belief in the impossibility to crush the vulgar terror, arising from the credence in the noises or gambling altercations with the devil, that the apartment was, *and is, walled up* with a double partition, in order that silence at least may be maintained, and whatever may pass in that deserted chamber be confined to those who have—if they have one—a mission to frequent it.

CHAPTER III.

THE LEGEND OF WEST WYCOMBE PARK, BUCKS.

PART I.

IT is very curious to recall to mind the many local tales we hear in our visits and wanderings over the fair face of what still must be merry England, if we contrast it with the grief which has fallen upon other lands, and especially upon the once boasted democratic paradise of America, and how much there is of the romantic and marvellous yet untold that would interest and delight the general reader. Surely if a theme of this sort were opened up in an established journal, and were well supported, it could not but prove a source of agreeable and amusing entertainment. While husbands and brothers were reading, for useful information, sporting intelligence, and matters of general interest in country-life, the ladies might glean a wide field of amusement from the perusal of tales once current in our ancient castles, baronial halls, and mansions. In my sporting wanderings I have never missed the trail of a legend, or even a stone, whose time-indented surface seemed to invite attention. In the wood, in healthful breezy Buckinghamshire, to the right of Dashwood Hill as you go towards Oxford, I have paused in the pursuit of game to sit down on the beech-grown bank of the old and now disused London and Oxford road, and muse over some of the occurrences which probably had happened in that lonely place, when the oldest stage-coaches pottered on their way, when the faster ones were once thought to fly, and where farmers bore their better halves to and from the market, or to Stoken Church, on pillions behind the saddle. Who knows, I said to myself, how many foot-pads and highwaymen have bid passing travellers on this very spot—" Feather-bed-lane," as it was once inaptly called — to stand and deliver; and what tales of love or signs of grief the battered stone now at my foot — brought here, perhaps, to be broken, or hurled at some-body's head — but still by time untouched, a tongue-tied evidence of the olden time, may not have heard and seen? How often have I longed to find a tongue in stones and trees, to tell me things forgotten, or hitherto unknown; and even for the appearance of a peaceful if terrific ghost, to sigh or murmur to a mortal of the past and future, that the mortal might have a *locus standi*, or immutable witness of the opportunities gone, or chances yet to come. In the woods of Wycombe, to which site I am about to confine my present narrative, there abound tales of shrieking ghosts, of women in white, and of those lights that have so lately filled the exclusive columns of *The Times* newspaper with discussions as wandering as the *ignis fatuus* with which those discussions sought to deal. Ghastly flickerings still haunt the swamp in Whittenden Park, and delight to flaunt their bluish vapour as the wisp demon seems to pause over the mysterious mouth of the cavern, said by the oldest inhabitant to hold its subterranean way to the river Thames, and which, for the purpose of the tale to come, I must at once introduce to the reader as the " Swilley Hole."

In wandering over the beautiful beech-woods attached to West Wycombe Park, which really amount to an extensive forest, I have come on spots so inordinately wild, that my mind misgave me as to their real distance from town, or whether or not civilisation and agriculture, in their rapid march, had not leaped, in a frantic jump, over certain isolated spots, resolved for once to leave Nature there alone, and again beyond to assume their sway. Who, in the midst of corn-fields, chalk, flints, and hollow beech-woods, would expect to come on so lovely and wild a spot, on one side of the estate, as Naphill Common? Heather, juniper-bushes, and fine oak-trees thickly interspersed, and the short, sweet greensward, give the common all the appearance of an ancient chase; and at every turn the wanderer almost expects to see the antlers of a deer, or, if in summer, the graceful doe and fawn grazing in the dewy glades. On the other hand, and to the southern side, what can be more unexpected or wildly beautiful than the almost forest, called Whittenden Park? or, at a little distance from it, the large beech-wood adjoining the lovely and shaded green, called Booker Common, all within the domain, and then subject to its manorial rights? Of all the lovely spots, deep-shaded, damp, and dismal perhaps to others—but not so to me—I never saw such a wood as that of Whittenden Park, haunted (as it happily is said to be) by a perceptible ghost, as well as by unearthly wails, when midnight gives mystery to sound, and timid pathfinders or dreaming ears start at the hoot or shriek of owls, the long yell of the vixen fox, or at they know not what. The fir-tree of all ages and of all kinds, the oak, the blackthorn, the bramble, and the holly, blend in one mysterious shade; and over little springs that spontaneously arise even in this, one of the highest portions of the county, gliding down almost inperceptibly and noiselessly through the ferns, the tell-tale mosses, and withered leaves, into dells where, of course, arise the alder and the willow to invite the haunting woodcock. In one part of this splendid cover there is a very considerable swamp, to which I must more particularly invite the attention of the reader, inasmuch as it will have to be referred to again and again. The swamp, in the midst of its reeds and rushes, mosses, ferns, and rank wild weed, locally known as the "cats-tail," and which in the lake at West Wycombe Park grows, as it struggles to the surface, to the length of from ten to twelve feet or more, extends a long distance from the higher to the lower level, and on one side terminates, and is confined by a chalk rock, at the foot of which there is a hole called the Swilley Hole, leading no one would have ever guessed where, but for the legend I am about to recount.

Into this mysterious cavern, small though the

orifice now is, that has been worn in ages past deep into the rock of chalk, any amount of water may suddenly rush from rain or thunder-storms, or swiftly-melting snows, when, with a few wild murmurs and gurgling groans, the very confined aperture at the bottom of the chalky cup ingulfs the temporary whirlpool, and carries it off to the depths below. From the situation of the wood, its many hollows, and at times overflowing rills, coupled with the last stormy feature alluded to, ·· no wonder that unearthly sounds, tender laments, and wild deep utterances, and even shrieks, arising, perhaps, from the sympathies of Nature with her children, whether vegetative, tree, or bird, vexed by unruly storms, should frighten the belated rustic, and scare even the marauding ruffian from his thievish pursuit of game. For myself I love the wood—its loneliness, and the loneliness of woods have been a part of my life; and though the woods of the Far West, those of the Alleghany Mountains, and thence to the extreme of the " backwoods" of North America, are still enough, I never met stillness more powerful than in the shades of Whittenden Park. I have stood beneath its firs as winter's night approached, my ear catching no sound but the whistling wing of the wood-pigeon coming to roost, and to within range,

perhaps, of my expectant gun, or my eye de-
tecting no other motion in the air than the noiseless glide of the sparrow-hawk as she sought the
warmth of the thicker fir, or the fall of a withered
leaf. If a contemplative mind needed a place for
reflection, let the man who owns it lean in winter
against its thickest trees, or lie down in summer
in the shady copse-wood of Whittenden Park, and
no earthly sound will reach him to disturb, save
those that I ever love—the sympathies and emotions, the sighs, the perfumes, and the wild min-
strelsy of Nature. Whittenden Park, its shades,
its silence, its deepened tints as night comes on,
affected my faithful dog " Brutus," since dead, as
they affected me, and as they used to affect both of
us when relying for sport and protection on each
other in the Western prairies. I looked at his intensely vigilant face as it ceased to be rid of the
lighter influence of game, and watched to guard
against some wilder intrusion; coming and sitting
up closer to my heel, he told me, as he did in
the Far West, that, with him, I could not be surprised. If I spoke softly to him and touched his
head, not an ear relaxed, nor did his roving eye
turn on me in thanks, or to be still. He would not
be interrupted in his careful guard; and, though
dreaming not of danger, I still felt thankful for his

presence. So strangely complicated and wild are the public paths that lead through this haunted wood, and so deep the self-arising mists and darkness that occasionally surround it, that the ancient possessors of the manor of West Wycombe used to erect over a conspicuous part of the locality an immense lantern, capable of burning for a given time, and set up and illumined at the expense of the lord of the manor, to guide the benighted tenants and peasantry to their houses. In height, the lantern, the roof of which is elaborately gilt, stands four feet five inches, its circumference nine feet three inches. But for such a beacon as this, a man indigenous to the soil, once in the wood and bewildered with intricate, and at night impossible-to-be-observed paths, and terror-stricken, perhaps, at the sounds and lights, deceptions or glares, above and around the great swamp and aqueous cavern, might wander in it all night, and, at the end of his perambulations, find himself as far from his home as ever. This lantern is in the mansion of West Wycombe Park at the present time: I have seen it, and, therefore, can vouch for the truth of this part of the legend; and there and thus it is a treasured proof, that if the old forest laws were stricter in regard to beasts of the chase than they are now, at all events the lord of the manor held himself responsible in a greater degree for the welfare and safety of his tenants and his men than he does now. There stands Whittenden Park Wood, a proud and sullen remnant of the ancient chase, defying aggression, and impervious at night, wild and dreaded in its deepened mysteries, and rejoicing in the phantom wisps that arise in blue effulgence from its very bosom — to quote from Burns, " a moment bright, then lost for ever."

Having thus introduced the scene of it to my readers, I proceed to tell a tale, not as it was told to me by any one person, but as I have gathered it from many an old rustic; aided in it, as I have been, by a young lady, to whose kind attention, gentleness, and good sense, I am ever indebted.

The Legend.

On or about the middle of the 17th century there resided in the county of Buckingham a family of the name of Barnwell, in the then little village of West Wycombe, where there rises from the foot — or even beyond it — of the hill called Churchdown, a beautiful spring, whence flows the stream called the " Wy," from which stream the village takes its name. It is this pellucid flow of pure water that feeds the lake and ornamental river in the park, sustaining the most splendid trout, and then, after being joined at High Wycombe by the stream from Hughenden Manor (Mr. Disraeli's), continues through the domain, giving employment to many mills, and watering the little valley of the Wy, by Wyburn, or Woburn, and on to the river Thames. The family of the Barnwells, thus about to be alluded to, consisted of a father and an only son, called Willie, who, like many an only, as well as an elder, son, was the idol of his house, and had been by his parents deemed a match for the highest in the land. Indeed he was of gentle blood, though not higher in rank than what sometimes is termed a " little gentleman"—or man rich enough to live without a trade; and thus, all things considered and looked at as I have accustomed myself to look at them, gentility once confessed, and *deserved*, a young man bearing that appellation in natural, not artificial rank, was and is eligible to marry the daughter of a peer. This view of the subject, however, was not then taken by some neighbours who lived in the vicinity of what is now called Booker Common, or rather nearer to Whittenden Park. Those neighbours consisted of a father (a widower) and an only daughter, who was to him the apple of his eye. Her father, known by the name of

Justice Wellrode, was, as may be supposed, a magistrate, and though a Jesuit, a sort of Justice Greedy, when, feasting at my lord's table, he could be jolly enough, as well as a thorough ally on all local matters; but he was apt to think that gentility in a sliding scale slipped from the shoulders of the duke to the marquis, earl, baron, baronet, and knight, and fell and rested, without descending an inch further, on his own. Stopping there, everything below his own state and station was deemed to be beneath any further notice, and not ascending to any rank at all. In addition to this he was an utter slave to the Jesuit priests, and squandered all he had upon them. Of course, as an only daughter always is, Marguerite was left a good deal to her own company—that is, she walked and rode alone, she was mistress of her father's house, of his farm, of his poultry, of his men and maids. She did much as she pleased, and she was thoroughly beloved by all; her duty, one for ever religiously kept, being to obey her father, to sing or play him to sleep at night, and with her own fair hands to put the sugar into his " nightcap," which was a simmering stoup of nut-meg, egg, and ale. In the day he shot or hunted, or delivered justice to delinquents brought before him; and in that lengthened space, when the soft summer glades of the woods, or the velvet turf of what is now Booker Common, invited Marguerite from beneath the beech-trees to inhale the breath of the wild violet and primrose, or the perfume of the wild cherry, then and in her own romantic thoughts she was left to enjoy herself or listen in Whittenden Wood—as I have said before—to the low sweet notes of the nightingale. The house of Justice Wellrode was situated not far from Booker Common, and about the spot where Grove Farm stands now. Not a stone of the old edifice, however, remains, nor a mark to indicate its site. It was very near the high road, and perhaps on the spot where the present comfortable farmhouse called "The Grove" was erected, every vestige of the old building might have been used up. As was often the case in those times, there was a Jesuit priest, commonly known as Father Crawl, in the neighbourhood; or, indeed, it might be said that he lived a great deal in the house of his patron the Justice, and certainly preyed on his finances as much as he prayed for his soul, and perhaps with greater effect: but as it will be our office in the course of this narrative to allude to him more particularly, for the present we content ourselves with but a passing notice.

The period of the tale was a stormy one. At one time the Roundheads had it all their own way, at another the Cavaliers, while at the same time the Jesuits and the Roman Catholics were often detested by both parties, and never thoroughly trusted by any, except for deeds of craft and hypocrisy. Indeed, the character as portrayed by Walter Scott in " Master Ganlesse," in his brilliant novel of *Peveril of the Peak*, was not only at the time a correct portrait of the Jesuit, but up to the present day those who have had any dealings with the priesthood of that guileful persuasion cannot fail to have conceived, that if the likeness of a serpent tempted Eve, the tamer and teacher of the serpent must have been a Jesuit priest.

As to any description of the heroine of this tale, so many heroines have been so well described that it would be vain to attempt a new one. I will, therefore, simply say, that her eyes were so beautifully soft, and yet so touched by sensibility and self-possession, that they seemed placed in her fair brow to watch over the graces of her gently-moulded form; an arm, an ankle, that would match the Venus, and a bosom tinted by the touch of driven snow. It was, then, in the bright balmy day of an old-fashioned May, late in that month, when genial spring really heralded the approach of hotter weather, that Marguerite was walking in the primrosed paths of Whittenden Park Wood, accompanied by a favourite little spaniel, "Jip." The birds were singing as they do sing in that most lovely and retired spot, and the nightingale was pouring forth its liquid lay in unison with thrush and blackbird. Aloft in the old fir-trees the cushat cooed; and in the willows and alders of the swamp beneath, innumerable warblers, willow-wrens, and white-throats, as well as the mellow blackbirds, were murmuring *sotto voce* their sweet melody, joined by the thrush, chaffinch, wren, and titmouse. Oh, it was beautiful on such a day to live! mere existence was a pleasure; the earth and woods around, in flower or in song, in one sweet sigh seemed murmuring of love; not sordid, selfish love—but in the unique sweetness of that mysterious passion appointed by nature, and hallowed by Creative will.

In a dreaming sense of security and solitary musing, Marguerite passed on, beneath the wood, and by the edge of the willow-bearing swamp, her little dog gamboling before her, when suddenly her companion, perhaps decoyed by the chase of a rabbit, vanished from her sight, and soon after she became alarmed by its plaintive whines for assistance.

On hearing solicitations for help from her little dog, Marguerite hastened to the spot, and ascertained that "Jip" had fallen down a deep chalk-hole, situated on the edge of the swamp; the steepest side of which adjoined the high ground beneath the beech-wood where she stood; the side of the chalk rock, or Swilley Hole, running sheer up from the small aperture below. To go round on the other side of this Swilley Hole, in the then wet state of the bog, was impossible; and Marguerite feared for the life of her little favourite, in danger as it was of falling into the hole, which at this time went beneath the earth no one knew whither; and had she got into it, it would have hurried her to certain destruction. To cry for assistance in so lonely a spot was vain, and in tears for the fate of her little favourite the sweet girl paused; a second Niobe, dissolved in tears. A slight rustle in the bushes, however, at this moment drew her attention, and she became aware of the presence of a black Newfoundland dog, who, seeming to comprehend her loss, peered down into the gulf at her foot, and then looked back into the thick wood, as if expecting some other assistance. The large dog seemed soon to grow impatient, and tossing his sagacious head back two or three times into the air, by way of preliminary, he gave a low and very peculiarly suppressed bark. The bark was at once answered by an approaching crash through the cover, as of an active and a hurried step, hastening to the summons given by the dog; and a tall, handsome young man, stood before Marguerite in the shape of Willie Barnwell.

At a glance a thousand things were then and there accomplished, which there is no need to tell. Eyes—though a beautiful pair of those eyes were still glittering in tears—as violets after a vernal shower, met with eyes as full of intelligence and quick sensibility as they were; and there are some that will understand me when I say, that in that one momentary glance were given and exchanged the seeds of a future destiny. Gracefully to doff his hat, and to step to the side of Marguerite, was the instant act of the young man, with the question of " What had happened?" The reply was a simple gesture towards the whining little favourite below; and the response to that gesture was an athletic swing by the arm from limb to root of the overhanging beech-tree: the young man leaped thence to the bottom of the chalk-pit, accompanied by his large black dog, who seemed to be as much interested in the matter as any one. How odd it is, that such little things so often lead, like stepping-stones, to great ones! Marguerite stood on the brink of the chalk-pit in anxious desire to receive her pet from the arm that held it somewhat closer than necessary to the bearer's bosom; and, in doing so, for a moment riveted the ascendant's gaze to insteps modelled in nature's truest mould; and faithful historian as I am, that ascending glance left the gazer in love with her from head to heel, and put him at once on a far different theme for thought than those in which he had left the old house at West Wycombe.

Landed once more in safety, "Jip's" gambols on her rescue upon reaching her mistress were soon excessive, and to such an extent did they affect the large black dog that he set off in playful gyrations round them, his master standing transfixed with admiration at the manner and method of Marguerite's caresses to "Jip," whenever she could catch her, and no doubt for once in his life wishing that he had been that dog. The excitement of the moment apparently ended with the safety of "Jip." Marguerite found time in words to thank Willie for his opportune assistance, and then it was that she first observed that she talked to one whose face and figure had for some time induced the girls of "Merrie Wycombe" to turn and look back at him as they passed him in their walks. Of course, next to thanking him for the act of saving her dog from its perilous position, came the desire to know who he was, when he replied that a house in West Wycombe was his home; his name William, or Willie Barnwell, as he was familiarly called. He cannot be a very shrewd observer who lightly treats even the glance of a woman's changeful eye; but when love, yes, the truest love of all, love at first sight, love that springs from the heart without bidding, that flashes forth in the unsullied purity of real and spontaneous emotion, that affects nothing, disguises nothing, that has no sordid nor selfish thoughts, but burns from a flame innate and at once kindled by what has suddenly assailed it — love such as that *has eyes* so quickly sensitive that they at once see, or think they see, even the very shadow of a cloud. What, then, was it, that cast a shade over Willie's admiring face? what for an instant shaded his brow, and made the eyes of the worshipper look down? Was it this,—Did he think that he saw what she at once felt, that she had made the acquaintance of one slightly below her own sphere of rank, or, as we should say in the present day, one who did not move in the best society, though still, for all that, a gallant gentleman? However, whatever it was

that thus affected them both, she thanked, and he
received her thanks so thankfully, courteously,
and well, that, alas, poor things! each step they
took as they proceeded through the wood, each
word and look they gave, but flung around them
another maze of the labyrinth by which they had
so suddenly become involved. Though Willie
was supposed to be leading the way towards the
open fields on the Dashwood estate, towards the
site which is now called " The Grove," somehow
he did not " run very straight," and through his
deviations they found themselves in sight of a few
rude stones supporting a cross, that marked the
sight of " Our Lady's Well." Above a small basin
in the highest part of the wood, formed by the
pellucid bubbling of a little spring, and defying the
hottest weather either to dry up its sources, or to
render its tiny waves less cool, there stood, and
still stands, a time-worn stone, exhibiting the
following lines:—

> "Drink, weary pilgrim! drink and tell
>   Thy beads beside Our Lady's Well;
> And thus beneath the greenwood tree
> The cross shall ever comfort thee."

On reaching Our Lady's Well, Marguerite became for the first time aware that she had not
gone the straightest way to her father's house,

and told the same to Willie, when he at once proposed a rest for a few minutes on a spot so inviting and so pretty. They sat down side-by-side at Our Lady's Well, while the large black dog drank the water, and there they continued to converse. "Oh," asked Willie, in an entreating and even a trembling voice, "do not, please do not hasten away the moment we have met; tarry yet a little longer. Often and often have I sat in this lone wood, but never till now was it so beautifully brightened." She sat by his side without speaking, yet she did not go. Accidentally, of course, Willie's hand, in seeking to rest on the stone between them, met hers, already resting there, each hand thus retaining its position, until the large black dog, who, after his draught at the well, had lain watchfully at their feet, growled. Marguerite did not hear it, or knew not its import, but Willie at once removed his hand from where it had rested, widened the very little distance which had been between him and Marguerite, and observing the look of his dog looked also in that direction, and then heard the sound of voices, and the rustle of advancing steps.

It was not long before the owners of the approaching steps disclosed themselves, in the shape of a very young and pretty cottage girl, accompanied by a priest in conversation with her. The effect of these strangers was to send " Jip," with her large full eyes, in terror beneath the dress of her young mistress ; while " Luther," for such was the black dog's name, stood up and manifested strong indications of violence on the male intruder. A sign from Willie, however, kept him quiet. Marguerite and Willie rose, and thus the parties became confronted. Father Crawl might have been of any age on either side of sixty approaching to that period, so light was the original colour of his scanty locks, and so pallid or leaden the hue of his emotionless features. Even his light grey eyes had a pallid appearance, and almost a set as well as an inverted immobility ; but when he did lift them, or fix them in momentary observation, such a glance of craft and cunning crept from beneath the lids, as at once gave the lie to honesty of purpose, and even made the person on whom his glance was directed feel as if compromised by the suspicion it conveyed. In height he was of the middle size, if anything below it; his figure was spare, and the action of it almost approaching to decrepitude, mingled with a sinuosity of gait that created the impression of a man writhing rather than walking, or moving in a snake-like fashion ; or, as his enemies affirmed, it gave the appearance of a man endeavouring to wriggle through his own neckcloth, like a serpent in the effort of casting off its skin.   As the priest and the cottage girl thus came up, Marguerite, as she rose, exclaimed in a whisper to Willie, "My father's priest !"   The priest took off his hat, and Willie had enough to do to quiet "Luther's" resentment. The girl then drew back with a low curtsey, but the priest advanced, and, in his usual imperturbable manner, spoke as if to both on the beauty of the day ; but then addressing himself to Marguerite he said, "I was glad to see your father so hale and hearty this morning ; *he asked me where you were.*"   When the Jesuit said this, had a microscope been directed to his eyes, it might have detected poison in the glimpse of their tiny balls ; but, other than a microscope could have conveyed, there was not an expression or the semblance of one upon his death-like features.

For some reason or other all seemed abashed, or ill at ease, in this man's presence, when, suddenly saying that she must at once join her father, Marguerite in haste bid adieu to Willie, and he saw her beautiful form receding down one of the paths of the wood, without the consoling know-

ledge of when, or if ever, they would be likely to
meet for the future. He was at once recalled,
however, from his unhappy trance by the voice of
the cottage girl bidding a good evening as she
hastened away, and then by observing the cold
impassive face of the Jesuit gazing at him.
Whether the cottage girl had received some hint
from the priest to go, while Willie was looking
after Marguerite, no one knows, but the priest,
bidding Willie then a cold adieu, sidled off in
another direction. Willie, when left thus to himself, beheld the now vacant seat by the cross, and
then cast his eyes on the ground as if to worship
the impression of the beautiful foot still treasured
by what seemed to be, in his eyes, the loving earth.
He felt, in short, that lonely sensation which many
of us, perhaps, have felt, not only in leafy bower,
but beneath the triter shelter of a hall or castle,
or a roof of any kind, when we see a room, a sofa,
or a chair, that but a moment before had been
tenanted by some loved form, whose lips we had
heard say good-bye, vacated for time indefinite.
Willie then walked in the direction Marguerite
had gone, perhaps in the vain hope that, rid of the
priestly presence, she might have lingered on the
way. But, no ! truth-teller as I am, those words
of the guileful Jesuit did the work of poison in

her ears. They were but commonplace—their import might be true, and yet said as only a serpent could whisper them; and stripped of their reptile cloak they seemed to breathe of mischief, and seemed in their subtlety to insinuate that, whether her father had asked the question or not, *he would now be told that Willie and his daughter had been in the wood together.*

CHAPTER IV.

SOME years ago Mr. Lomax, of Netley in Surrey, and the late Lord King, the father of the present Earl Lovelace, were walking on the lawn at Netley, and, great cronies as they were, they were deep in the discussion of politics, scandal, and passing events; or such topics as in the year on or about 1838 were available to ventilation, and likely to interest men of their standing. Suddenly a voice, considerably imbued with the graceful taint usually on the tongue of a native of the Emerald Isle, sounded close to the elbow of Mr. Lomax; and in a whining tone those syllables prayed for " the laste taste of a bit of vittels." Startled out of propriety, and turning short round upon a tall beggar-man, and without much choice of expression, Mr. Lomax told the suitor for charity " to go to hell;" thundering forth, at the same time, " that he had relieved such a constant succession of beggars that he had resolved to do so no more."

As Mr. Lomax made this annunciation, he and his friend Lord King faced about to take another turn on the lawn; and the Irish beggar-man, leaning on his stick, came face to face with them.

" Lord love yer honour!" said the beggar; " is it to hell you bid me go? I've just com'd from it."

Mr. Lomax, amused with the cool, sly twinkle of the old man's eyes, as he stated whence he had so immediately come, asked him, in a more good-natured tone of voice, " Well, and what were they doing there?"

" Down on their knees they was," replied the beggar-man, " every mother's son on 'em, a-praying for the arrival of Mr. Lomax, who, they said, had long been due, and a-swearing as he'd give 'em a shilling all round in the way of drink, to pay his footing, as soon as ever he come."

" Here, you old humbug!" said Mr. Lomax,

laughing, giving him a guinea for his wit. "That's better than the shilling, should you be there to meet me."

I was walking out one morning with my brother-in-law, Mr. Robert Berkeley of Spetchley, when, as we egressed from the grounds into the high road, a young beggar-lad ran against us, coming in. Grasping a forelock on his sandy forehead, the mendicant commenced a pitiful whine, but was cut inconceivably short by my relative, who exclaimed, in a voice of thunder, "What! you here again? Why, you've been here every day this last week! How dare you show your face?"

"Please yer honour," replied the suitor for broken victuals, "I 've nowhere else to go to !"

I roared with intense merriment at this reply; in which, though he turned the beggar back, my relative could not help joining. As to the beggar's religion, if he had any — whether Roman Catholic, Established Church, Dissenter, Nonconformist, Puseyite, or Puritan, I cannot say — but as Spetchley is the great Country-house for Popery, no doubt for the time being the beggar — it tallies with the conduct of the priests — was to his lips a Jesuit.

In these anecdotes of "the Upper Ten Thousand" it will be, perhaps, but fair that I should recur to all the muscular practices that were in vogue, not only before but when I was a boy, and even when I grew to manhood; and in noticing such accomplishments, of course I must refer to "the art of self-defence," as it is called, or, in more homely phraseology, to the bout with fists.

At one time, everybody who was anybody, from the Prince of Wales to the son of an esquire, practised with the gloves; and I really think that I may safely say, that through "sparring," as it was called, many a young gentleman has received from his inferiors in everything else but fighting a sound thrashing. Sparring and fighting are very different things. If a would-be pugilist thinks that by flapping, dodging, and stopping, with the gloves on, he can lick a rude, game, untaught man, he is very much mistaken. The rude, round, unwilling-to-be-denied man, will "mow" him (to use the phraseology of "the ring") "into the middle of next week." To be a good judge of distance, and to stop when necessary, as at cricket you would stop a ball, are admirable things to be possessed of; but, after all, just as it is the spur that wins a cavalry engagement, not the sword, it is the hitting that, in a boxing-match, wins the battle, and not the " stop " or " parry."

I can remember poor dear George Fitz-clarence, the eldest son of William IV., when in the 10th Regiment of Cavalry, — at least, I recollect hearing my brother speak of it, — being one of those in company with the Duke de Grammont, who, with his brother-officers, was always sparring, being taken out on the highway purposely to pick a quarrel with some wayfarer, in order to get up a boxing-match and prove his prowess. They met a quiet man with a bundle of umbrellas under his arm, whose peaceful occupation it was to mend those cumbrous things which protect your hat, for they don't screen your person, from rainy weather, and who, until quar-relled with, had nothing on his mind but the comfort of his fellow-creatures and the turning of an honest penny. I forget now how they pro-moted their difference, whether George Fitz-clarence hit the wayfarer's hat over his eyes, or knocked his patched-up umbrellas from under his arm, and then dared him to battle; but, at all events, the combat commenced, and in three or four successive rounds George Fitzclarence was knocked down.

Whatever might be the falls of their friend, his brother-officers, like good seconds, rose to the emergency, as, in truth, poor dear George did; the difference between the belligerent and his backers being, that the one rose to punishment and the others only to the occasion, for the more George bled, the more clamorous they were in assuring him of victory.

At last this little episode in the afternoon's diversion arose. For the fourth time when they picked their brother-officer up, and set him on his legs, and when they all joyfully exclaimed,—"Well done, George! all right! you're winning!" he turned to his friend who had given him his knee, and in rather a desponding tone of voice, though still right willing to "toe the scratch," remarked, *sotto voce*, — "If *this* is winning, I wonder what losing is!"

The upshot of the encounter was, that they took George away, and with that generosity which I hope ever will be the principle of a soldier and a gentleman, and, therefore, the principle of "the Upper Ten Thousand," they liberally rewarded the poor umbrella-mender for thrashing their brother-officer!

"Billy Duff," who was at one time celebrated for his eccentricities and his wonderful museum, at

his lodgings, of knockers, bell-pulls, watchmen's
staves, rattles, hats, handkerchiefs, and lanterns,
&c. &c., really could, for a slight, lathy man, fight
and hit—for, as I have previously said, the gist of
fighting is hitting—had a favourite dodge when
he had succeeded in the pleasurable task of picking a quarrel, and it was this: just at the moment
for the commencement of hostilities he would
feign a something wrong in his shoe, and stoop
down to adjust it, and then, suddenly rising from
beneath his foe, administer the “upper cut” to the
unexpected nose of his enemy, and knock that
prominent feature up into the forehead of the
man, who, of course, was totally unprepared to
protect it.

Billy Duff assured me that he had done this
often, and the recipient of the assault “never
came again.” I do not admire this proceeding,
and it is not one in any way recognized or governed by the old rules of the ring; for there,
where fair play is ever patronised, the combatants
meet at the “ scratch,” shake hands, and, similarly prepared, at once fall back into position
for offence.

Made to spar as I was when a boy, with boys
older and stronger than myself, it gave me a
considerable insight into the intricacies and best

rules of self-defence *and aggression.* Self-defence is not the only thing ; the chief thing is deter- mined, resolute, and quick aggression : and the best way to defend yourself from, or to stop a coming blow, is to step in and hit the hitter out of his intended aggression, particularly when you have to deal with a round man, or a giant, and therefore, if very big, most likely a slow man.

If you let a huge, slow, muscular coalheaver, brewer's drayman, or rural labourer, stare at you with both eyes open, and concentrate his huge arms for a slow hammer-like blow, it is one thing ; but if you step into the giant left and right, between his round-coming arms, with quick, straight blows, and close his eyes, or, better still, catch him on the under-jaw, and knock him off his legs, it is another !

Nothing could be more appropriate than the remark of a ruffian named " Bill Gibbons," the sworn " pal" of " Huffy White," who was hung, to a friend of his whom he was seconding in the ring. His friend was all on the dodging, stop- ping system, and never assailing.

" I say, old pal," said Bill, " if you stand there, a-taking of every think and a-giving of nothink, *you can't win !* "

" A little knowledge," we all know, " is a dangerous thing," and more young gentlemen have got thrashed from having flapped about with the gloves on, and supposed, therefore, that they could fight, than there would have been if they had never sparred at all.

For myself I have never abused either of the two accomplishments, boxing or swimming, but been contented with the unostentatious knowledge that I could defend myself with no other weapon than my hands, and save myself from drowning by the aid of the same members, jointly with my feet; for in boxing and vigorous swimming, hand and foot should go together.

I never purposely got into a row : every combat I have ever had was forced on me, or arose in enforcing the law in protection of my property, or in defending the weaker sex from villanous aggression.

It is high time now that such affairs should be avoided. It is sufficient when you arrive at a certain time of life to be able to defend yourself when forced into acts of violence, and to be willing to do so : increasing years should inculcate a desire, at least, for an armistice with all the warring world.—This latter is certainly a wise remark, but very difficult to maintain to the letter, as insult or impertinence is apt to make a man forget that his best boxing-days are over.

Swimming, as with boxing, is a very useful art; but as there have been more young gentlemen licked from having sparred with the gloves and thought that they could fight, so I believe more men have been drowned by knowing how to swim, than have been saved by the knowledge. The reason of this is, that they take liberties with the art they possess, and go out in dangerous salt-water tides, or in fresh water, among cold springs, that often give the cramp; and long, cumbersome weeds, which, as they grow in the Avon and Stour, and other rivers, would, if he got well into their midst, in deep water, drown the best swimmer that ever was. As it is always the best plan for a woman whose dress catches fire from beneath, to sit down on the flames instead of running about in them; so every swimmer, finding himself overpowered by a tide, should not endeavour to stem it, but should swim with it, but slantingly across it, for the shore. If in a running river, where very long weeds grow, and of course in their length trend down the stream, then the swimmer, when in danger, should recollect to direct his course for land with the incline of the weeds. Unfortunately, in the nervous excitement of the moment, all the man in danger thinks of is to make at once for the land, without considering which would be the best way to obtain the desired safety.

CHAPTER V.

A DEVONSHIRE GHOST—THE DINNER AND THE GUESTS.

IT is very difficult to prove that the ghosts or apparitions that have so frequently been said to appear are mere delusions of the brain, particularly as in my own case at Cranford, when two people at the same time see the same thing, and when describing to each other what they saw they do not vary in any respect whatever.

If we are to be guided by religious lore, and by the doctrines maintained by divines regarding the soul in the future state, a spirit could not come back to this world without especial permission from the best or the worst of places; or, if the soul was in an unjudged state, it is folly to suppose that in death, and in the severance of the ethereal essence from the clay, death could go masquerading at will in the body and clothes of life, to make the living miserable and to visit the sins of the father upon the children for many generations.

In all the legendary lore that I have collected on this abstruse subject, for the life of me I cannot meet with a single narration wherein a ghost comes back to this world for a good or a beneficial purpose.

If, for argument's sake, it be asserted that to warn a living creature of approaching dissolution is a kind and Christian act, and one of which a benignant Heaven might approve, for the sake of a prepared or unprepared soul, why, then, is not the communication more direct? Instead of being direct, in nine cases out of ten the apparition is seen by some second or third person, and not by the one for whom the warning must be supposed to be intended; and it was so in the tale now narrated, told to me by a most excellent friend of mine, who knew all, and still knows, many of those concerned in this strange transaction.

" Mr. D." was a gentleman of an old family, and the owner of considerable property in the beautiful county of Devon, and very much addicted to field-sports. While on a visit at a friend's house he met a young lady, considerably his junior, clever, pretty, and attractive, and in good time bore off his youthful bride to his ancestral home. Mr. D. was not only devoted to horse and hound, but he extended the most liberal hospitality to all his brother-sportsmen, and whenever the fixture of hounds was nearer to him than to the houses of his friends, it was his custom to ask them to dine and sleep, to be ready for "the meet" on the following morning. At times he would ask his friends from the hunting-field of that day to send word home by their hacks for their things to dress, and return with him when the chase was over. Thus, on hunting-days, his wife never knew how many there would be to dinner, nor how many beds would be required; so she took a graceful care in ordering rooms and roasts sufficient for all comers, so that she could never be taken by surprise, let her open-hearted and open-handed husband bring home whomsoever he could. It is possible, I grieve to say, that this sort of uncertainty would have been disagreeable to some mistresses, but not so in this instance. Mrs. D. was always glad to see her husband's friends, come when they would; so all went comfortably and happy. Of course, on very many occasions when the gentlemen came in late from hunting, Mrs. D. was dressing, so that occasionally she did not know how many guests had arrived till she came into the drawing-room immediately preceding the announcement of dinner, and found them thus assembled.

It is my wish particularly to impress this state of affairs upon my readers, because it accounts in an extraordinary degree for what I am about to relate. One day, when her husband had gone to a very distant meet, knowing that he could not be home till late unless the fox had run in the direction of their woods, Mrs. D. took a long round of visits to some poor people in the village, who were ill; and on coming near home, just as it was getting dark, she heard the half-hour dinner-bell for dressing, and knew by that that Mr. D. had returned: so, fearing to be late, and making all the speed she could, she ran through the hall and up-stairs, throwing off her shawl and unfastening her bonnet as she ran along. When half-way up the stairs, and in advance of her, she saw a man, who, as she came nearer to him, moved aside to let her pass. On she went, aware that he was a stranger to her whom she had never seen before, and she subsequently remembered that she had uttered to herself, ere she reached her own door, " Who can that man be, so oddly dressed, and *whose face is so remarkably pale?"* settling it in her own mind that he must be one of the guests brought home by her husband. She also remembered thinking to herself as she dressed, " How strange that pallid man's attire! *He belongs, perhaps, to some hunt I have never seen."*

Dressed and arrived in the drawing-room, there she found her husband and three guests, all of whom she knew, and then the butler entered and announced dinner to be " on the table ;" leaving the door to the hospitable board invitingly open. She had seen the three guests, but she *expected to see a fourth ;* so she still lingered in the drawing-room, under a desire not to sit down without him; till she was surprised by her husband saying to her, " What are you waiting for? *we are all here."* On this, and marvelling much as to who the man could be whom she had met on the stairs, she took the arm proffered to lead her in, and they sat down to dinner. So convinced was Mrs. D., however, that she *had met a guest on the stairs,* that she counted the chairs placed at the table as they sat down, and though there was no vacant chair she could not disabuse herself of the idea that *her husband had forgotten somebody.* Every time the door opened she looked in expectation of the entry of a belated guest, and during dinner she was absent in manner and distant, and not in her usual power of conversation.

When " curtain-lecture" time came, and she was alone with her husband, then she was eloquent on the apparition, and she said, " What I saw on the stairs was not a servant—of that I am certain; it was a gentleman, and very strangely dressed.   Who could he be ?"

To this direct question, and reft of his usual calm and affectionate manner, her husband replied rather sharply, or as if annoyed,—" Oh, nonsense! If you saw a man at all, he must have been the servant of one of our visitors; but no doubt it was a delusion: so, for the future, don't be so fanciful." Having said this, Mr. D. at once, and with evident haste, changed the subject of conversation; but his manner and method of doing so rather increased her curiosity, while at the same time she felt certain that she had not in any way been mistaken.

Some weeks after the strange occurrence thus related, Mr. and Mrs. D. went on a visit to a neighbouring mansion in the same county, and when the gentlemen came from the dinner-table on the first evening to the drawing-room, watching her opportunity to gain his ear alone, Mrs. D.

said,—"You remember my telling you of a mysterious man I met on our staircase some weeks ago? *I have seen him here to-night.*" (Her husband started.) She continued—"His picture, I mean; it hung on the dining-room wall opposite to me as I sat at table: the same white face and strange attire. I should know that face among a thousand." To her astonishment her husband seemed strangely disturbed at this intelligence, but after a moment's thought he said,—"Do not speak of this to any one; the subject to me is most painful: but to-night, when we retire, *you must hear the truth.*"

Retirement and truth that night, as they often do in phases of the world's history, came together; for her husband, after requesting her to dismiss her maid for the night, came into her room greatly excited, and depressed in mind and manner, and at once told her, that "as she had become in a manner possessed of the secret, she had better now hear the whole truth in regard to the apparition she had seen, for the truth ere long would be sadly and terribly made plain."

"A hundred years ago," he continued, "the man you saw, or thought you saw, on the stairs, was killed by one of my ancestors in a duel. The facts which led to the combat were most painful. It was his picture that was opposite to your seat at the dining-table. When any great calamity is about to happen to any of my family, the appearance of that man foretells it, by his presence either in the hall or on the stairs, precisely about the spot where you met him."

The joyous-hearted sportsman and the jovial and hospitable host the next day was in his usual spirits, or, if a shade of gloom was seen for a moment to darken his brow, the sight of the twinkling sterns of the dappled pack, and their rattling melody on a flying fox, chased each mist away, and sent him as a leader among the fastest and the gayest of the gay.

I wish that the story could close here; but the sequel must be told, as it is a fact that can be attested, and which bears the moral.

A few weeks after that semblance or apparition was seen by his wife on the stairs, her husband lay dead, killed by an accidental fall while hunting. Then, and not till then, was all the truth disclosed,— he had not told her the entire truth, for, in deference to her feelings, he had disguised the fact, that the ghost came alone to warn the head of the family that he was about to die; and though the apparition might be seen by relations, or even by other people in the house unconnected by blood, still the portentous messenger from the grave had but one fatal mission, and that was to the mortal in possession.

CHAPTER VI.

QUEEN ELIZABETH'S UNINVITED VISIT TO BERKELEY CASTLE —THE EARL OF LEICESTER AND THE "STATELY GAME OF RED DEER."

IT was in the reign of Elizabeth, when the Lord Berkeley of that day had come in from hunting, and was crossing the inner courtyard of his Castle, that a messenger was announced bearing despatches from the Court. A royal letter was then put into his hand, announcing, by the Queen's command, that on a given day it would be her Majesty's pleasure to pay her right well-beloved subject and cousin a visit, and to be entertained by Lord Berkeley for several days at his Castle in the vale of the Severn.

Now it so happened that it in no way suited the finances nor the pleasure of Lord Berkeley to entertain his sovereign; the latter, because he did not like some of those among her court: therefore this proposal from the Queen, which he well knew to be tantamount to a command, disconcerted him exceedingly; and, undecided what to do, he took it to a guest then staying with him, Sir Arthur Chichester, who had so brilliantly distinguished himself against the rebels in Ireland, and consulted him in the matter.

"Your lordship must receive her," was the reply; "and I see no way for you to escape. Her Majesty is going on a round of visits; in short, she cannot be still: a vein of melancholy has seized her, and her physicians recommend a change of scene, so make the best of it, and return an answer stating your deep gratification at her Majesty's command, and that your poor Castle of Berkeley — Gad's my life, it's large enough! — will only be too much honoured."

"But, my dear Chichester," exclaimed Lord Berkeley, "I can't and won't receive her! The stables are under repair; the roof of the kitchen wants looking to, — I can't afford the expenditure of so much money just now: so I'll be ill; or, better still, I will be from home, — I'll urge an engagement abroad which I must keep, and plead that as an excuse to deprive me — Heaven save the mark! — of so much honour."

It was useless then for Sir Arthur Chichester to attempt to shake Lord Berkeley's resolve. A letter was despatched to the Lord Chamberlain, expressive of Lord Berkeley's deep regret that he should be unable to receive her Majesty at his Castle in her progress through the county, not only was his Castle not in a state to receive his Royal Mistress, but at the time at which her visit was proposed he was necessitated to be from home.

Now it happened that Lord Berkeley and the Queen's chief and all-powerful favourite, Lord Leicester, had had a difference of opinion in regard to Sir Harry Nevil, who had been unjustly accused by Lord Essex with conspiring against the Queen, her crown and dignity, and high words on that subject had passed between the peers, which ended in Lord Berkeley sneeringly saying that Leicester was a better man at a ball than a bull-fight, and that he valued a scissors more than a sword, and his tailor better than his armourer. This was a sneer which, with ninety-nine men out of a hundred in those days, would have induced to single combat; but Leicester, perhaps thinking that he could afford to pass it by, or deeming it safer to note it down in his memory for requiting at some other time, took no notice of the insult, and the matter seemed to be forgotten.

Carrying out his resolution not to receive the

Queen, in spite of all that could be urged by Sir Arthur Chichester, Lord Berkeley closed the portals of his Castle, and, I believe, went into Wales, but not to the Castle of Chepstow, of which he was then the Governor.

Nothing could exceed Queen Elizabeth's displeasure when the Lord Chamberlain laid before her Lord Berkeley's excuse not to entertain her. So angry was she, that the physicians in attendance declared that it had done more to rouse her out of her desponding and dyspeptic melancholy than all their advice or all the pageants she had lately witnessed. Her ruff trembled with indignation, and the harsh lines of her face and prominent forehead seemed to open and close again through nervous excitement.

Leicester was sent for, and he added fuel to the flame: the time was come for requiting Lord Berkeley's sneer at his warlike propensities, and a word put in here and there induced Elizabeth to pay a visit, with all her retinue, to Berkeley Castle, and to entertain and " disport " herself there, no doubt with much pleasure, in the absence of its Lord.

On a beautiful afternoon in September, ere the foliage of the oak and elm had begun to wear the golden tints of autumn, the towns-people or vil-

lagers of the collection of houses beneath the
walls of the old Castle were out in their holiday
attire, and thronging the sides of that portion of
the road which led in the direction of the ancient
city of Gloucester.

Messengers, seneschals, butlers, cooks, and
caterers of every description, had arrived some
days before, and, much to the old grey-headed
janitor's astonishment, demanded from him, in the
name of the Queen, the entire keys as well as the
exclusive possession of the Castle. The park-
keepers had forthwith to kill stags and bucks for
the royal larder; game of all kinds were ordered
from the manors, and poultry from the farms; and
the extensive fisheries of the Severn were desired
to send in their salmon—then, as now, famed for
the richness and delicacy of their flavour.

And here, in passing, let me correct at least
one of the myths that have mystified the shallow
brains of the Commissioners under the recent
Fisheries Act for the protection of the English
rivers. It is a fabulous idea that salmon at one
time were so plentiful that the apprentices were
guarded in their articles from being obliged to
eat that delicacy at certain periods within the
week. It was not as to the fish in season that
this prohibition alluded, but it was as to the

black fish, or fish out of season, or what even to this day in some rivers is called the "duty fish," that the 'prentices refused to eat. I wish with all my heart that this was the only folly promulgated by Commissioners, by Philosophers, and by pretended Naturalists, whose only right to the term is being "naturals" themselves. But I must return to the advent of Queen Elizabeth to Berkeley Castle.

The occasional blast of a trumpet, and the rise and fall of martial music, had for some time floated on the air around Berkeley, but now a loud fanfare heralded the approach of England's single Queen, and shortly after the vanguard of the royal procession came in sight; now afar off, and dimly seen; now nearer, and more distinctly flashing, as the bright coats and arms of soldiers and the royal retainers glided between the stems of forest trees, till all at once, where the road came straight upon the town, the full panoply of the procession of England's Royalty broke gaily, proudly, and musically into view.

Although the retainers of the house of Berkeley inhabited every house by which the procession passed, and though each tenant on the domain was aware of the rumour that the present royal visit was distasteful to their Lord, still the crowd assembled cheered the Queen as Englishmen can alone cheer, and husbands, wives, widows, single men, and children, shouted and waved their caps and handkerchiefs, as if the cavalcade was as agreeable to their suzerain as it was to their sovereign, and as welcome to the Castle as it was gay and gallant to behold. Queen Elizabeth reclined in a species of litter, or open car, and rose occasionally to acknowledge the greeting of her subjects; and by the side of her car, the head of his splendid steed about opposite the hinder wheel, rode her favourite and minion, Leicester. Ascending the hill leading from the town to the outer lodge and portcullis, the head of the procession passed the archway, and the long retinue following soon filled both the inner and the outer court of the Castle; the Queen, leaving her carriage at the door of the great hall, proceeded through that spacious saloon to the dais, on which was served " a slight refectory," to refresh her and to enable her to bear with time until the tables groaned with supper. In those days they supped at our hour for dinner.

On the following morning, and ere the Queen required his attendance, Leicester stood on the leads of the Castle, and viewed that wide domain of rich meadow which surrounds it. Immediately beneath the Castle walls lay the Castle meadows, but not so smooth and green then as they are now, for they were more subject to floods, and in places the water had given to the grass a sour or yellowish hue.

Far away, but still plain to the view, could be seen St. Michael's, or Micklewood Chase, the higher ground and its phalanx of huge forest trees rising darkly against the horizon. Nearer still, or seeming to be nearer from the abruptness and height of its elevations, arose from the vale a spur of the Cotswold Hills; and Stinchcombe, with its precipitous side, called Breakheart Hill, loomed grandly over the town of Dursley, which gives to the family the second title. " By my faith," said Leicester to himself, " a goodly prospect! But stay! what have we here on this, the more northern side? Ha, by my life! a stately " game " of red deer, a portion of it splendidly traversed by avenues of elms. This noble lord, so full of his sneers and gibes, who cannot receive his Queen, keeps all in splendid fashion. Good! we'll see what the Sovereign says; and, by my faith, yon stately park of red deer would be a fine place for her to disport herself in chase of the antlered game."

Now it so happened in those days that parks of red deer were few: they, the larger deer, existed chiefly in forests and chases, and in this park, known to this day as the " Little Park," to distinguish it originally from those of more extensive dimensions, Lord Berkeley had taken, and still took, the greatest delight: in short, according to the family historian, Smith, " he set more store by ye great stags in ye park adjoining unto ye Castle," than he did by any other of his possessions.

Towards noon on the first day of the royal sojourn at Berkeley Castle, the fine herd of red deer were unwontedly aroused from their luxurious lairs among the rich herbage of that portion of the little park now called " the Worthley," by the presence of strange men fast assembling in the hitherto (from interruption) sacred scene of their haunts. The deer, whisking their many twinkling " singles," and tossing their antlers at the flies, little dreaming of what was about to happen, walked idly off to a more retired spot; but again they were moved from every station they assumed by parties of strange men, and now by the setting up in many places of huge nets, used for the purpose of taking deer, and called the " toils," as well as by the eager baying of gazehounds held in leashes.

All being in readiness, the Queen, with Leicester at her bridle-rein, and followed by a mounted retinue of lords and ladies, who had feasted and revelled the day before at the absent lord's expense, entered the park, and at a signal the sport, if it could be so called, commenced. When the line admitted of it, the deer were shot down without reference to age, sex, or condition; while the dogs, slipped upon the terrified animals, drove them in tangled confusion into the nets; when, as their throats were being cut, or as they were held by the royal followers to receive the *coup de grâce* from the hunting-knives of the Queen's guests, the roarings of the dying red deer sought the royal ear — a meet and appropriate greeting for the abominable and spiteful use of coarse, despotic power.

While the Queen and her minion were enjoying this wholesale destruction of the creatures of the man against whom she was piqued for his refusal to entertain her, and of whom Leicester was afraid, as well as sore from Lord Berkeley's sneers, hereinbefore previously mentioned, a huge stag, mad from being baited and desperate from distress, his splendid eyes prominent from passion, and his antlers lowered against everything alive, broke through the lines of his immediate assailants,

and charged full into the courtiers surrounding
the Queen. Narrowly missing the Queen's palfrey,
as well as the steed of Leicester, the noble hart,
"royal" by age, at length countered with the
steed of one of the attendants, bearing horse and
rider to the ground, and burying his brow antlers
deep into the horse's flank. A panic seized the
crowd, the cry arising of " Beware! another and
another stag! the old male deer are breaking from
the bay and charging right and left! Take, take
her Majesty away!"

It is not for the historian to assert things he
cannot vouch for, but rumour still lives; and
perhaps, in this instance, rumour does not lie,
when it says that there was an unseemly rush,
or *sauve qui peut*, among the royal crowd, to
escape with and in the royal presence, and that in
the rush to get out of the way of the charging and
infuriated stags the steed of the Queen was not
the first to get clear of the enclosure, and that her
Majesty was considerably jammed against a post,
and that, too, by her favourite minion, Leicester.

After that day of wanton slaughter, the few
sullen old stags that had held their own were
destroyed or maimed by innumerable devices;
and as a last and crowning despotic act the Queen
gave orders for the scene of the gentle pastime to

be disparked, and the few deer that were left alive escaped into St. Michael's Chase.

During the short time of the offended Sovereign's sojourn at the Castle, not only was the " stately game of red deer," as Smith calls it, exterminated and laid waste, but with a like view to injure the lord of the acres as much as it was in her power to do, everything he possessed was more or less injured, and the wines and strong beer tapped and let out to run wastefully over the stones of the before amply-stocked cellars.

The day at last came for the Queen's progress to Bristol, and all sorts of rumours having reached him, the outraged and indignant Lord of the Castle hastily returned, and found his noble halls, his park and his chase, his poultry-yard and his farm-yard (for he was an amazing patron of agriculture), his cellars, his game and his deer, all laid waste, and suffering from the presence of an offended Sovereign—from the revengeful feeling of that worst of all enemies, a piqued and a slighted woman—and from the bitter instigations and intrigues of a favourite courtier, who feared to assail his foe in any way other than from beneath the robe of royalty.

It is not to be supposed that Lord Berkeley was kept long in ignorance as to the covert hand

which Leicester had in these inflictions, or that
he was inclined to be still under so flagrant a
breach of all law and courtesy as had been put
on him by the Queen: his first act, therefore,
was to make it a personal affair with Leicester;
but, according to Smith, a friend about court
wrote to Lord Berkeley, and told him not to stir in
the matter of his wrongs in any way whatever, for
that Leicester, well knowing his aptitude to resist
oppression and insult, had devised a scheme that
should induce Lord Berkeley to violently commit
himself far enough, as against the Crown, to warrant the forfeiture of his estates; and remembering
the tyrannic act that Elizabeth had done, in for-
bidding an elected member of the House of Commons to take his seat, Lord Berkeley's friend
at court prayed him to be quiet, and to thwart
Leicester's ultimate view, which was no other
than to obtain a grant of the Castle of Berkeley
and its lands at the hands of his royal mistress.

With many a shrug and many a growl of dis-
content, however, Lord Berkeley constrained himself to adopt this wise counsel. The Castle and
estates are still, if for a time usurped, in the entail
of the family; but the outraged Lord never again
took delight in his " stately game of red deer,"
or attempted to restore the confines of the " Little

Park." The deer have since been in St. Michael's Chase, or, as they are now, in the ample park on the hill, at the foot of which stands King William's Oak, still bearing acorns, although at " Domesday Survey " it was a tree so remarkable among its fellows for its size, that it was then selected and set down as a landmark for the hundred of Berkeley.

CHAPTER VII.

PART II.

PREVIOUSLY to introducing the reader to the home of our heroine, it will perhaps serve to elucidate her position if I say that she had for some little time been regarded as the *belle* of the vicinity, eligible to intermarry with any family, not only on account of her beauty and accomplishments, but from the gentility of her birth. Her father, I believe, was connected with the very old family of the Darrells of Millend, whose estate was at Toweredge. The mansion at West Wycombe Park was not then the beautiful and elaborately ornamented structure that it is now. All we know of it is, that it had been an old-fashioned house, and that at a more recent period Sir Francis Dashwood, the father of Lord Le Despencer, who succeeded to that title in right of his mother on the death of John, Earl of Westmoreland, rebuilt it again in the old red-brick fashion. It was left to his lordship to remodel it all, and to this hour stands the mansion in the purest style of the Italian villa, probably the only specimen of the kind in the United Kingdom. Lord Le Despencer was as magnificent in his ideas of architectural embellishment, paintings, and statuary, as he was versatile and able in his mental accomplishments; for he filled various situations in the Cabinet of the day, including the difficult one of Chancellor of the Exchequer: not so difficult then, perhaps, as the neighbouring possessor of the adjoining manor to West Wycombe Park —Mr. Disraeli—has since found it to be; for in the days of Lord Le Despencer there were not quite so many schoolmasters abroad; accounts were shorter, the returns no worse, and the broth the better for the cooks being few.

But to return to the immediate progress of the legend.

When Marguerite reached her father's house she found him in his study, in no way unusually desirous of seeing her, nor could she learn that he had asked for her during the period which had expired in her adventure in Whittenden Park

Wood. She told him, however, that her four-footed companion had fallen down the Swilley Hole, and that a gentleman accidentally passing had extricated "Jip" from her perilous position. Had a close observer regarded Marguerite's face when she thus hastily touched on the past occurrence, he might have seen a tremulousness in her beautiful upper lip, and a slight flush of the rose on her cheek, when she uttered the word "gentleman;" but as her father had got his spectacles on, and was at the moment endeavouring to read a letter from Lord Carnarvon, he did not take much heed of what his daughter said.

Her interview with her father having thus passed, Marguerite resumed her accustomed occupations until the hour of the evening meal, or supper; at which time, to her very great discomfort, the priest as usual put in, to her, an unwelcome appearance. During his stay, for the first time in her life, Marguerite felt ill at ease. Though educated to deem the priest a deity, and an ignorant man—as in truth he was—infallible and gifted with heavenly inspiration, it seemed as if that leaden face before her had in it an absolute power for evil, if not for good, as well as the will, under some circumstances, to do her grievous injury with her father—an injury thoroughly vague and undefined, but yet in being. So strong were her feelings on this head, that, though fatigued with the excitement of the day, she was resolved not to retire while there was a chance of her father being left alone with the Confessor Crawl. She had previously had cause to dread the priest's influence with her father, for the "infallible" not only assumed complete sway over all matters touching religion, but also sought to direct in all mundane or worldly things, which in his craft he thought he could twist to his own advantage, always appearing to consider that whatsoever benefited him was similarly serviceable to the interests of Heaven. To give a more homely illustration, in craving gifts from his patron or patroness, if he asked eleven boons, the first ten would be for his own creature comforts in beer, spirits, wine, and food, and the eleventh for a vestment in which to appear before the altar.

Marguerite had, as I have previously said, already tasted of his meddling and mundane interference; for among her suitors—it could be justly said that she had several—was one especially pleasing to Father Crawl, a Sir Caldwell Hunter. This man was rich, unscrupulous, depraved, and intemperate—by profession a Jesuit, and, at an advanced time of life, as little calculated to make Marguerite happy, or to understand, treasure, and cultivate the refined sensibilities of her nature, as a bear would be to comprehend the tender sweets of a budding rose. The priest had repeatedly endeavoured to back this man's suit; for he had thrust his attentions on the reluctant girl, and even openly spoken of them to her father : but it was so obviously against the feelings of both, that the tempter, or the worldly adviser under the garb of Heaven, felt at some loss to pursue the subject further, and was forced to content himself with biding for a better time. The evening of which we are speaking wore on; night-prayers over, Marguerite, with great relief to her mind, saw the priest depart, and then only did she retire to rest.

The morning following proved the forerunner of a completely wet day, and Marguerite did not leave the house. The next day, however, was fine; and why—alas! I cannot tell *why*—but Marguerite, with "Jip" frisking before her, walked as if musing and hesitating around the garden at the grove, and then suddenly took the direction of Whittenden Park Wood. The face of May was as the face of childhood after tears; the sun put forth a cloudless smile, lit up the dewdrop that the night had left, and flashed in pendent diamonds over the jocund woods and fields.　Oh! but the very bees were so awakened to their honeyed loves, that from the lowliest flower, up to the trilling and ascending lark, the earth seemed chanting praise acceptable to Heaven!　What a lesson to the mind of man!　Well, O most suspicious, or most sensitive reader, what harm was there in Marguerite's walk to her favourite wood ?　What wonder if, when she came to the prettiest spot in it, "Our Lady's Well," she then again encountered Willie, who accidentally came there before her ?　They had made no assignation, given and exchanged no promise to meet beneath the greenwood tree; yet there they were; and, after taking a turn or two, once more they became seated on the stone beside the Well.　I must not delay the progress of the tale by repeating all they said. Love—yes, love at first sight—is the best picklock to the box of discretion, and the best breaker down of the crude conventionalities set up by the regulations of society.　It is enough for my readeresses to know, how down the beams of their eyes and into each other's hearts there slid, without their being aware of it, little liquid stars of fire, that would go nowhere else but to each heart, there to thrive to greater volume.　Thus, alas! it was; and thus for days, and day by day, with but little interruption, it continued. To the dangerous and dreaming bliss of these stolen interviews—for so, I suppose, they must be termed —there seemed to be but one drawback; and that came from Father Crawl. He had again resumed his favourite theme of suggestion as to Sir Caldwell Hunter. He talked to Marguerite of his riches; glossed over his faults; and said, as many a foolish mother since has said, that "if she married him, he would amend:" hinting that even if he continued in one of his worst, most disgusting, and most miserable of faults, and drank himself to death, she would be in a position, after but brief suffering, to choose for herself; and, should she be so disposed, to confer benefits on the house of God.

It was in vain that Marguerite looked up into the leaden face, and asked if it would be right in her to approach the altar, and swear to love and obey a man whose mind and body were loathsome to her in every meaning of the word; and by whom she felt she could not do her duty. The priest replied, that if vows were made to attain a good end, a vow so made was covered and excused by the intent; and as to vows so fixed by legal rule, they were not binding to the better spirit, and from all such vows he could give her absolution. The deep penetration of the wily priest soon saw, however, that his case was hopeless; and that the bribe the rich man had, in truth, offered to him personally, if he could induce Marguerite to become his wife, was lost, unless he could devise some other way of working her to his will. It was then that, in the sly bitterness of his reflections, he remembered the first day on which, at their first accidental interview, he had surprised Marguerite and Willie together in Whittenden Wood; and now he made up his mind, obstinate as he deemed the lovely girl to be, that the cause of her determination was to be found in the fact that her affections had become engaged. So often had this priest succeeded with the female mind—by sophistry, dark insinuations, and impious tales of supernatural signs and miracles—that he was astonished, piqued, and even angered, at one so lovely and so young resisting all his importunities and exhortations. It was not long before the cogitations of Father Crawl bore the fruit he wished.

One morning Marguerite was sent for into her father's study, when, pushing his spectacles from his eyes high up on his forehead, he thus peevishly accosted her:—

" How now, minx ? What is this I hear? Word has been brought to me that thou hast picked up a wandering acquaintance in Whittenden Park Wood."

" Dear father," she cried, " I told you of the acquaintance I had accidentally made the day it happened:" and as she said this, she leaned fondly over the back of his chair. " You do not wish me to drop the acquaintance, without some reason, I am sure, papa!"

" Reason ! no. I ever tell thee, child, that everything should be governed by reason; and I am sure no child of mine can be a fool, *or lose her self-respect.* There, go along with thee to thy chickens: I can, I know, *trust thee* not to make idle acquaintances, nor rashly do anything to displease thine old father. There, kiss me, Madge, and begone to thy chickens: go."

She kissed her father, and, calling her favourite " Jip," went forth for her woodland walk. Poor Marguerite, like thousands of her sex before and since, had permitted herself to drift through many happy interviews with one who really was her lover, without staying a moment to think in what it all could end. Matters were changed now. This short interview with her father cast her back into most painful reflection, whence she could discover no extrication. That her father could ever be brought to consider Willie as a connexion suited to her, and to his own rank in life, she had very little hope; and, besides this, she was well aware that the priest had been gradually working on her father's mind to assist him in wedding her to the old, the dissolute, and even the diseased, man of riches. These painful reflections lasted till she had ascended the lawn amidst the brakes of furze leading from the grove to the wood, now clad in the gorgeous hues of green and gold; the air so sweet, and the scene so sunny, the songs of birds so blithe, that the dear girl almost burst into tears from the very contrast the world without afforded to the sorrowful intelligence within. Once in the wood, the more sombre hues of the old fir, and the darker shadows of the foliage beneath, though the bright young leaves of the beeches were just bursting to perfection, seemed more in unison with her saddened spirit; and she proceeded in her accustomed walk towards Our Lady's Well, resolved on an explanation with her lover. Even then there had been no assignation between them; not a word as to time or place: but that Willie would be there at any time that Marguerite might chance to come, was just as sure as that at a certain hour of the morn the light of heaven, whether the face of the sun was clouded or not, would illume the eastern glades. A turn in the walk brought the lovers again together, and a few steps further placed them seated side-by-side.

" Oh, Marguerite! dear, darling Marguerite!" Willie exclaimed; "what has happened? Thy sunny brow is clouded; nay, thine eyes are tearful; and all over there is sorrow. Speak, love! speak, and tell me!"

Marguerite had deemed that she had nerved herself for the coming explanation; but when the time arrived, thus so suddenly and unexpectedly addressed, to have spoken would have been to have wept; and with her eyes cast down, her beautiful lip quivering, she sat motionless and speechless, her arm then clasped in Willie's hand; while in the deepest anxiety he paused for a reply.

At last she spoke. " Oh, Willie, I never thought it would come to this. Foolishly—yes, foolishly—we have met together, day by day, since our first interview, without thinking to what a precipice our steps were tending. Some one has told my father that we have been often together in this wood, and he has spoken of it to me to-day."

"Well, Marguerite; and if he has spoken to you, what has he said? Has he listened to the vile whisper of the Jesuit snake — from thence he has his information — and has he bid you to cease all communion with one whom he calls his inferior, not worth a place in your affections? Has he ——"

"No, no, Willie," interrupted Marguerite, in anxious haste; "he has said nothing against you — he never named you. Had he done so, and mentioned you to me disparagingly, I would have defended you from insult. No, he did not mention you, but, despite all he had heard, he only said *he trusted in his daughter*, and that *in that trust he felt he never should be deceived.* Oh, Willie, it is best for us both that we should meet no more, or — or — at least see each other less frequently. We have yet time to extricate ourselves from the difficulty into which we have so heedlessly rushed, and I know that you will aid me in schooling my heart to better things."

"To school your heart to better things, Marguerite!" replied Willie; "strange and false preceptor I should be to bid you hate me!"

"No, not to hate you," returned the now weeping girl; "I meant not that. I wished you to look upon what has passed between us as a vain dream — to regard me as a sister; yes, Willie, as a loving sister; and avail yourself of these stirring times to seek your fortune in the world, and to forget the hours we have passed in Whittenden Park Wood."

" Oh, Marguerite, do not, dearest girl! deceive yourself in thinking that I can ever forget you, or that I will try to do so; but," he said, springing with a bound from his almost kneeling posture at her side to his full height, " any sacrifice that you can demand from me, that you even think is for your happiness, I will devotedly endure. Let mine be the grief, mine the wretched side of life, if I only know that I suffer for your sweet sake."

" Oh, Willie, this is what I had hoped from you; yet think not that you are the only sufferer. In obedience to the father who has *ever relied on me with trustful affection*, I must try to do his will. I suggest these harsh terms to you, not because I do not like you, Willie, but for fear that I should love. Look at our little robin: he has become so used to our presence, and even to that of " Luther " and " Jip," in his woodland haunt, that he comes to us now, and even perches on our feet to take the crumbs I have latterly brought with me on purpose for him. He used to eat them thankfully by our side; but now, you see, he fills his little beak, and hops away beneath the brambles, to feed the young in his leafy nest, and then returns to us for more. He, ere he knew us, had no human friends. A few short weeks, and he will forget that we have ever been. Oh, Willie, we must forget each other!"

As she uttered this, a low, long-drawn alarm-note from the robin — as if it had seen a hawk — uttered as it flew into the thicket, and an anxious gaze and growl from "Luther," warned them of an approaching step. The lovers rose: for, in spite of all sophistry and self-denial, still they were mutually so; and the cottage-girl, of whom we have already made mention as having been in the wood in company with the priest, stood before them. She was out of breath with haste, and her pretty plebeian features were flushed with news, as with a low curtsey, and in some bashful confusion, she addressed Willie, and said,—

" Sir, I thought you'd like to know as Father Crawl is in the wood: I see him peering up and down the rides, and all as knows him knows he never looks for nothing."

Marguerite only coloured; but Willie said,—

" Thanks, my good girl; I am glad to hear the

priest is out for a walk, but I have no particular wish to see him. Good-bye."

He said this, for Marguerite had taken his arm; and he felt she desired to hasten away, when, having left the girl, she said,—

" There, Willie, is a further proof we have been here too often. You see my poor Mary "—she was a great favourite with Marguerite — " thinks that we have reason not to wish to be seen where we are. Oh, Willie, Willie, we must sever; it is not for me to create even a suspicion of impropriety in a vulgar mind, and I am sure you would not wish me to do so. Here," she cried, stopping where a path led different ways, we must bid adieu to each other."

" Oh, if for to-day," cried Willie, " but not for ever!— you will not, cannot, doom me to such undeserved misery! Say, Marguerite, we shall meet again. Say, at least, that if anything prevents our meeting — for I dread the interference of that accursed priest, who hates me for my Reformed faith — you will find some means of communication. Beneath the spot where that sweet foot of thine first pressed the moss on the edge of the chalk cliff of the dell, down which poor little " Jip " had fallen, and on which spot I lifted her to your hands, I will carve a little shelf,

which will faithfully conceal any written communication, and be discoverable only to ourselves."

As he said this he held her hand, but he suddenly dropped it, for he caught a glimpse of a
black garment not far off; and she, too, started at
the same thing, and sped away from the spot she
had fixed on for their severance. He gazed at her
receding figure, and then turned to where he
deemed that he had caught a glimpse of the
priest; but whether he had or had not been deceived by the waving of some dark bough, he
could not tell. At all events, there was no one to
be seen. Still clinging to his momentarily formed
hope of at least a written communication, Willie
walked to the Swilley Hole where they had first
met, and with his knife made a sufficient vacancy
in the edge of the chalk rock beneath the overhanging moss, safely to conceal any little thing
that might be intrusted to its safe - keeping.
Leaving him thus occupied, we must follow the
steps of Marguerite.

We left Marguerite hastening from the wood,
where she had so suddenly and so sorrowfully
taken leave of Willie, towards her father's house;
but ere she left the verge of the high trees,

on nearing the furze-brakes on the lawn, she
fell into a slower pace, and eventually almost
stood still, to review the circumstances in which
she found herself, and to decide, if she could,
upon her future line of conduct. The Jesuitical
tenets in which she had been brought up, so
calculated as they always are to make, at
least, a strong impression on the plastic surface of a child's mind, had done their office
on her, but not so deeply but that, at the thinking age at which she had arrived, there was
a struggle to free herself from superstition and
the daring assumption of infallibility by the
priesthood.

She was too sensible not to see, but that
in the method taken by Father Crawl to induce
her to countenance the overtures of Sir Caldwell Hunter, there was much that was worldly,
in direct variance with truth, and opposed to the
free exercise of conscience. Infinitely too pure in
her own heart not to feel, that in the face of
Heaven there ought not to be, and in reality
there could not be, deceit of any kind, she might
be said, for some time, to have been in a frame
of mind to have embraced the purer doctrines
of the Reformed Church had not another obstacle
intervened, and that obstacle was her father.

Bred up by him since her mother's death with great affection and indulgence, and implicitly trusted by him, as we have already seen, the generous sensibilities of her nature, so apt to be so thoroughly developed in the female mind— save in some instances, when the utter loss of all that is good may be said to be *the* exception— would not allow her to contemplate for a moment running counter to his will, where a direct contact with his wishes could be avoided ; and hence she came most seriously to consider what course it was her duty to adopt. Moving thus, and musing thus, her downcast eyes resting on the ground, with their silken lashes on her lovely cheek, she had stepped from out the wood upon the lawn, when something touched her arm, and starting from her reverie, with an exclamation of almost terrified surprise, she found the priest at her elbow.

" Mistress Marguerite," he said, " will it please you to give me—to one so humble, and yet I trust so heavenward as I am—a few moments' conversation ? From infancy I have taught you, or tried to teach you, the way to heaven, and have endeavoured, under the Supreme Will, to render you a blessing to your father, and even to our holy Church. May the

Holy Virgin forefend that I have failed in a mission so dear to all my wishes!"

Marguerite stopped, and fixing her eyes upon him as he said this, in that slow and measured tone which never left him except when at his ease, and free of the artificial cloak that screened his real nature and his innate vulgarity, paused for further speech.

"I come to speak to you," he continued, "on that topic to which I have so often referred, and zealously to endeavour to bring you not only to a knowledge of your duty to your father, but also to a devout sense of Heaven's will; aye, and my dear young lady, to the knowledge that in you lies, not only the rescue of your father from impending difficulties which beset him, but even the almost heavenly power to serve your Church in the essential way which she at this moment most needs. I need not say that I plead the cause of Sir Caldwell Hunter."

As the spur to a mettled steed, as the report of the rifle to the scared doe, the mere reference to this suitor, through the cold, passionless lips of the priest, made the sweet girl start as from a thought at which her very soul recoiled, and she commenced a hasty retreat towards her home ; but Father Crawl laid a detaining, even a forcible, grasp upon her arm, and again addressed her.

" Mistress Marguerite," he said, " you know not what you do. Hear, then, the impending danger to your poor father from my lips—*he is a ruined man!* Nay, start not; and do not attempt to fly till you have heard me out. A thoughtless and lavish expense far beyond his means has cast him into debt ; he has béen temporarily rescued by loans from Sir Caldwell Hunter, but his last resources are failing him ; and unless you come to the rescue, he—your father—is a lost man, *and you are his destroyer!*"

Stricken to the heart, scared and miserable, poor Marguerite mechanically permitted the priest to lead her to a seat by his side on a fallen tree. He saw the effects of his words, and proceeded : " I have seized on the present opportunity to open your eyes to this, even at the moment when *I know you to be fresh from the vows of a forbidden lover*, and to use every effort in my power to save you from that perdition which will inevitably attend you and yours, if you continue these clandestine meetings against your father's commands, and forbear to embrace the only line that can save his grey hairs from a prison, and perhaps from consequent death. Your own reputation, too, must be saved from the wild whispers against it which these woods have engendered ; and there is *but one remedy for all this*, and that is your acceptance of the hand of the rich suitor !"

Father Crawl again paused ; but stunned, almost heart-broken, and in tears, as yet Marguerite made no reply : he saw, or thought he saw, the advantages he was gaining, and was proceeding to follow them up, when, from the midst of her sobs and tears, as if to enable her to realise the terrible idea, Marguerite murmured,—

" My father, my poor father ruined ! Oh, tell me what it is you mean !"

" Then, listen," the priest replied, " and you will see the force of all I say. Your father has ever been a zealous supporter of our faith ; in times when the maddened hands of all men were against us, he stood forth as far as he dared as our defender. His sword in former years, his life, his purse, were ever at our holy will ; and light enough has been given him to know that the servants of our Holy Mother must be sustained in strength to do their duty. He has been gifted to see the necessities of Heaven, and on his wealth the priests have lived ; and the body and soul of our shattered convents and churches have been kept together by the pittance he was given the grace to supply. If you serve him not, the misbelievers of the Reformed faith, as they call it, Roundhead and Cavalier alike, will glory in his downfall. Oppressed by debt, you will see your father dragged to prison ; his hearth deserted ; and his name a by-word in the place where once it was respected. You have to choose between your father's ruin or his rescue by your hand—to select between the approbation of Heaven or a reward in hell. A word, and *you can save him.*"

" Oh, father, is this the horrible alternative?" asked the weeping girl. " Must I wed the man my heart abhors, and stand before the altar with a guilty soul, breathing falsehood at the throne of truth? I cannot, cannot do it!"

"Marguerite, you can do it, and *it must be done!* The Holy Mother will forgive and even bless you for the sacrifice you make—for the means by which you attain the end. Hush! for I have not yet done. You are—at least you were—acquainted with Sister Susanna, who, in the odour of sanctity, is lately dead. She charged me to deliver a message, and it shall be given to you in her own most blessed words. For three or four days she told us all 'that she experienced a profound desolation of spirit, to which was also attached an internal and external disgust for ordinary occupations. On one of those mornings she felt more than usually depressed in soul and body, and somewhat cold in recovering herself to receive the bread of life. She was lost in astonishment how the Lord could bear with her with so much patience. Having communicated, she seemed to feel herself more than ever distracted and without recollection—a thing which always occasioned her much grief during the precious time in which Jesus was with her. On this morning, however, His goodness drew her to a Divine union, notwithstanding all her coldness; but at that moment, when she saw Him full of goodness and love, His irritated justice was shown to her; and, to her unbounded horror and fear, something was represented to her so terrible and frightful that she knew not to what to compare it, for the idea remained in the superior part of her soul, not communicating itself in the least to the inferior portion.*   At the moment when she perceived the Divine justice thus irritated against her, and as if all in earth and heaven were moved, the angels and saints cried out,—' Let the systems of nations be changed; let the terrible plague come; let there be no place 'twixt the heavens and the bottom of the sea that shall not have expiated the crime of man; and let the daughters of the earth wed with the rich that remain uncleansed, to bring their wealth as a sacrifice to the holy altar, and to desire and to win for themselves the Saviour's love.   Let her once earthly friend, sweet Marguerite, hear this, and bid her be the first to sacrifice her sinful desires to the throne of mercy. In short, tell her to wed whomsoever the priests shall name.' "

The priest concluded, and up stood the re-

---

* I have transcribed so far nearly *verbatim* this revelation of the dying Nun, as it came into my possession, and as it was handed about at the time from female to female of the Jesuit thrall, to impose more strongly on minds that did not seem to the most bigoted to be sufficiently impressed or blinded by what I cannot but term the implous rule of Self, not Heaven-elected men.   There is much more of it; but in no way wishing to touch too elaborately on a subject that should never be lightly approached, I have abstained from further quotation. The document will remain in my possession, among others of a similar nature.— G. F. B.

awakened girl! Not weeping *now*, though a trembling tear-drop still clung on the flushed cheek beneath her flashing eye.

" Sir," she cried, " I will no longer mock thee with the term of ' father;' thou hast, indeed, dashed from my sight the veil of sophistry flung there in my earlier years, and shown me how the behests of Heaven can be perverted when interpreted or read according to the selfish will of man. I have long seen that the creed which the Jesuit preaches substitutes the worship of the priest for that of Heaven, and that man is to be idolized instead of the Great Creator. My poor father may be involved in difficulty; at present I have it only from your lips. If he should be so, there is no sacrifice that I can make in this life, and which interferes not with the world to come, that shall not be freely rendered; but I will know more. I fear, however, that, little scrupulous as you have shown yourself to be as to the means to attain an end, you have already done much to set my father against me — the daughter who designed to be the prop of his failing years — and you may yet do more; *but, so long as he trusts me*, I will enter into no engagement which he disapproves. Speak to me, then, sir, on this subject no more; tempt me not to the most loathsome and false vows in the face of Heaven, and which if made I feel would be but as a chain of thistle-down to restrain me for the time to come. I leave you, sir," she said— her graceful figure seeming to dilate with the scorn and resolution of the moment—"to seek the fullest explanation with my father, and then to guide myself as becomes his daughter and a Christian girl."

She turned from Father Crawl, leaving him as pale and motionless as ever, but, if possible, stooping and cowering still more in his position upon the fallen tree. For some moments after she had left him, the Jesuit sat resting his forehead in his hand in a state of deep reflection. He then looked up and looked after her, but she was out of sight.

"So, so!" he exclaimed, in a rough, natural, and therefore vulgar tone; " that's it, is it, my pretty mistress! Then we must take some sharper means yet to bring Sir Caldwell's wilful falcon to his will, and there is not much time to lose." So saying, he arose, regained and passed through the wood, continued his writhing gait across some open ground beyond it, till he came to a few scattered cottages at Lane End, at the door of one of which he knocked. The little dwelling belonged to a labourer, the father of the pretty cottage girl whom we have previously introduced to our readers as " Mary;" and in that cottage, to which he was at once admitted, for the present we must leave the Jesuit priest.

CHAPTER VIII.

NATURAL HISTORY—NATURALS, AND FLOCKS OF WILD-FOWL
—PHILOSOPHIC BLUNDERS AND ERRORS OF EVERY DE-
SCRIPTION.

IT is a strange power, that which the love of natural history gives, to the really practical observer, over the four-footed and feathered creation of the wilds; and often and often have I laughed—not in my sleeve, for I hate such melancholy merriment, but outright, at the published folly I have seen *spawned* and palmed on the listening multitudes who throng the Zoological Gardens in the Regent's Park, and the lecture-rooms of innumerable societies. People listen to the accounts of fishes from men who all their lives have been surrounded by walls, instead of by the waters, and who know as much of the instincts of piscatory nature as they do of the harem, or eunuch-guarded seraglio, of a turbaned Turk.

We have seen the multitude officially invited

to the most absurd sights previously alluded to by me : to snakes sitting like hens on eggs; to snakes, said to be foreign, which cannot be found out of England; common minnows in little tanks doing duty for the young of salmon ; deer in the Zoological Gardens without one pliant bough on which gently to rub the fading velvet from their new and tender antlers ; the Prairie dog without a hole in which to lay and to conceal its young; deformed foals made to represent a hybrid between the deer and horse ; and young ducks with the webs clipped from their toes, asserting themselves to be mules between the drake and barndoor hen; horns of many deer stuck together, and proclaimed as the enormous antlers of one; and large, cumbrous monkeys, depicted as the tyrannical athletæ of forests, roaring the scared lions from their dens!

There is no sort of mare's nest in which philosophers will not believe; and so mystified is the present and rising generation with the consideration of what is true and what is false, that their hours are passed in doubt instead of progress; and in science of this kind there is a dead lock.

Owen pronounced a whale's tooth to be the " canine tooth of a badger." Other philosophers declared some skulls of wild cattle, brought by me from Haddon Hall, to be skulls of the *Bos-longifrons* of the ancient Britons: but that was an error, because each skull had been perforated by a bullet, and powder and ball were not then known.

I will now state some interesting facts which occur to me every day when amusing myself with my creatures at home, in this the year 1866. Where there never was any open water before, I have cleared away the mosses and made ponds, and reared all sorts of wild fowl in their vicinity. In doing this, a wonderfully small and pretty little milk-white bantam hen, whose name is " Betty," and who knows her name as well as any dog ever knew his, reared one of the finest broods of fowl of the smaller kind, and was taken with her callow young and placed in one of the swamps in the valleys on the moors. " Betty " had no place to roost in other than the heather, and she so adapted herself to the necessities of her foster-children that she might be seen wading in the swamps up to her breast — her clothes, so to speak, held very high, or kilted — and catching insects for them as assiduously as if she had been on dry land. She remained with her brood of ducks till they took flight away from her, and then she was *brought home.* Since then she has reared both pheasants and partridges on dry land; and her conduct when her covey of twelve partridges one day, in the September of 1866, flew away from her, immensely amused me. I saw it happen, and therefore had a right to be amused. She stood up as erect as she could make herself, and watched their flight as if she desired to mark them down, and then pretended to find food, and for a few minutes called them to come to it as loudly as she could. Finding they did not come, she leisurely, and in an offended manner, walked home to my lawn, never looked for her birds again, and very shortly after knocked at the window of the kitchen to be let in, to lay under a boiler in the scullery not in use, where she has invariably deposited her eggs for the last two years; laying more frequently than any hen in my possession, and continuing to lay throughout the summer and winter.

I have on my manor four decoys, or feeding-places for wild fowl, and at each of these places the fowl are fed twice a-day. When I am at home and disengaged I generally feed the last time in the afternoon, at each of these places myself, and they are at a considerable distance apart. The one which is called the "Round Pond" has been selected by the flock as their chief home, and there the larger proportion of fowl of all kinds during the day resort. I never pass this spot without a little corn and bread, and a few acorns, in my pocket, and attended by my black retriever, " Diver," who has succeeded my late poor, dear old companion, " Brutus." From his being of the same colour as " Brutus," and much about the same size, the fowl did not recognise the difference, and therefore the only slight difficulty I had was to make the dog of eleven months old be fully aware, that when seated by and guarding my gun while I was at work in the vicinity, the strange birds that came close to him from the water had no intention of touching it, and that he was to consider all life as perfectly sacred unless I desired that it should be otherwise. At times when at these ponds, and there are several in the vicinity of the Round Pond, I have come to the place unobserved by the wild fowl, and occupied myself in planting or in widening the water, leaving my gun and dog at some distance, and nearer to the water. I have then been highly amused to hear the congratulations of the ducks to each other, and the odd croaking sort of cry of the pochards, mingled with the voices of other and rarer fowl, all having found out and recognised my dog, and forming a levée all round him, evidently under a very distinct impression that where the dog and gun are I must be; and so they waited by him in expectation of my arrival. At one time I used to feed at the Round Pond, where the chief flock was, first; but in a short time the ducks became quite aware that, after feeding there, I went to another place, and when I did so darkness was setting in. The consequence of this knowledge on their part was, that as I walked through the fields to the next feeding-place I was accompanied by the whistle of wings in the air, and before I reached my destination a considerable flock, that had already been fed, were waiting to eat the food from those who had not been so fortunate, and who, being of a much more wild humour, were not such greedy feeders while I stood by. To obviate this difficulty, I ordered one of my men every afternoon to bring down the food for the ducks, the box and the pail, or the conveyance that carries it, being well known to them, and to remain by the Round Pond till my arrival. While this was being done I fed in the other places, and so secured to the wilder birds their share of the entertainment. Some distance on the other side of the Round Pond there is a small piece of water in the woods, and this is inhabited by some pochards who never leave it;

and this pond, being nearest to my house, I feed last. With these pochards a pintailed drake, or Chinese pheasant as it is vulgarly termed, has taken up his abode, flying backwards and forwards as he lists to the Round Pond. He will be in the Round Pond when I feed the flock, and he feeds slightly in their company; but so sure as I conclude matters there, and go through the wood to the pochards, there he is again, and there he makes his supper.

A great many of these pets are very much attached to me, and they answer to their names. A large eider drake, who feeds from my hand, answers to the name of " Thomas." This bird is now in St. James's Park; and a little nondescript from an egg laid in St. James's Park comes to the call of " Tiney." What it or she is — I believe it to be a female — I cannot tell. It is not so large as a moorhen, it is a little larger than a dabchick, but not so large as a tufted duck or po-chard; it takes in its plumage of something between the female pochard and female tufted duck; — a beautiful diver, and immensely quick in action on as well as in water. It is so elastic in its con-formation that in rushing to catch a bit of barley-meal I have seen it run over and trod on by large ducks and mallards, and once I saw the large eider duck stand on it for a brief space: it never cried, and, while struggling to get free, never lost sight of the likely spot to find the food. This made me take an immense fancy to it, and the upshot of my endeavours to promote a good understanding has been crowned with success. It now feeds from my hand, and takes up a position between my feet so that nothing can interfere with it; and I must say, that of all birds I ever knew, for its size, it has the largest appetite.

I can remember people asserting in my presence, that tame pochards and tame tufted ducks were not to be obtained; and more, that they would not breed in England. At Newstead Abbey the tufted ducks in the lakes breed by hundreds, and I have known an instance of the crested grebe breeding there too. Now, however, all the assertions of would-be ornithologists, as to the breeding of the rarer wild fowl in England, are set at nought; for everything, duck, pochard, widgeon, and teal, and all sorts of water-fowl, breed in London, in St. James's Park.

A great many of my friends have asked me to write a description of my flock of wild fowl, their treatment, and their food; for, though in sight of Poole Harbour, when taking their flights at "flight time" they do not go away.

The request is very easily complied with in that phase of its relationship: the varied sorts, from the Pernambuco goose to the Bahama duck, the pintail, the shoveller, the pochard, the tufted duck, and the American wood duck, the gadwall, and the eider duck, and the widgeon, they comprise my flock.

Their food is boiled rice, barley, Indian maize, boiled and mashed potatoes mixed with toppings or barley meal, and acorns. The rarer kinds of this food are distributed to individuals by hand, but the potatoes and barley-meal and acorns are placed in quantities collectively for their general acceptance. A stable-pail full of the meal and potatoes twice a-day, at a given hour, morning and evening, disappears in no time; and it is amusing to see how they leave the coarser food in a long trough untouched, as long as there is a chance of getting anything better from my hand.

There are a thousand things too minute, but still amazingly curious in the study of my flock, which might tire some of my readers to narrate; but every hour of my study of nature brings to light new phases and fresh beauties to admire in the gift of an Omnipotent Creator, whose wisdom is seen even from the smallest insect to the elephant, from the meanest creature to ascendant man.

If Heaven gives me life and health, I hope to make the little waste on which for a time I am located a model farm as regards fowl and fish, and perhaps the culture of the willow. I have yet to test the real value of trout-hatching, but during the winter of 1866 I hope to enlighten myself and my friends on that subject; for if I had wished to have selected a spot, with shallow springs to the sun, unsubjected to floods, I could not have done better than have chosen this wherein to have watched the ova to perfection, if to useful perfection it can ever attain.

I confess that, in *regard to trout*, I am sanguine of success, after seeing the methods so well carried out by my friend Mr. Webb, at Newstead Abbey.

CHAPTER IX.

PART I.

IN these days, when it is the fashion fondly to assert that "intellect" is on its march, and "civilization" ameliorating the mental condition of man, it is curious to contrast the annals of crime and the foot-and-hand way in which learning and moral laxity tread the highways of life together.

It ever has been said that "a little learning is a dangerous thing," and my own observation leads me to the conclusion, that if man or boy be let loose, with nothing more of knowledge than the power to apply his A, B, C, it is like putting a razor into a child's hand, the keen and misdirected edge of which is sure to cut his own fingers.

To minds of a certain calibre and of a certain age, let the calibre be what it may, there can be

no doubt but that the understanding, in its first
and strong use of letters, gets more fun out of the
Newgate Calendar than out of the Prayer-book or
Bible; and that fiction — the more tragically or
disreputably horrible the better — far surpasses in
interest *The Good Boy's Little Book*, who takes
the apple that he picks up to his nurse to ask her
if he *may* eat it.

The system, too, of teaching the youthful
mind the way it should travel, even in the highest
and best-regulated families, is, perhaps, as sillily
erroneous as anything can by possibility be; for
instead of pleasantly schooling the mind at its
most malleable or plastic period in the direction
and in the ways of truth, the very first books the
child is given with which to amuse its leisure are
lies from beginning to end — fictions, deceptions
in themselves, and inculcating the most lament-
ably ignorant and false conclusions on the most
commonplace subjects, which never need to have
been thus grafted on the callow brain of the
beginner. *Jack the Giant-Killer* and *Tom Thumb*,
and a thousand other little lies, are followed up
by *Robinson Crusoe*, the *Fairy Tales*, and the
Arabian Nights' Entertainment, and other larger
fictions of the kind. All in all fiction, and not a
word of truth as a foothold on which to save the

misguided swimmer from a drowning and menda-
cious grave.

Surely, in these days of reformation, this mistake at the commencement wants revising. Why
should children from the first not be taught in the
language of truth, and be induced to study from
the amusing book of Nature? The butterfly and
the bird are attractive enough to the child; the
beautiful shell and the gleaming pebble are similarly so: then why not devise a little amusing
work, full of truth and beauty, holding out a daz-
zling path to research? and instead of the seven-
leagued boots of falsehood, which in time grow
hard and painfully oppressive, put the foot of the
child on an expansive sole, which by use becomes more easy, and every instant entices to
wider fields and to mysteries *so* lovely, *so* supreme,
so unfathomable, and *so* glorious, that the inscrutable veil which seems to hide, really just shadows
forth enough to lead the young beginner on, and
to make the child a man.

Boys and girls, when nine, ten, or twelve years
old, are as well up in a hundred literary lies, of no
use to any one, as the ridiculous books I have
alluded to can make them. They know little or
nothing more of natural history than that birds
lay eggs for boys to blow, and insects like flowers.

They have no idea that the length of their step, from stone to stone, really contains innumerable instances of bygone volcanic power; or that in the bosom of the hills they see lie evidences of former creations and of long-forgotten worlds — strange and mighty, obdurate, imperishable witnesses, upsetting the methods of the monkish scholar, outliving time, and settled to eternity!

A far better and a fairer, a more alluring, yet a firmer choice, might be made to amuse and lead the young beginner on, from " the queen of insect spring " to flower, bird, and fossil, and thence to commune with the great Creator of it all.   In every little thing it needs no microscope to see the Master-touch which passes all comprehension, which gives the splendid hue, the wondrous form, and leaps from chaos to vegetation, to reptile life, to beast and bird, and, lastly, to the soul of man, leaving to us yet a dome illimitable on which to speculate and try to dive into the mysteries of the sphere above us: a sphere as to which the first and monkish historian knew nothing, and from the appearance of which he, in his ignorance, expected nothing, and therefore wrote as of *one* world, to be condemned or saved; nor for an instant thought that in the constellations there was infinitely more than a lamplight duty, and, indeed, that there was much more in heaven and earth than was dreamed of in his philosophy, or that of his self-dubbed infallible Church.

A thousand questions might be raised on the present accepted history of the globe; and a practical naturalist, thoroughly versed in the habits, haunts, and conduct under danger of beasts of whatever kind, might take a different view of the varied bones, and the why and wherefore *they* become thus conglomerated in *caves beneath the hills*, from that loudly descanted on by the philosophers ruling the ears of the listening multitudes, who take for granted all that the big-wigs say.

A practical naturalist knows that a *flood* or *deluge* drives all living things, from the mouse to the largest creature, *out* of their holes and caverns, and *on* to the tops of the highest ground.

Passing over the terrible loss of that most important link to the ,asserted theories of the day, the fact of fossilised man, and his cousin the monkey, neither of which in a fossil state, though often claimed, *has ever been found*, it is competent to an inquiring mind to suggest the possibility of a general destruction coming from above, instead of from the rising of the waters, by stupendous rain or otherwise, and the earth—our earth—having been overwhelmed by a falling star, or hemisphere of much greater size.

Astronomic philosophers have ruled that *there are worlds* in the vast hemisphere above us which we call stars, infinitely larger than this our so-called terrestrial globe, and our personal experience has made us acquainted with the fact, that *substances*, or stones, have fallen from other worlds above us, and been picked up; and therefore, at some era of this our world's existence, it is not impossible that an overwhelming mass should have descended to crush out all existence below, and to drive beasts into caves as a natural safety-place from the overhanging ruin; safe, apparently, or at the moment, but eventually to be closed up or crushed by the superincumbent weight.

The reader's pardon must now be requested by me, inasmuch as that I have been led away, as it were, from the ridiculous to the sublime, from the living child to the fossil; so now, by permission, I will again return to the subject, with a glance at what is often given now as "the child's ball."

I never am seduced to one, but that perfect sketch—I think by my late friend Leech—in

Punch is brought to vivid recollection. I allude to the one where a little girl, about up to the bottom of the waistcoat of a moderately tall man, rushes up to her mamma with all the uncontrolled expression at that age pervading the features, and with eyes almost starting out of her head—in a voice, too, loud enough to be heard by all the room, she screams,—"Oh, mamma, there's that gentleman been and tickled me, without being properly introduced!"

It is strange, very strange, to look on and see these things; to see children, who, but for a certain vanity instilled into them by their mammas, would have been much happier in bed and asleep than capering about and aping the follies of their elders, and doing that which they would have been certain to have learnt in good time, without the application of hothouse forcing to make them bud unseasonably. If the little partners show an over-fondness for each other, and they kiss, their mammas go into ecstasies at the fun; and as they move about, dressed precisely like little fairies in a pantomime—only at balls they have no wings, but stick out behind, and show as much leg as ballet-girls—the fond mammas *in their hearing* exclaim, " Oh, has she not beautiful legs !"

The child is therefore taught to do, at an age most susceptible of impressions, all that wise mammas, at least those under an assertion of wisdom, think it right to undo the instant the child verges on the full-grown girl. Legs, like fruit, are netted when they are in perfection, and lips warned off with all the zest that game-preservers show against the trespasser. Under the present system of education, or "bringing up," it is a miracle if the mamma finds a path unencumbered with thorns or free from scratches.

The word "miracle" reminds me of a fact in the Emerald Isle, and takes me away from a subject that is too serious, and might be made too long. Blessings, then, on Ould Ireland! Why she should bear that ancient definition more than her sister, Scotland, for the life of me I never could discover. But, "yer honour, it is the word 'miracle' that now lades to my discoorse."

A young Irish peasant, or "pisant," as it is more properly pronounced, was induced from curiosity, as *he* asserted, but more likely, as *I* think, on account of some "famale" inducement, to attend a series of controversial lectures given in his parish by a busy agent of "the Irish Church Missionary Society." At these gatherings the subject of miracles was discussed, disputed, and taken to pieces—" Oh, by me faith ! all over I don't know how."

The "broth of a boy" was puzzled; " bedad, he was all abroad;" but by no means convinced that the Church in which he had been brought up was wrong as to the doctrines that had been hammered into his head and tail. " If she 's wrong," he said, " on my soul I 've been a suffering innocent." Still Paddy, with all his slavish subservience to the Romish Church, had too much shrewdness in his composition to deem that it was impossible that the Irish Church Mission should be right. "Faith," he said, " we know our priests are right; but, divil's in it, but t'other may be right too:" so, after pondering over the matter for some days, he resolved to seek a thorough explanation from Father Tom, his burly parish priest. " Bedad," he said to himself, smiting his thigh with his right hand, "ould Father Tom " (he was not much older than Paddy was) "shall give me, by the powers of snuff, the full explanation of the term ' miracle.' "

One fine morning, about eight o'clock, bent on this intellectual explanation, Paddy presented himself at the door of his priest's house; but as he did so, at a glance through the parlour window

he saw that his Riverence was eating his breakfast.
"Be my soul," he said, "it's not me that'll disturb
the good father just now, and make him, like his
loaf, a bit crusty."

Thinking thus, and being a civil fellow, shy
of intruding on privacy, for the moment he contented himself with walking up and down on the
little gravel-sweep that led through the grass-
plot to the door; when, by-and-by, the priest,
surmising that Paddy wished to speak to him,
came forth, and accosting him said,—

"Well, my man, you want me, I suppose?
Nothing wrong, I hope?"

"Yes, your Riverence—no, your Riverence,"
replied Pat, pulling off his tattered or crushed
hat, and answering both questions at once. "I'm
in throuble in the mind of me, yer Riverence,
and I am come to see if you will help me
out?"

"Certainly, Pat," rejoined the priest; "let me
hear all about it!"

"Well, then, yer Riverence, I'd be a'ter axin'
you to explain to me the meaning of a 'miracle.'
I want to hear what it is, and what it isn't!"

"Pat! Pat!" exclaimed the priest, severely in-
terrupting him, and shaking his head, "I'm grieved
to think that you have been led astray to some

of these Irish Church Missions—temptations, Pat, delusions of the devil!—and that your mind has been upset."

" No—yes—no—yer Riverence."

" Come, come!" exclaimed the priest, again cutting him very short. "Come, come! now Pat, no lies! tell the truth, ye vagabond! for, by the holy Virgin, I'll get it out of ye!"

" Well then, yer Riverence, it *was* at them lectures, as they call 'em, that, be my faith, 'ris up the difficulty; that made me wish my holy father to explain to me the maning of the word 'miracle,' what it was, and what it was not."

" I'm sorry to hear it, Pat," replied the priest. "Ye'd no sort of business there; but, never mind, I'll explain what a miracle is. Turn round!"

Pat obeyed at once; when, on turning his back to the priest, who was a hale, strong man, he found himself propelled several yards by a well-directed and powerful application of the holy foot, where, according to *Hudibras*, a kick well-placed

> " Hurts honour more
> Than many wounds laid on before."

" Did you feel *that?*" inquired the priest.

" *Fale* it, yer honour?" echoed Pat, with a

rueful countenance; "fale it! Begor I did, yer Riverence; and, faith, there 's no mistake!" rubbing away to ease the pain.

"Well, Pat," exclaimed the priest, "*it would be a miracle if you didn't;* and that 's all I can do for you!"

I shall never forget a scene that happened on Lord Sefton's ground at the great coursing meeting at Altcar, when the greyhound of a Roman Catholic priest, widely known at that time at all the English and Irish coursing meetings, was running well in for one of the largest stakes.

The Irish greyhound was having rather the best of the course, but with all the work yet to do, when, on a sudden turn of the hare, while he was holding her in check, and thought to kill her, he made his rush, missed his catch, and with a tremendous impetus shot well into one of those deep watery ditches that intersect the lands. For an instant the holy father, the owner of the dog, stood silent and transfixed, in an impatient expectation to see his dog get out again and catch up his opponent, who was, in the meantime, gaining point on point with his hare, and sweeping out all that the priest's dog had previously gained. Instead of getting out, however, the greyhound, with his forelegs, head, neck, and chest, on the edge of the bank, remained there, struggling for no apparent reason, but just as if something had hold of his hinder legs beneath the surface of the water, preventing him from ascending to dry land; and thus he remained till the other dog had won, what, in the last part of it, had become a single-handed course.

All I now remember beyond the position of the dog is, that the priest suddenly became natural, which, being interpreted, means violently vulgar; and his expostulations, anathemas, exorcisms, and exhortations, were of the most curiously violent kind that it is possible to imagine. He accused the devil of being in the ditch, and under water, holding on to the hind legs of his dog; excommunicated my noble relative the landlord, and the land, for having a ditch of that description; and made one of the most drunken, unworthy servants of one of the best masters—my poor, dear, departed friend, William Lawrence, of the Greenway near Cheltenham—exclaim, "Well, that is something like swearing! *Did* any one ever hear tell of such a priest?"

While on this subject, and speaking of drunkards, I must tell an Irish tale, which may well have for a heading, "The Fruits of Experience."

An incorrigible drunkard had been sent to jail for an assault committed in one of his whisky insanities on some unoffending creature unfortunate enough to come in his way. While in prison, of course, he did not get the "laste taste" of his beloved comfort: so, on the morning of his discharge, he felt himself, as he expressed it, "lost for a dhrop of the rale thing." "Divil a stiver," however, was in his pocket to prevent "the fiend from dancing there;" so, as he had not the money for a "dhrop," he drew on his wits, having no banker, to see if, by any possibility, he could raise the wind. In coming up a street that shall be nameless, he saw a spirit-dealer whom he knew, and *who, unfortunately, knew him,* standing at his shop-door, and on the instant a happy thought struck him.

"God and the powers above bless you, Misther ——! an' give us a glass of whisky. By me sowl, I niver got the laste taste of a dhrop these last three months in them dry stone walls!"

"So best for you, Mike," shortly replied the spirit-merchant; "and I'll give you none now."

"See now, thin, Mr. ——, if you did, you wouldn't be sorry; for it's meself can tell you something that may be, or might won day, sarve you yet," rejoined Mike.

" Sarve me!" exclaimed the spirit-merchant; " where could you have heard anything that would sarve me?"

" There, begaut, in the ' Stone Jug,' sure weren't we always talking of you?" replied Mike. "Come, Mr. ——, jest one little glass. Begorra, it's a quart you'd give me if you knew what I had to tell!"

The curiosity of the spirit-merchant became excited; just a toss-off of the creature comfort would not ruin him: so he took Mike into his shop and gave him the glass of whisky he asked for.

" Now," said the spirit-merchant, as Mike, with a smack of his lips, handed back the glass, " I have done my part, now do yours. What is it that you can tell me, that I would give a quart to know?"

" Well," replied Mike, sideling away to get near the door, and be ready for a run, "it's jest this,—the first time *you* are put upon the treadmill keep to the right of all, and *you'll* be able to lean your shoulder agin the wall."

Off Mike started, leaving the enraged, duped, and insulted spirit-merchant at the end of an

empty kick, which he had aimed at his victimiser,
and at his door, swearing at the flying vagabond
as long as he could trace a rag on his retreating
limbs.

CHAPTER X.

PART II.

I MUST now take my readers into the drawing-room at Berkeley Castle, wherein Lady Betty Berkeley — before she became Lady Betty Germaine—was sitting with her mother, when the door opened and in came Dean Swift, in a state of furious excitement; and holding an open letter in his hand, which he had received from Lord Berkeley, who was then for a few days at Cranford, near Hounslow, thus addressed Lady Berkeley,—

" Oh that I was but a Captain of Horse, my lady!" exclaimed the Dean; " if I did not make you a widow, I'd be d——d!"

" Hush!" cried Lady Betty, holding up her hand.

" I'd be divided into fragments to feed the crows, then," continued Swift, " ere I put up with

such a letter as this! God's sooth! has not a man
a right to do as he likes with his own? and yet
here's my Lord blackguarding me like a pick-
pocket!"

"And what have you been doing now?" exclaimed both the ladies at once: "what has called
down on your somewhat irreverent head my
Lord's anger?"

"What!" cried the Dean: "no more than this.
I asked his Lordship to pay the principal and interest of some money due to me into the hands
of my friend Gay; who, with his usual desire to
serve himself, and his friends too, with my consent intended to invest the interest in lottery-
tickets about to come out; when we should stand
a good chance to win ten thousand pounds. I told
Gay, too, to do something—or, in fact, whatever
he thought best—with the principal sum: and just
hear what the husband and father says to his spiritual adviser and chaplain, commenting, as he
proceeds, on a letter he had previously received
from me!"

These are his Lordship's sentiments:—" I
never designed to have wrote to you any more, because you bantered and abused me so grossly in
your last. To flatter a man from whom you can get
nothing, nor expect anything, is doing mischief for

mischief's sake; and, consequently, highly immoral. However, I will not carry my resentment so far as to stand by and see you undone, without giving you both notice and advice. Could any man but you think of trusting John Gay with his money? None of his friends would ever trust him with his own, when they could avoid it. He has called in the 200*l.* I had of yours; I paid him both principal and interest. I suppose by this time he has lost it. I give you notice you must look upon it as annihilated."

" ' Now, as I have considered, your Deanery of St. Patrick brings you in little or nothing, and that you keep servants and horses, and frequently give little neat dinners, which are more expensive than a few splendid entertainments; besides which, you may be said to water your flock with *French* wine, which altogether must consume your substance in a little while: I have thought of putting you in a method that may retrieve your affairs. In the first place, you must turn off all your servants and sell your horses (I will find exercise for you). Your whole family must consist of only one sound, wholesome wench. She will make your bed and warm it; besides washing your linen and mending it, darning your stockings, &c."

There! there! exclaimed Swift, there's a

pretty sermon from a Lord!   And he concludes a lot more of such-like stuff and his letter by the following words:—" Adieu; continue to be merry and wise, but never turn serious or cunning.' If his advice as to my household and state of affairs is not enough to turn a man serious, I don't know what is."

" Well, my good Dean," replied Lady Berkeley, " you must settle all your differences with my Lord: we women will have nothing to do with men's quarrels.   And now to other matters.   Betty has long thought of taking the Beauty of Berkeley, Biddy Floyd, as a companion on her marriage; she has been with her here at the Castle a great deal, as you are aware, before her marriage, and now she says she must have her at Drayton."

"What!" cried Swift; " rob our hamlet of its loveliness at ' one fell swoop?'   Why, there'll be no youths at church to hear us pray if Biddy is not there, and the ' reens ' will be full of drowned and disappointed lovers!   Take her away, my lady! In God's name consider what you do! it will be a loss to the community."

As the Dean thus delivered himself, Lord and Lady Bolingbroke, the Duchess of Queensbury, and others, who were guests at the Castle, came in, when the conversation became more general for a short time, and then again reverted to Lady Betty Berkeley's expressed intention of having the rural beauty with her as her constant attendant.

" And is she, this friend of yours, *so* beautiful," said her Grace of Queensbury, " that it would drive the men of the Berkeley Vale mad to take her away?   My life on it you overrate her powers, and underrate the great capability that all men have of consoling themselves with new faces. What is she like, most reverend Dean? there are no better judges than you are.   Come, Dean, were we to tell you to give us a recipe from which to form a beauty, would you borrow a lineament from the face or a limb from the fair form of your rural enslaver, or would you seek elsewhere for ingredients for fascination ?"

" No, on my life," replied the Dean :. " give me but a few moments and I will write you out a recipe to form a beauty."

So saying, the Dean went to a writing-table a little apart from his friends, and with scarce the delay of five minutes produced and read the following lines :—

> " When Cupid did his grandsire Jove entreat
> To form some beauty by a new receipt,
> Jove sent and found, far in a country scene,
> Truth, innocence, good-nature, looks serene ;

> From which ingredients, first, the dextrous boy
> Picked the demure, the awkward, and the coy.
> The Graces from the court did next provide
> Breeding, and wit, and air, and decent pride.
> These Venus cleans'd from every spurious grain
> Of nice coquette, affected, pert and vain;
> Jove mixed up all, and the best clay employed,
> Then called the happy composition—Floyd."

Pending the marriage of Lady Betty Berkeley to Sir John Germaine, there was asked to the Castle a very large amount of visitors, as well as a constant succession of them, and Biddy Floyd was frequently by the side of Lady Betty, and came in for an immense amount of admiration. She was not only beautiful, but there was a freshness and vivacity in her conversation, though still governed by a retiring modesty, which sat very well upon her; and being very beautifully dressed under the supervision of her patrons at the Castle, and Lady Betty taking great delight in what is termed " bringing her out," and putting her forward, all the best young men of fashion of the day were often at her side, and doing that by her which in these days would be called " flirting." For myself, I confess I do not know the exact definition of " flirting," unless it be a predilection for pretty and agreeable society: if it be so, then I am a flirt, and have been so all my life.

Poets, infinitely more modern than Swift, have spoken of a sailor's grief being so poignant " that his head was turned, and so he chewed his pigtail till he died." In respect to Biddy Floyd, her delight was so great that, her head being in some measure turned, she might similarly and pleasurably have masticated her back hair till she died : more luxuriant and less hard would have been the end, and less difficult the rumination. Still, still, in those brilliant and splendid *réunions* in the old Castle, in the midst of a profusion of light to make gay the dim tapestries of the chambers, and the old black oaken beams of the great hall, Biddy's mind used occasionally to stray to the emerald fields of the Vale, to the primrose banks and cowslip meads, to the fields and little brook near Thornbury Castle, and to the stile where she last parted from George, and told him " that she could make no promise." If she were carried away for hours, and for days and nights, by the scenes of the higher gaieties in which she now so constantly mixed, and gave a delighted ear to the whispered nothings of her titled admirers, still, occasionally, a small murmur in her heart would seem to ask if she had utterly renounced George, and if they were never to meet again in those calm, those sweet, those well-remembered scenes, where he was so eloquent, so happy, and she seemed so pleasantly to listen ?

As Biddy drove through the hundred, through the hamlet, through the Chase, here, there, and everywhere, George very frequently saw her— saw her surrounded by ladies in the highest ranks of " the Upper Ten Thousand," and sedulously paid attention to by the splendidly-dressed and well-looking gallants of the day. She did not write to him, and he had no opportunity of speaking to her; and poor George's love was too mighty, too sincere and honest, to be lightly dealt with. He felt it to be so, and resolved to " put it to the touch, to win or lose it all."

Whatever is talked of in the castle is sure to be talked of in the town. Lord Berkeley was about to go to Ireland as one of the Lords Justices, and to take Swift with him as chaplain and private secretary ; but Swift lost the chaplaincy by conduct alluded to in the letter from Lord Berkeley, already quoted : and indeed his conduct generally, with " Stella " and others, was not at all in accordance with high clerical position. To the broad, or what would now be called blackguardism, of his witty but coarse epigrams, as seen in *Swiftiana*, in Scott's *Life of Swift*, and in many of his doggerel lines on persons and on places, conjointly with other things, no doubt is due the interference of Dr. King, in regard to his being presented to the rich Deanery of Derry, then in the gift of Lord Berkeley, and intended for him by his patron.

The Lord of the Castle and his chaplain being about to depart for Ireland after Lady Betty's marriage, was a stirring topic in the hundred of Berkeley, and over the lands between, and in the cities of Bristol and Gloucester.

The marriage, too, of Lady Betty was deeply interesting to the vicinity ; but underneath that great ruffle on the local tide of affairs there was a little under-current, of not half the width of the commotion above, but, as regarded one young man at least, of deeper and tenfold more force than anything else that met the superficial gaze.

Poor George felt, in spite of himself, that Biddy Floyd liked the Castle and its society better than his cottage and the dairy, the orchard, and an association with the middle class. Still, though against his will he was aware of this, he resolved to bring matters to a point the first opportunity, and one was not long in placing itself to his acceptance, for in one of her walks in the Castle meadows he met Biddy Floyd alone, and unattended.

Poor George’s handsome face flushed up as he took Biddy’s hand ; and so did her face, too : but, alas ! their manner of greeting was widely different. His bearing was replete with the sincerity of settled purpose ; while hers was that of timidity, or, so to speak, of a commandant of a fortress forcibly and seriously beleaguered who contemplated a capitulation. Not in any way touching a surrender, but an honourable evacuation and retreat, carrying off side-arms, horses, and swords. In short, Biddy found herself face to face with an interview she would rather have avoided, and obliged to give some sort of explanation on points which, in unguarded, and therefore happy hours, she had conceded to her undoubted lover.

I will not tire my readers, as county chairmen and judges of assize tire a conclave of stupid men, yclept “ twelve honest jurors,” by pretending to sum up, or, in legal phrase, to confuse their obtuse intellects ; but having to do with a more enlightened jury, in a much wider sense of the word, many of whom, no doubt, have been in similar situations as the one I have described with other Biddys, I will simply go on to say, that the interview in the Castle meadows was painful to both. Painful to Biddy, because she had no other way of retreating save by referring to the fatal words at Thornbury,— " She could not or would not promise," or by directly telling George that high place and lofty preferment had induced her to change her mind. When they came to a spot where they were to separate, " Well, Biddy," exclaimed George, his broad chest heaving with a hurricane of woe and immediate and prospective misery, " at least may God in His goodness bless you ! For myself, the sun of my life has set : I gather more from your manner than from any words you have spoken, and I know my hopes are crushed. As to my staying here in the once sweet and happy Vale, your footstep impalpably impressed on every path, your breath in every flower, and your presence out on the view wherever the scene is loveliest, that I *will not do*. Look to Stinchcombe height yonder," pointing with his outstretched arm as he spoke. " Biddy, it is called ' Breakheart Hill,' and as it now from the distance throws its Cotswold frown on us, it seems to echo the name of its steepest hill in my poor distracted breast."

As he said this, Biddy Floyd, with slow and hesitating steps, took a path leading directly to the Castle ; while George, with the precipitancy of insanity, rushed in the direction of the town.

The gaieties at the Castle were over; Lord Berkeley was gone to Ireland, taking Dean Swift with him; Lady Betty's marriage was consummated; and after the honeymoon Betty Floyd had left Berkeley and joined her as a permanent friend and companion, and the Vale of the Severn was reft of its chief female attraction. George had left his town, and the Vale too, and no one knew in what direction he had gone; for when a hale and athletic young man once gives himself to the breeze of Misfortune, with Despair at the helm, it is a wild guess as to what port he will steer for.

Many weeks had not elapsed before there was an account in the press, though the newspapers then were infinitely fewer and primitively diminutive in comparison with what they are now (I have *The Times* in my possession when it was not much larger than a sheet of foolscap paper), that a vessel had been wrecked at Puffin Island, a site much visited by tourists from Bangor, and an eye-witness to the *débris* of the disaster wrote to his relations at Berkeley in substance as follows :—

" I was one of those, when the weather moderated, to land on Puffin Island, and to search for the relics of the sad catastrophe that had happened. Still dashing against the precipitous side of the island were portions of the wreck, sea-weeds and a sail, sea-weeds and a mast or rigging, and fragments of wood rising and falling with the swell of the subsiding sea. Around and above us were thousands of gulls, shrieking their varied and discordant cries, and gracefully, as if without an effort of the wing, floating in the air close over our heads. All at once our attention was called to the opposite side of the island from its cliffs, to where it simply rises above the water by a steep bank; for there the air was absolutely crowded by all sorts of fowl of the sea-going tribe, but chiefly by gulls, all screaming in portentous and mournful clamour, and all dipping in their hovering flight at some object beneath the bank. Ornithologists or not, we all at once had our attention riveted to the spot, and, without a word expressive of such intention, all my companions in breathless silence hastened to the scene indicated by the birds. A strange and curiously sad spectacle awaited our inspection. Just above the level of the water, then calm and still, but until that morning washed by the heaving waves, in a sort of crevice in the bank lay the corpse of a fine young man. He seemed in the energy of despair to have clung with his hands to a projecting stone or boulder, and in the last agony of death to have turned on his back, and been kept in that position by the stiffened muscular arm that had held a point of the stone or rock in the curve of the elbow-joint. The face was handsome, calm in its expression, but deeply impressed with what I can only describe as confirmed melancholy; but the curious and strange part of it was, that a little puffin, in its spotless purity of down, washed from its nest at some point, and in its callow state unable long to contend with the boisterous waves, had found a resting-place in the bosom of the drowned man, in which it nestled with the tenacity of a tiny object clinging for its poor life."

After inspection proved that the corpse thus given back by the sea, the only one recovered, was poor George, the handsomest and most amiable young man of the town, or hamlet, or hundred of Berkeley.

And how fared it with Biddy Floyd, or with "Mistress Floyd," as it was the fashion in her new state and station to call her? In a letter dated June 5th, 1733, from Lady Betty Germaine to Dr. Swift, her ladyship says,—"You are angry if I do not mention Mrs. Floyd to you; so I must tell you she has gone for a little time into the country, to try if that will cure her cough." In another letter she had written,—"Mrs. Floyd has been excessively bad and dispirited, but country air may revive her." In other letters, again, Lady Betty alludes to her dulness, and that "she never says a word." The account from Berkeley had reached her of the death of her handsome and rural lover; she thought, perhaps, of the days when she reigned the queen of the wall, the wall-flower, or flower of perfection, when her walks in the sweet fields on the banks of the Severn were as fresh and free from any annoyances, as her life in the sumptuous halls were full of them; and many an hour and many a night she pondered over the scenes she had left and the lover she had discarded, contrasting the impetuous honesty of his professions with the cautious whisperings and dubious promises of the many that had essayed her ear since she parted with George in the meads beneath Berkeley Castle.

I am not apt to sermonize, or give unsolicited advice or caution to lovers, yet if, on parting, the loved one tells the lover that " she can make no promises," if he asked my advice I should tell him instantly to rush forth into the gardens of Eve, and to court snakes and serpents to give him the apple of forgetfulness; for if he continues to cherish his unrequited and hopeless passion after that iced assurance, his peace of mind is irrecoverably gone, and his enjoyment of the splendid blessings of this life, among them all the sincere and implicitly trusting love of woman, is not worth the purchase of a single hour.

CHAPTER XI.

Part III.

When Marguerite parted from the Jesuit priest, leaving him still cowering upon the trunk of the fallen tree, as if to some extent stricken by her displeasure, she repaired instantly to her father, whom she found seated in his study with many papers and letters before him, apparently of a disagreeable nature. It was, therefore, easy for her affectionate eyes at once to read, though considerably discomposed as she had been, that something had seriously annoyed the Justice, and that he was in no humour to be trifled with. Hastily pushing up his spectacles — his usual wont when he wanted to look at anything—he somewhat testily exclaimed on her entrance,—

"Another time, my child; I can't be teased with trivial matters now."

"It is no trivial matter, dearest father," she replied, "that I come to speak of. I hasten to tell you that I have obeyed your commands, and parted with Willie,"—she checked herself—"with Master Barnwell for ever. Oh, papa, papa, forgive me; we did at times meet in our walks, but after the last interview, when you showed your trust and affection in and for me, I resolved not to see nor to speak to Master Barnwell any more, *and I have told him so.*" As she said this she threw herself into her father's arms, and sobbed upon his bosom.

Justice Wellrode clasped her affectionately, while he parted her beautiful but dishevelled hair upon her forehead, and kissed its snowy surface. "I knew, my child," he said, "that I could trust thee not to encourage a stranger, nor in any way to transgress my wishes; you have then set my heart at rest, and you will think of that young man no more." Her father seemed to take this as a fact accomplished, and continued,—"There are higher destinies, my child, for thee. I have been thinking that the good knight, Sir Caldwell Hunter, though sorely maligned, is not so bad."

"Oh, father, father!" almost shrieked the girl in an agony of terror, as she clung more closely to him, "speak not that horrid name now

—not now! I have done all I could in obedience to your wishes—I will do all I can; but pray, pray tax me on that distressful subject now no further. Let me rest; give me time for rest and thought: the priest has been urging the dreadful alternative on me till he has made me almost mad. I think—I *will* think of Master Barnwell no more; there is *no pledge*, there has been *no gift between us*, and he will forget me: dear, dear father, I will not disobey you. Please, then, pardon your obedient child; and as she loves you, and attends to your commands, be merciful to her, and outrage not her heart and soul."

It would, indeed, have been a hard heart, and a father made of strange and obdurate metal, who could have resisted an appeal so urgent from such a lovely creature. Justice Wellrode folded his daughter once more in his arms, and kissing her again and again with the utmost affection, said, " There, there; hush thee, my child; thou shalt not be vexed, and I will not now tease thee any further: thy happiness is very dear to me, so let us change the subject. Thou hast pledged thyself to obey me—so now be as happy as ever."

The afternoon then wore on; night came, and Marguerite, wearied with the scenes she had undergone, retired very early to rest, and sank in deep slumber on her pillow. When lovely youth and innocence thus sinks to sleep, to dream perhaps of happier hours, or, like the rose, to gain that healthful strength that makes the flower scent the air, and give sweetness to the world, and draw around it the richest wings that sunbeams call to life, surely there should be some waking angel on the watch to stifle villany, to crush the corroding worm, to save the beauty of the flower, and scare the mischief-worker from his evil deeds, the plotter from the path. Was there no Power on high, so frequently evoked by him for ill, to warn the Jesuit priest against a deed so dark and mean, that felon low might blush to do it? There was, or there seemed to be, none! Ill, for the time, *was* given any length of tether, good kept back, misfortune revelled high, and chance, as chance so often does, stood firm the friend of crime, and Father Crawl prevailed; but how or when he did so, a return to the evil-doer alone can show.

We left him, then, after his interview with Marguerite at the fallen tree, an admitted guest to the cottage of Mary's father, at Lane End.

Father Crawl found the old man seated at his frugal table with his wife and daughter. The trio rose respectfully when they saw the priest, though, if the dark eyes of Mary had been closely watched, they might have been seen to emit a considerable, though a carefully-suppressed flash of hatred and indignation, not unmixed with awe. The priest motioned them to be seated, talked of the weather, and then, as if by accident, spoke of Willie, saying how much addicted to sport he was, and what a pity it seemed that he did not do something to earn his bread. "By-the-by," he added, addressing the old man, "was he not concerned in some scrape which you and your daughter got into?"

"Scrape, sir!" cried Mary, blushing up; "no, there was no scrape, sir! he saved the life of father and myself, and I'm sure we must for ever be thankful to him for it."

"Thankful to him under grace!" solemnly remarked the cold, inanimate voice of the priest, crossing himself, and now guarded and schooled as usual.

"What was it in which he thus befriended you?"

"Why sir," said the old man, "Mary and I were coming home one night, when 'twas very dark and foggy, guiding our steps by the Beacon Lantern in the distance, then lit on the verge of the wood, which we could see, though it was ar beyond our cottage, looking from the direction we were coming, when suddenly two ruffians sprang out of the bushes, one of whom struck me down while the other seized on Mary. The girl cried for help, while I endeavoured to struggle to my feet; but the robber, or whatever he was, was too much for me. Just then there came such a blow—I think I hear it now—right on the head of my assailant, which laid him sprawling over me, and then such another blow to the villain as had got hold of Mary, and she was safe too. Then we found ourselves all alone, except Master Willie and his dog, who gave one of the villains a good grip, too: it was them that came to our rescue!"

"Truly," replied the imperturbable priest, "truly a drunken brawl, no doubt: but, well, what happened then? Did you thank your deliverer next day?"

"No, sir. We thanked him then and there, and he saw us home; but the next Sunday as ever was, me and my old woman, and Mary here, took him down to West Wycombe some nice new-laid eggs, and said all we could to show our gratitude."

"Well, and what said the nice young man?" replied the snake-like priest. "Did he make you welcome, and give you anything in return?"

" No—yes; leastways we did not want anything," replied the labourer: "but Mary saw a little picture of Master Willie hanging on the wall, and, girl like, she admired it very much: so, seeing she was greatly taken with it, he said he'd give it her, and she has got it now. I warrant it's safe enough, for she sets great store by it."

"His picture, indeed!" rejoined the priest. "I like to look at pictures. May I see it?"

" Run, Mary! run upstairs!" cried her father to the now still more reluctant girl; "go fetch the picter, and let his reverence see it, for 'tis very pretty."

Mary did as her father commanded her, but the keen glance of Father Crawl detected a desire on her part to disobey, had she dared to have done so. She being longer away than seemed necessary, the priest made himself unusually conversable with the old couple; and observing a pack of dirty cards on the mantel-piece, over the little fire-place, he suggested " a game." While thus playing with the old woman his restless little eyeballs occasionally peeped from the corner of his half-closed lids, as it were impatient for Mary's appearance. When she came, however, with the little portrait in her hand, much about the size of one of the cards with which he was playing, he seemed to lose all interest in her. She put the picture by his side, hoping devoutly that he would forget that it was there; when, scarcely looking at it, he put some of the tricks he had won on it, his handkerchief as well being on the table. The old people sat up, taking turn-about to play with his reverence, and more than once suggested that Mary should retire to rest, or she would not be up with the dawn of day to cull some water-cresses. In obedience to this reiterated command, she approached the table to look for her treasured likeness; but her parents asked her why she tarried, and ordered her at once to bed. It was indeed most reluctantly that Mary then left the room; and as she did so, she fixed her bright, dark eyes on the priest, in a look that, coupled with suspicion, bordered on the most intense distrust. The old people were now fast nodding to sleep over their games: so the priest rose, and casting the cards down with the words, " One, two, there's luck in my shoe," as a sort of interjection, perhaps, to show that *he had won*, he, at the same time, gathered up his pocket-handkerchief, gave them his blessing and a good-night. and went away.

Leaving the priest to wend his course to the Grove, we must request our readers to abide with us yet awhile in the now deserted little cottage room. The cottage had become perfectly quiet, the only noise being a duet of snoring diversely played by the respective noses of the old couple, accompanied by the ticking of their clock, when quietly, and with great care, a little door, which shut Mary's room from what might be called the parlour, was seen to open. The crack between the door and the post at first only admitted the eyes of the gazer—had there been one—to a light and narrowed view of Mary's dark eyes and pretty face. She then stepped lightly to the table, and turned over the cards. Suddenly a look, not only of anxiety, but even of horror, suffused her features. She searched the cards again and again, then looked upon the ground, and then on every shelf, and all over the little apartment, and then, with a sigh of alarm, she uttered, " He has stolen it!" Whatever she sought for not being to be found, like a statue she stood stock-still, the tears streaming down her face, and whispering to herself in agony,—"The snake, the snake has got it!" She then turned softly to her room, and going to bed sobbed herself to sleep.

When the priest reached the Grove he found that Marguerite had retired to her room, but that her father was still up, and busied with his papers. He knocked at the door, and was admitted to the study.   When an old man has sat for a length of time at his desk, and has had an already wearied brain, vexed by written communications and figures of the most confused as well as annoying import, he is rather apt to be angry with an interruption of any kind, more particularly if the intruder brings further unwelcome news; and thus he received Father Crawl rather ungraciously, because that worthy but rather difficult-to-be-understood divine, had taken it into his head to put on some expression to his features which he wished his patron to read as real concern at being the bearer of the painful tale he desired to tell.   The Justice saw this, and was proportionably peevish.

" What now, father?" he exclaimed; "what's in the wind now?"

"Alas!" replied the priest, " it is my sad duty to tell you that your daughter is *not* obeying your commands; that she keeps up clandestine interviews and correspondence with the young scapegrace, Master Barnwell; and having accepted him as her lover, that, sir, is *the real reason* why she will not listen to the proposal of our good friend, Sir Caldwell."

" Tut, man!" replied the Justice; " you bring me this intelligence, founded on you know not what; you are not used to the ways of girls, and you start at trifles, and shrink at every light cloud that passes.   Marguerite has but just left me; she has told me all—I know all about it; she met this young man more than once; but when I expressed my wishes in regard to the matter, she obeyed me like a dear, good child as she is, and severed the connexion.   It arose by accident, and now it's all forgotten.   *I can trust her;* aye, aye, sir priest, she never told an untruth in her life, and always abides by what she says: and as to marrying her to the Knight, we'll talk of that some other time."

The priest at once saw that it was no use to attempt to reason with a weak, and therefore an obstinate man, and that a man of that calibre was as likely to be accidentally obstinate for good, as he might have been, and often had been, blindly attached to evil.   So, with a blessing, uttered in the very reverse of the usual temper of that term, he crossed himself; and grossly vindictive, and bent on an especial and vile purpose, he returned, for the time, to his little dormitory.

The blessed, blissful sun of summer rose in unclouded brilliancy on the following morn, and even before his beams had given brightness to the world around the Grove, the lark and partridge had begun to sing and call, the first of the feathered creation to herald the approach of day. Marguerite had arisen calm, sorrowful, but refreshed by that sleep so bountifully bestowed on youth, had met her father at breakfast, and was now trying to amuse herself with the flowers in her garden, while the Justice was again busied in the details of accounts and letters. The morn had reached that age when domestic or household arrangements had for the day been done; the house was set fair, and the sleeping apartments opened to the summer breeze. Marguerite in the garden, her father in his study, the domestics occupied below, why stood the priest on a landing-place on the stairs in listening attitude, as if to assure himself that all were away, and that *there he stood alone?* That landing-place led to two rooms. The one was the apartment of the Justice Wellrode, the other of his dearly-loved and obedient child, who, in a matter as near to her heart as anything earthly could be, and only the day before, had obeyed her father to the letter, and because *he* *trusted* to her truth and obedience, had severed from her lover. It was to the lock of this door that Father Crawl stretched forth a presumptuous hand, and, after a moment's pause, " with ears laid back to listen and the beard on his shoulder," he writhed his stealthy gait noiselessly into the apartment, and approached her bed. Was there nothing sacred about that snowy pillow and neatly and smoothly-arranged counterpane, to whisper mercy to him on the lovely form for whom it was intended in her innocent rest, and to evoke his pity? Was there in his inmost soul no reference to, no fear of, the holy goodness of the Name he so often loudly appealed to—no dread of the symbol he so often signed? None. He had neither dread of nor compunction for the deed he was about to do. A breathing illustration of " Peru," his eyes were tearless, and for any softer current in his thoughts, they, like the air in Peru, had but one. That one current, unencountered by any other air, ran on — arid, pitiless, tearless, and dry: it carried its wretched possessor to the neglect of all true religion and to the extreme of selfish design. He approached that snowy and hitherto sacred little bed, drew from his pocket the picture of Willie which he had stolen from Mary in her father's cottage, and carefully deposited it beneath poor Marguerite's pillow, and *then* sought her father. He knew where to find the weak and deluded victim, entered his study, and thus accosted him, for he dreaded the discovery of

the picture ere he had had time to work out the
value he attached to its present position:—

"Sir," he said, "I have come to you on a
serious matter, because I know you to be deceived.
You think—in fact you assured me but last night,
that your daughter had broken off her acquaintance with Master Barnwell. *Indeed she has not.*
I know they are betrothed, and in a blessed revelation made to me last night by one from among
the holiest dead, I am confidently and fully assured that they have plighted their troth to each
other, and *that your daughter sleeps each night
with the picture of her lover beneath her pillow.*
If you have any sinful doubt of what I tell you,
come with me: you have a right to enter her
chamber, and you may convince yourself."

Justice Wellrode rose from his table with
cheeks livid with rage. He was angry at being
disturbed, and violently incensed by the idea that
he had been deceived in the faith he held in his
only child. Ill in health and disordered in mind
and body, he would not have been displeased to
have had even the priest himself, by way of a
channel on which to wreak his wrath. While his
child was sorrowfully yet innocently employed
attending to her flowers, Justice Wellrode ascended
the stairs, followed by Father Crawl, rushed into

her room, and rudely raised the pillow from her bed; then, *there indeed was Willie's picture!* The concentrated essence of human rage, the picture of fury, the Justice, for an instant speechless, glared upon the portrait; the priest, with crossed hands and an affectation of deep humility, stood looking on from his half-closed cold grey eyes; but at that instant Marguerite came in behind them, and beheld in astonishment the scene that was presented. Her father at once turned upon her with the blind and temporary insanity of a weak man.

"So, so, minion!" he cried, "this is your obedience! this is the reward of affection and faith I have ever had in you! You told me no engagement, no gift had passed between you and this young man," rapping the picture violently; "and here I find his gift to you, a treasured pledge, beneath your pillow!"

Completely bewildered at what she saw, she could only exclaim,—

"Oh, papa, you wrong me!"

"I wonder not," he continued, "at your confusion; but there, away with this accursed bauble!" Thus saying, with the utmost fury he flung the picture out of the window, and then rudely pushing his daughter further into her apartment, said, —"I'll teach you to disobey and to deceive me.

If good faith and affection cannot keep you within
bounds, we will see what lock and key will do;
henceforth you are a prisoner."

Thus saying, he quitted the room in company
with Father Crawl, and, locking the door upon
her, descended to his study.

While these events were passing, Mary the
cottage girl, carrying on her head her freshly-
gathered water-cresses, with the usual freedom to
the premises assigned her had entered by the
garden-gate. As she neared the house something
struck heavily on the soft contents of her basket,
and she turned round under the impression that a
mischievous boy had flung a stone at her; but
seeing no one she passed on, in time to catch the
few last angry words of Justice Wellrode, the
slamming of a door, and then the heartrending and
hysterical sobs of the sweet girl, whom she had
been accustomed to call her young mistress. With
that quick perception that servants invariably have
of anything "gone wrong above-stairs," she found
the female domestics gathered in a knot of whis-
perers, and all of them listening for a further elu-
cidation of the circumstances which were now
taking place. Mary, therefore, entered almost
unnoticed; when, instead of being questioned for
news, as if she represented a living epitome of

the village events that took place around her, she was permitted to set. down her basket without a word, and to join in the circle of her friends. She soon heard that there had been a "terrible row," as the servants expressed it, and that Marguerite was locked a prisoner in her own room; the key of the door being in her father's possession. What the events were that led to this, no one could tell her; but Mary recollected the sobs she had heard, and acquainting the servants with this fact, they stole hastily into the garden to listen up to the window of their young mistress; and there they heard enough to induce them to believe that Marguerite needed assistance. Frightened to death, one maid said she was going to swoon; another exclaimed, that it had given her such a turn she had not any power to move without some beer; while the Abigail whose duty it more particularly was to attend to Marguerite lost her head completely, and stood in the middle of the kitchen like a helpless statue. Mary alone had her wits about her, and at once counselled the girl to repair to the Justice, and tell him that her young lady was very ill: and in giving this counsel she urged that, unless she did so, she might even become answerable for her lady's life. Thus exhorted and roused to action by the energy of Mary, the Abigail did as she was desired, and her knock interrupted the interview between the Justice and the Priest in the study, which was still going on, and elicited such a " Come in!" from Wellrode, as nearly to send the girl back into the kitchen.

She contrived to open the door, however, and to stand stock-still between the posts; while she stammered forth, " The key, sir, of my young mistress's bed-room; I fear for her life."

" Her life, indeed! And what if she did lose it?" was the insane, the brutal reply, of the still furious father. " Here, take the key; but, hark you, Mistress Abigail; you are the upper servant in my house: take the key to minister to your young lady's wants; but on no account is she to quit her apartment. You hear me; and I will at least be obeyed by you."

More dead than alive, she soon presented herself to her young mistress, whom she found hysterically affected, and lying on her bed almost insensible. Having done all she thought necessary to give relief, she hastened below for other remedies, and among them ordered a cup of tea; which, as she remained still upstairs with her mistress, Mary volunteered to take to her: she was permitted to do this, from the fact that with their young lady she was known to be a favourite; and

for the moment all petty jealousies were forgotten.

Well, Mary — faithful, affectionate, simple
country girl—why beam those pretty dark eyes of
yours with so much satisfaction? Is there anything more than usual in the longing desire your
eyes seem to evince to be within speech of your
young mistress? We shall see. As Mary ·as-
cended the stairs with the tea, the Abigail was
descending for something else she wanted; so that
Mary came to speak to her mistress alone. There
was but little time for talking, for a returning step
was heard; so from her bosom Mary drew forth a
little billet, and whispered the words, "It is from
Master Willie." Almost unconscious of what she
did, Marguerite's trembling, snowy hand, clasped
upon it, and the servant came in. Mary remained
for some little time assisting in attentions to the
sufferer; and when she saw her young lady more
composed, not desiring to create any suspicions
that should interfere with her future ingress to
the Grove, with the simple assurance that she
would ask to see her young lady again when she
brought a fresh supply of water-cresses, and at
the same time receiving a look of thanks from
poor Marguerite, Mary quietly withdrew, and was
proceeding to the kitchen, when in the passage

she encountered Father Crawl. He stopped, and regarding her intently, asked " What she did there?"

The reply was, " That she had come of her usual errand with her basket."

" With the basket, and what besides?" was the searching interrogatory.

" I haven't got anything, sir, but cresses," was the reply; and Mary passed on.

The priest stood still, and when she was out of sight he shook his head and murmured to himself, " So, so! another messenger of evil! but I'll look to it, though the time is not yet come."

When Marguerite had been put to bed, and left to herself, from beneath her pillow she *did* withdraw a communication from her lover; yet half hesitating, and still to some extent swayed by the promise she had given to her father, she paused ere she broke the silken thread that kept its folds together. The pause was not of long duration. The face of things, under which the pledge had been given, had utterly changed. No longer trusted, the faith between the father and his child, rudely, coarsely, and wrongfully severed by his deed, the inclination of her head and heart kept pace and time together, and soon taught her to believe that the force of circumstances had absolved her from her vow; and that she had—but not from any seeking of her own—been made free to act for the future as she chose. She broke the thread that bound the intelligence; she even pressed the billet to her lips. The letter, written immediately after her parting interview with Willie, ran as follows:—

"Then Marguerite, dearest Marguerite! *has* that dreaded hour come, and hast thou said adieu? Ere it came to this, I saw thee, heard thee, drank of the cup of love thy soft sweet eyes had filled, and my dreaming soul was steeped in rich forgetfulness. My love for thee came with succeeding suns, rose blandly with the rising moon, and even fell in tender showers; for still, in rain or shine, dear Marguerite, we were one! How changed the spirit of my dream is now! To-morrow gives us not a time to meet; the day drags on, and we have been, alas! we scarce know whither. No gentle voice to sing; no calm, if self-possessed, yet tender glance to bid me live and hope. No accents bland to touch those heavenly chords that lie so deep in my devotion. If I whisper to myself thy name, some stifled echo tells me 'tis pronounced by others. Oh, Marguerite, listen to me, for I speak the truth! The earth holds but *a* summer! Heaven wills it, and

the wild birds sing; the sun grows warm, and
blossoms deck the fields. As that bright solace
gladdens all the world, so thought on thee or
love for thee drives winter from my frozen door,
and makes me breathe the summer of thy presence. Oh, say not 'I 'll forget thee.' If the
wood where we have been forgets its leaves to
bear, if the moist ground around Our Lady's
Well refuses primrose birth, if violets never
grow, and flowers die for ever, then mayest thou
tell me I forget, and thou hast ceased to charm
me! Marguerite, if thou dost not relent, I cannot
but write, although, compared with what *I feel*,
words are but empty sounds. Forget not the
secret cleft beneath the moss in that chalk cliff I
told thee of. Mary will place it there, if thou
wilt not come, and it will reach me safely. Oh,
come thyself; let me but see and hear thee; if
forbidden, I will not speak of love."

Marguerite read this letter, nay, pressed it to
her lips again and again, read again and again the
last line, and then, with a deep, sad sigh, said to
herself,—

"Oh, Willie, we must not even now deceive
each other; nor can I so hurriedly force myself
to prove faithless to that firm trust my father so
long assigned me. No, Willie, it must not be, or

—it.must not *now* be; my poor father may yet be kind to me again."

Thus saying, Marguerite's pale, yet lovely cheek, sank upon the pillow; when, as if for ever hovering over youth, that soft renewer of earthly strength, and at times the beguiler of each present sorrow, sleep came in its bland oblivion, and for a time stole her from the world.

CHAPTER XII.

ALL Englishmen are more or less taunted by foreigners with a love of country and of home, and with being bigots to roast beef and plum-pudding; and yet, when I divest myself of all national proclivities, and sit down to deal in an unprejudiced manner with what really belongs to Englishmen and their country, to "the Upper Ten Thousand" and to the moving millions that till the soil or expend their brief lives in the manufacturing districts, in the midst of the " devil's dust," and terribly minute chips from needles and pins, brass, copper, iron, and lead, I am forced to admit to myself that there is no higher class in the world, none in courteousness, good breeding, chivalry and liberality, that can surpass the nobility of the United Kingdom. If a famine spread its misery over the land, whose hand goes more readily or deeper into the pocket than that of the peer or peers, the baronets, knights, and esquires, of the afflicted region? Who answer more liberally and profusely to the cry of starvation and distress that the members of " the Upper Ten Thousand ?" or who show more feeling, more charity, or a greater amount of Christian fortitude and gentleness, than do the ladies of that upper class ?

To the English castle or hall, when the land is free from famine and wide-spread distress, come the local poor that live within the manorial acres, every morning or every week, for the broken bread and meat, and clothing, and such alms as the presiding genius may deem to be requisite. The clergyman has only to report distress, and the rich coffers find the means of relieving it; and in the whole course of my experience, an experience neither short nor limited, I never saw " a great house" where Charity, more or less, did not reign over the threshold, or to which the afflicted poor might not turn as to a friend invariably good at need, and who was never blind nor deaf to just and timely representation. I have loved to see the red cloaks of the old women, when coming to the Castle in their clanking pattens for the morning gifts, and to hear the "God bless'ee, sirs!" of the clean old men, who, on their sticks or crutches, came up for a share of charity. To me there is something so nationally and so gracefully comfortable in these scenes, that I am never more proud of my country, countrymen and countrywomen, than when I see them open-handed to the really suffering and really honest poor. I guard myself by saying to "the honest poor," because, as a country gentleman and justice of the peace, I know that there is nothing more mistaken, nor of greater evil, than an *indiscriminate charity*, moved as much by ragged, drunken idleness and roguery, as by the rent and worn-out garments of the honest and industrious poor. Because a man or woman is in rags, that is no reason why they should have assigned to them the wherewithal to live on. The reason why they ought to be relieved lies in the conduct of their existence, their industry, their honesty, and their unmerited distress.

There are rags of guilt, rags dark to be reviled, and there are rags for pity and relief, whose every fissure really is a "poor, poor dumb mouth!" to pray for and to pity. Country lords, ladies, and gentlemen, generally require the pastor's report to confirm them in their graceful gifts to the poor, or they themselves judge from personal observation; they ought never to trust to vague rumours, set about by servants or by some who thirst for the outward and visible signs of charity, and care not for the inward and spiritual grace of it. In short, lords and ladies cannot be too careful never to misapply their charity; and never to pass by the wants of the really deserving poor.

As a local illustration of this, I venture to narrate an occurrence which happened to me when resident at Beacon Lodge. I give it, not with any vain wish to puff my own charity, but as one of those facts that are always the best props to argument.

It was on one of the first cold days of October that a great muscular under-keeper of mine came to me, to report that there was laid up in a little sort of gravel-pit willow-bed of mine what he termed a "rummish customer," in the shape of a "tramp," who had replied to his question of what business he had there with the intelligence that he had passed the preceding night where he was, and intended to remain there for twenty-four hours longer. "And why did you not then expel him from my private territory by the collar?"

was the next question. " Go and do so now."
My servant left me, I thought rather unwillingly, on
this service, muttering to himself that he thought
the "rummish customer" might be inclined to hold
his own. It had previously been a suspicion of
mine that this under-keeper was much too big
and muscular a man to be in possession of the
best pluck, for I had often noticed that Pro-
vidence was usually inclined to make things as
even as possible, by giving the greater courage to
the moderate sized. Or giants might really have
ruled in "Asgard," in the absence of lesser "Thors"
and effective "Hammers." These thoughts up-
permost in my mind, I came to the resolution to
run a trial of my man and this "roughish customer," as, to try them, men often run their
terriers at a badger. I say " men," instead of
" we," because I never do; for I detest the baiting
of an animal, or the combat of animals where
there is not a fair and open option to surrender.

As we were going to the spot, the thought came
across me that, before any violence was permitted,
I would judge of the " roughish customer" myself.
With this end in view I went down into the
gravel-pit, but the willows and brambles were so
thick that I could only dimly define the outline
of a recumbent figure.

" Holla, my man!" I exclaimed: " you must not stay here; get up and be off!"

" Humph!" replied a gruffish voice; " that's easier said than done."

Angry at what I took for insolence, and at the moment forgetful of my intention to try my under-keeper, all impediments were burst through, and I stood over the still passive form: The man was enveloped in long grass, showing only a considerable length of limb, and in the vehemence of the moment I stooped to pick him up by the collar with the words,—

" Get up and go you must!"

" Very well, sir," replied the voice, now in tones of obedience, and as I thought, too, with a touch of sorrowful regret and a melancholy acquiescence in the command. As he crept out of the longer grass, and came fully into view, I saw him adjusting a tattered bandage and an old broken shoe on a terribly lame foot, — his whole bearing so different from what I had been led to expect, that the tone of severity in which I had first addressed him seemed to recoil on me, as a harsh act of heartlessness; so, putting my hand gently on his shoulder, I told him to " sit down and be still." The change in my voice and manner, I suppose, was too much for him in his then forlorn condition, for he at once sat down and burst into tears. It was a good deal too much for me, and I could not help what my eyes did too; so, to divert the feeling, I called on my man to make in, but he either did not, or would not, hear me; therefore, bidding my poor friend to remain where he was, I ran off to my house, and obtained some nice bread and meat and a soda-water-bottle full of beer. With my hands full, and I hope my heart the same, I returned to the gravel-pit, and sat down by the poor fellow's side. The homely viands were soon spread before him, and he tried to eat some of them, evidently to oblige me more than from any appetite; but at last he frankly told me, that if I would let him he would keep the refreshment for some other time. Receiving a ready acquiescence in this, and an additional half-crown, he then rose, and said he would continue his journey in the direction of Lymington, having told me that by trade he was a compositor, and, if I remember correctly, a native of Preston in Lancashire.

It is a curious anecdote relating to the management of the castles and halls of "the Upper Ten Thousand," and regarding servants, that though close inquiries are made into the character and antecedents of a butler, none in any way so searching are made as to the previous life and condition of a gamekeeper.   Now, as to those two places in a household, there can be no sort of doubt but that the man more to be trusted of the two, and on whose sobriety and good conduct depends so much, is the gamekeeper; and for these reasons: — he is more out of sight, and less under the control, of his master, and has it in his power to annoy or to render more comfortable every tenant-farmer within the manor or manors of his superintendence.   Even the respectful conduct of the labouring population depends on him, for he is either a just and vigilant and sober servant, overlooking little faults and punishing flagrant innovations, or he is a feverish annoyance to the entire neighbourhood, making it very unpleasant to individuals against whom he feels some petty spite, and favouring rogues lest they should inform against his intemperate or drinking habits. With some lords of houses anything will do for a head-keeper.   If a man of a life of bad habits, but supposed to be reformed — reformed in pretence only, and to obtain the place of keeper — he is regarded as a thief set to catch a thief, and mistakenly glorified accordingly.   He may have two hundred pheasants in a wood, and take half of them as his own perquisite, and his master will not miss a feather. On the other hand, if the lord and master have a cellar-book, and once a-week checks the quantity of wine that is uncorked, he can at any moment miss a bottle, and come to a settlement accordingly with his butler upon that very bottle.

A manor with game is either the scene of disquietude and a sort of guerilla warfare, or it is a large, well-arranged acreage, where crime is justly repressed, and where the poor are taught to see that in good conduct and a desire to oblige lies the way to ample fare at Christmas, and charitable gifts to them and theirs when sickness or accident has demanded graceful consideration. For myself, as one of "the Ten Thousand," I am more careful in the selection of a keeper than in that of any other servant; but in no instance, and in connexion with servitude, would I tolerate a drunken man or an inveterate smoker on my premises, for either would in time corrupt a whole household.

There is a system widely disseminated in numberless households, the toleration of which surprises me. It is that of permitting large fees to be given to the servants. Many noble lords and guests at some houses give a sovereign or more to the groom of the bedchamber, who, dressed like a gentleman, simply lights for them their bed candles when they retire for the night. At a *battue* they present the head-keeper with a five-pound note, and so on to all who do not do more than pick up their glove. Some men fee the butler wherever they dine; and thus when a clergyman comes —

> " A man to all the country dear,
> And passing rich with forty pounds a-year "—

as an invited guest to dine, sleep, or share in innocent sport, he is scowled at simply because with, say a few hundreds a-year, he cannot afford to do as much as a man with triple that number of thousands. I think this is a state of things derogatory to the heads of great houses. The upper-servants in these large establishments are, or should be, so well paid as to render the reception or expectation of fees utterly beside their notice. If a domestic serves me, I consider that it is just that I should pay him sufficiently, without reference to perquisites from strangers; and the only fact to which I would shut my eyes would be, when little remunerations were offered to servants who were put to additional trouble from the guest not bringing with him a servant of his own. It is in such a case pleasing to the guest to think that he may reward those to whom he gives trouble not contemplated in the daily avocation, and it is a spur

to those who attend on him, to make him as comfortable as they can in *little-great things*, that do
not come directly within the verge of their appointed duty.

In regard to the breakfasts in the castles and
halls of " the Upper Ten Thousand," they are ruled
in two ways. One system is to have an appointed
hour for breakfast, and all to assemble at the given
time; the other is to have no set time of meeting,
but for every guest to drop in as he or she may
select, and each guest to have a teapot and coffee-
pot, breakfast-cakes, toast and eggs, broils, fish,
and made dishes, at their individual disposal: the
mighty side-table at the same time garnished and
groaning with every sort of cold *pièce de résistance*,
game and fowl, that the season or the spit can
set upon it. Of the two usages I like the latter
the best, because it ties not to time, which, in my
opinion, is one of the vilest bonds that humanity
can bear.

In an English castle, hall, or mansion, all is
beautifully delicate and clean, warm, comfortable,
and profuse, well attended to, and replete with
luxury. I cannot say so much for establishments
I have seen in the French châteaux, or in houses
in the disunited States of America. Hospitality,
liberality, and kindness most profuse, you may meet

with anywhere, but there is no country in the world where splendid entertainment and superb magnificence go hand-in-hand with ease and comfort, to the same degree as they do in the houses of "the Upper Ten Thousand" in the United Kingdom of Great Britain. France is famed for gastronomy, but out of Paris I never saw a really *récherché* or good dinner. In Paris I never saw a really well-roasted roast, nor, in the entire of my travels in the land of the forests, anything approaching to a well-dressed or a fat haunch of vension. The same in America: there I have never tasted venison better than that of one of our wet and, therefore, lean does.

At the best-arranged breakfast-table no one ever thinks of awaiting the advent of the master or mistress of the mansion. Breakfast having been said to be ready at a given hour, there it is, and the guests come in and sit down to it without reference to anything but the viands before them. Scotland has ever been lauded for her breakfasts, but in England, and in some of the castles and halls of Ireland, she has found her match; and of all the meals in the twenty-four hours, to my mind there is none more luxurious than that of an ample and well-arranged breakfast, whether it be in England, Scotland, or Ireland. Where I have been, there always was an hour announced for breakfast, to suit the sporting arrangements of some of the guests, but beyond that hour guests not pledged to time came down as they pleased. This used to be the case at Woburn, at Taymouth, at Berkeley Castle, and, indeed, at every other place of large established notoriety.

I know nothing more disagreeable to a guest than to be tied to time in regard to breakfast. He may have had a sleepless night, and, at the moment of being called, find that that most fickle thing, Sleep, is willing to settle on his lids at the very moment he proposed overnight to have risen. Let the hour of dinner be fixed to the minute of projection, and let no one be waited for; but as to breakfast or luncheon, let the guests partake of them as they please without form or ceremony.

CHAPTER XIII.

PART II.

THE following is a ghostly legend, the truth of which was, and I believe is, vouched for by a Roman Catholic Priest: so it may have some weight at least with those of my readers who profess to have faith in priestly assertion, and in the power of the priesthood to hold spiritual communications with heaven, and things alike beyond the grave, and not within the power of man. In this, as in similar well-authenticated facts, however, I see no good in the supernatural visit.

The priest—I shall give him no other name than Father H. (H *is* the first letter of his surname)—a name so celebrated in drawings, that it may have caused him to draw on his own fertile imagination for the following story, or it may not. It was told me by a young lady, for whose graceful truth and sincerity, disposition and attributes, I have unbounded admiration and faith, and I could not have received it through a prettier channel. She was not, and is not, of the Romish persuasion, therefore I am not "telling tales *out* of school," however much so Father H. might have been doing, when *he* professed to see what it was not given *others* to *see*, and then only saw a mystery, which Heaven gave him no authority to unravel. The ghost, by his own account, was as silent, and cut the living priest as dead, as ghosts generally do the clergymen and sinners of other creeds who venture to ask them questions. Ghosts never speak: the father of Hamlet was dumb; and the most sweetly poetical and erring ghost of all, Byron's " Astarte," could only articulate the name of her brother and her lover. No disparagement, then, to Father H.: he was just as much cut as the rest of us, and I simply allude to *that* fact as militating against the pretended power and direct communication of the Romish priests with heaven. Urbanity prevents my alluding to any other place.

But to proceed with my legend.

To those noble halls, those still aristocratic

halls and noble domains, where the merry hound and joyous horn, profuse hospitality and the ready steed, have so often gladdened the hearts of numerous guests, I must introduce my readers. Some of the circumstances around them may have changed, and changed regretfully; but the site still stands ornamented by all its mute attributes, and the deeds of ages cannot remove the grace attached to walls and woods, or make the mind forget where once the highest grace presided.

About the year, and about the month of October, in 1857, on her way from the north, a young lady, attended by her maid, went to pay a visit at B—— C——. I may as well leave out the first letter of the alphabet, as not needed on this occasion. She arrived at the noble mansion too late to dress for dinner. There was a large party staying in the house, and her hostess, Lady ——, had but just time to show her to her room. It was a small room on the ground-floor, and situated in the left wing of the mansion, almost at the end of a very long passage.

Having hastily ushered the young lady into her bedroom, Lady —— then as suddenly exclaimed, " Perhaps I ought to tell you that this room is said to be haunted! No complaints have been recently made to me by any of my guests that have slept in it, and I do not think you need be in the least alarm. I only mention it in case you should hear exaggerated accounts by any accident, through other sources. Good-bye, my dear. Come down when we have dined."

With these comfortable assurances to a girl just arrived in a fine, old, rambling, strange house, my lady skipped from the room, and left her guest in horrified dismay.

Now it so happened, that if there was one thing more horrifying to the young lady I allude to than another, it was the idea of sleeping in a lonely, an isolated, and a said-to-be-haunted chamber, everybody, including her own maid, far away. My friend did not like to confess this very natural feeling, so she concealed her horror, dressed, and, after the dinner was over, joined the party in the drawing-room. She joined the ladies there as graceful, or more so, than any, and she was gay; but still her thoughts would recur to the "haunted room;" and, though she veiled the depression at her heart with a semblance of hilarity, there seemed a constant foreboding on her soul that she would see an unearthly visitant before the break of day.

On going to bed, as to falling asleep for any length of time she did not do so, and a restless night was passed in expectation of a thing that did not come. Night after night succeeded, and no ghost haunted her chamber, till time made her cease to fear the thing she once dreaded, and she became anxious to hear the particulars, if any, of the reputed apparition.

Having expressed her desire for further information to my lady, her ladyship at once referred her to Father H. To the priest then, on the first opportunity, she applied, and, of course, received a Roman Catholic answer. At first Father H. declined, mysteriously, even to talk on the subject, in no way allaying the interest in the female mind by the boding assurance " that it was very wrong to put her in *that* room."

" Why ?" asked my friend; " why wrong?"

"Because," replied Father H., " you might have been frightened."

" Oh," rejoined Miss ——, " no fear of that!" putting on a laugh when she said so; her words and actions governed by that curiosity for which women are said to be so famed. " I don't believe in ghosts."

" You *don't believe* in supernatural sights ! Do you not ?" exclaimed the priest; regarding her very gravely, and putting on an *empressement* frown of serious expression. "My dear young lady, do not say that! Because *you* have not *seen*, you do not believe. Some there are who are not permitted to see: it is not to every one to whom that privilege is given. Such things to you, perhaps, are not permitted; but still they are, and may be at your elbow: but, by the merciful blessing of Our Lady, spiritually *you* may be blind."

All inclination to laugh or to put on laughter, all approach to hilarity, then left the young lady: for the manner assumed by the priest had so impressed her with the seriousness of the matter in hand, that she felt almost sad. Nevertheless, the beautiful buoyancy of spirit, so often an inheritance of the female heart, and so frequently and cruelly crushed by those—God forgive them!—to whom her finest, and most innocent, and delicate sensibilities are intrusted, rose triumphant, even in the presence of a gloomy priest and reputed unearthly apparitions; and Miss —— exclaimed: —

" Well, though it is a satisfaction not to be one privileged to see a ghost, still, most reverend sir, I am not to be thus put off. Tell me, I implore you, about this ghost; as my Lady has referred me to you, and I am curious on the subject."

"Well," replied Father H., "do not say in jest that you do not believe in things because you have not *seen* them—things which, if seen by you, and not by one privileged to see, expound, and understand, would be regarded, perhaps, as the delusions of a dream; or, maybe, the inventions of the devil. If you hold that disbelief in Omnipotency," he continued with startling emphasis, "*a ghost, even to-night, may be sent from the other world to undeceive you.*"

It is ever dangerous for the sensitive mind of a girl to talk of ghosts, or to attempt to deal with the mind of a subtle priest, whose prey so often is the mind and belief of woman. And in this instance my young friend found it so. All the horror she had previously felt as to sleeping in a confessedly haunted room returned, and fell on her with a weight of depression not to be understood by minds of a more resisting quality. At once she retracted all her disbelief in unearthly apparitions, and, as far as I gather from her description, she asserted herself a convert so far; but, thank Heaven! no further. By this she hoped to render the apparition in her room of the ghost, with which the priest had threatened her, needless; and to gain his good-will, as well as elicit from him further information.

What she said, or was induced to say in the matter, she could not, when in conversation with me, remember; but she gained so much good-will from the old priest, that on parting she obtained his promise, that if she would meet him in the library on the following morning, at an earlier hour than the guests generally came down, he would then confide to her *what he himself had seen in the bedroom she then occupied.*

Of course she was punctual to the appointment, and he narrated as follows:—

" When I first came," said Father H., " professionally to reside here, I was put into one of the bachelors' rooms; but finding myself continually disturbed at all hours by guests, who slept to the right and left of me; some of them coming rather noisily to bed about the time when I got up; some earlier, some later; some singing, and some swearing at furniture which did not move out of their way—I applied to the head of the family to move me into quieter quarters; and I was put into the room you now occupy.

" On being put into that little lonely room, I had at first sight every reason to be satisfied. It was lone and snug; and, as you know, almost at the end of a passage on the right-hand side, leading out of the long passage, nearly at the end of which your room—my room then—is situated. At the further end of the long passage you may have remarked that there is a green-baize door: that door leads only into a stone cellar, used as a housemaid's depository for coals to supply the rooms.

" For the first two or three nights I slept most soundly: the novel quietude of the place probably induced sleep; but on the fourth night an unaccountable restlessness seized me; and, turn which way I would, sleep fled from my wakeful eyes, and I seemed as set on a continuous vigil. Thus I remained, as nearly as I could determine, till about the third hour of the morning. Suddenly, and close at my bedside, there was revealed to me the figure of a woman clothed in white; and at the first glance she seemed to me to be carrying her head under her arm, for it did not rise above her shoulders. On gazing intently at her, however, I ascertained that she had a head, but that it was hanging down on one side, as if the neck was broken. I spoke to her, and enjoined her, in the name of Our Lady, to reply; but she made no answer: when, after regarding me for a brief space, from the peculiar position of her eyes, she slowly retreated and passed out—apparently *through* the door. Strange to say, strong in my faith, I was not the least frightened—-oh! no!—by my morning visitress. But I wondered whether this was the first visit she had paid to my room: and if not, how long she might have been in it without my knowledge, when in the profound sleep enjoyed by me on the previous nights. To clear up the point, my courage and the support accorded to me by Our Lady made me determine to lie awake on the following night and watch for the appearance of the ghost, and when she left my room, to follow and see what became of her.

"On retiring to rest I had not long to wait, for I had scarce kept my vigil for an hour when the same figure again suddenly appeared at my bedside. Again I spoke to her, but in vain; so I lay with my eyes riveted on her strange appearance, and on her face and eyes, pendent and askant; and it seemed—I must confess it— as if there was the length of a lifetime in that brief space, or until she again moved towards the door.

" When she moved to go away, the same way which she had gone on the previous night, I sprang from my bed and followed. She passed the door, and I pursued and arrived in the passage just in time to see her turn the corner into the other passage. I hastened on; and then to my horror, hanging by the neck from the green-baize door,

I beheld the pallid ghost that had haunted me.
The passage and all about me was dimly dark,
but a sort of pale and lambent flame played
around rather than lit up the ghastly head ; while
above, in characters formed of the same pale
blue light, in large letters, I read the name of
' Anne ——.'   Even at that moment, my dear
young lady, I was not frightened—oh! no!—but
I must confess that a very strange and potent
sensation came over me, which utterly prostrated
all power in my legs to move me from the spot.
I never felt the like before ; nor could I stir a
hand to relieve the figure from, no doubt, its
painful position, its meed of penitence and pur-
gatory.   How long this state of things continued
I cannot attempt to say ; but at last, as quick
as lightning, the figure and the unearthly light
which surrounded it, and the handwriting on the
wall, vanished, and I was left in comparative
darkness to grope my way back to bed.

" For the rest of that night I lay awake, pondering over that which I had seen, and at last
resolved to say nothing about it to my friends
in the mansion, but to go quietly forth among
my poor parishioners and see if the elder people
in the village had ever heard of a haunted room,
or the why or wherefore that the ghost appeared.

My inquiries for a length of time elicited no information ; but at last I found an old man, truly " the oldest inhabitant of the parish," who, when I asked him if he had ever heard the name of Anne ——, ' Yes, sure,' he cried, ' I mind hearing tell of her all my born days. Anne ——! Oh, she was the housemaid ; I knowed her, too, as a boy. Anne ——! she it was as hung herself over the green baize-door as now is, at the mansion, more than sixty year ago!' "

As may be supposed, this tale, solemnly told by the priest, had considerable effect on my informant's mind; as, indeed in a lonely room at the end of a long passage, and away from all other apartments in that large and fine edifice, it in all probability would have : so she ordered her maid to sleep in the room during the time of her stay, and resolved to leave her relatives and friends as soon as an opportunity offered. This she did, and thus while she was at the mansion she never saw the ghost, nor heard more of it.

CHAPTER XIV.

THE LEGEND OF WEST WYCOMBE PARK, BUCKS.

PART IV.

WHEN Marguerite awoke on the following morning, she felt that her nervous system had experienced so great a shock that she was unable to rise. As she lay, reviewing the painful transactions of the previous day, not a sound on the stairs, nor a footfall in the passage, but made her gentle and affectionate heart beat at the hoped-for — nay, expected — visit of a repentant father. Had that weak and mistaken man presented himself by the bed of his loving child, she would have stretched out her snowy arms, and clung around his neck, with obedience and love; but he came not, nor did he send even to inquire about her, contenting himself, we will suppose, with the knowledge that she was alive, and under lock and key. What wonder, then, that thus left in neglect, harshly treated, wronged in her most delicate sensibility, and alone, the tearful eyes of the poor girl should seek for better comfort in the assurance contained in Willie's letter? Still, in such undeviating habits of obedience had she lived, so fond was she of her father, and so bound to him from her sense of propriety and duty, that, even under the cruel circumstances in which she was placed, she yet hesitated to renew her correspondence with Willie. It needed but a kind look and word from her father — an assurance that she was still the trusted child of his heart — to confirm her in the forced severance from her lover; that look and word were, however, wanting, and she recurred to the billet brought her by Mary. Had she not been depressed in body and mind, that resistance to tyranny — to undeserved wrong — with which the gentlest female heart is so often heroically imbued, would in all probability have acted powerfully in Willie's favour; but as it was she seemed stricken down from all strength in action, and at the moment constitutionally as well as habitually inclined, perhaps with a lingering hope that her father would yet be kind to her, to obey the course to which she was in some degree pledged. Her writing materials being within reach, she wrote to Willie as follows :—

"WILLIE—I have received your letter at a time too sad to tell you. That I am unhappy I will not disguise; nay, that I am miserable. So far, Willie, had I written, when something whispered that I had better tell thee all. I am locked in my room a prisoner, and on thy account. I cannot further explain, the matter is so far beyond my comprehension; so indelicate, and so strange. The priest has much to do with it, of that I am too sure. Upon the whole, Willie, do not deem me weak; but if I dared trust myself to do so, it would now be a comfort to me to know that I have the means of communicating with thee: the more so, because in these inexplicable circumstances we seem to be similarly wronged: but, Willie, even now it must not be. Mary shall place this letter in the cleft of the chalk cliff you have described. If I err in doing this may Heaven forgive me, for I intend no wrong, but cannot rest when wrong seems done to thee.

"Communication, Willie, perhaps but prolongs our pain; besides, to keep up a clandestine correspondence through the hands of a cottage girl, however good she may be, can neither be safe nor just to me. Canst thou blame me then that my lips refuse to utter words of sin; refuse, under any circumstances, to say that I will meet thee (alas! it is out of my power to do so now), and by meeting thee so break my father's stern command? Thy love, Willie, which has sprung so suddenly into life, will die as quickly; and in after years, if, from the midst of those who have become more dear to thee than I have ever been, thou shouldst ever look back to these days, I would that thy remembrances of them should be pure and bright, and mine without a tinge of shame. Let us then part as friends. Were it in my power to meet thee, which it is not, I might yet learn to love too well. Oh, if thou lovest me, come no more to those dear woods; for if thou dost come, some fatal fascination would be sure to draw me to thy side and tempt me into error. Oh, if thou lovest me, then, Willie, make my struggle less. If ever happier times *should* come! . . . but 'tis madness now to think they will, and so adieu. I can meet my father still with a clear conscience, and, Willie, we must part. That all blessings may attend thee shall ever be the prayer of   " MARGUERITE."

Leaving poor Marguerite lying exhausted on her pillow, by the exertion necessary to write these lines, we must revert to the previous day, and accompany Mary home, where, having left some of the contents of her basket with the servants at the Grove, she emptied the rest into a pan of fresh water at the back-door of her father's cottage. Had a mine sprung beneath her feet, or an adder leaped from among her cresses, she could not have jumped higher, or been more startled than she was, when Willie's picture made a splash as it plunged into the water! To rescue it, and to very carefully wipe it dry, was but the work of a moment, and then she began to consider how it came into that extraordinary position. It was not long before she remembered that on her passage through the garden at the Grove, something had seemed to strike her basket; but then, if thus the picture had come there, whose was the hand that flung it, and how came it out of the priest's possession?—for she was well convinced that no one but the priest had taken it from her father's cottage. Quick-witted as she was, and as country girls very often are in the common-place occurrences which surround their rural lives, though an ill-defined idea might possess her, that perhaps the picture had something to do with the scene she had lately left; still she could come to no conclusion as to the facts of the case, nor dream how or wherefore the grief of her young mistress could have been produced by Willie's gift to her. Having resolved, however, to take her basket on the following day, as an excuse again to be admitted to Marguerite's chamber, delighted with the possession of her treasure, she kept it and her intentions to herself. The day—the next day—that running and succeeding grain of sand that slips through the glass of life, and so swiftly marks the progress to the end—that is but an atom to look back upon, but which looked forward to at times seems an almost illimitable period, came, and Mary again presented herself at the Grove, and again was ushered to the bed-

side of her loved young mistress. There she was
not left for a moment alone, nor could she find an
opportunity to open the conversation about the
picture. Oh! *why* did chance thus thwart an
opportunity for a few words which could so easily
have reconciled a father to his child, and have
closed all difference between them? And *why*
did it screen the cold-faced villany of one whose
means were in this world, *but not for ever*, supposed to be sanctified by the end in view? But
so it is, so has it often been, and often will it
again be. It is as if the fallen angel yet held a
blighting power upon earth, to thwart the good
and prosper the bad; to choke, to stifle up the
few explanatory words that under heaven would
have set anger by, and united Christian people,
the offspring to the sire. Mary was never given
a chance at explanation; the one boon in store for
her was, that when she took leave of Marguerite
the latter held out her hand, and as she took
Mary's, she pressed into its palm the letter we
have already described, and with that the faithful
cottage girl was forced to be content.

In great haste to carry the billet to its destination, Mary set off, and gained Whittenden
Park Wood. She came to Our Lady's Well, and
there she tarried some little time in the hope of

seeing Willie. Her haste, however, and the little converse she was permitted to have with Marguerite, had brought her back to the given spot much earlier than Willie had anticipated; so, not desiring before she had performed her errand to meet with Father Crawl, whose terribly acute eyes she feared as capable of " seeing through a stone wall," and which, of course, would therefore enable him to detect, through the simple handkerchief that crossed her breast, the little note with which she was entrusted, she hastened on to the cliff above the Swilley Hole. The speed at which Mary had come through the wood had given an additional bloom to her healthful cheek, and added fresh brilliancy to her dark eyes, and caused her pretty lips to open freely to the quick breathings of her bosom. On reaching the Swilley Hole she paused, out of breath, ere she stooped to look for the secret cleft, and to complete her mission. Having gained her breath, but still in dread of the priest, she went a few steps down, and stooped towards the edge of the cliff with the note in her hand, when a stick cracked, apparently very near. It made her start and listen, but all seemed safely still; a stick might have cracked beneath the foot of hare or rabbit; so, hesitating no longer, she knelt down and deposited the note in its hiding-place, taking great care to re-arrange the overhanging moss so as to conceal the spot with the greatest nicety. Matters being thus settled to her satisfaction, Mary tripped off as lightly as a little doe, and was soon far on her way to the cottage. She had not, however, left the place two moments, when a stick again gave notice of pressure, and crawling, writhing, serpent-like, through the rank herbage of the morass, which he had reached by a shorter cut than Mary had done, while at the same time to some extent he had kept her in view, the form of Father Crawl came up the side of Swilley Hole, from below the little adopted spot about which he had seen Mary busied. It took him some little time to discover the place; nor were his cold, clammy hands without some degree of tremulation as they groped among the moss, nor his passive features free from a nervous expression; for he, too, feared the advent of a strong arm, that might by possibility requite his present occupation with a blow. The moss above the little cleft was at length lifted by his trembling fingers, while the other hand clutched the note. Oh that Willie had been there to strike down this traitor to heaven and earth! or that "Luther," the faithful dog "Luther," had been on the watch to pull him down, ere he had read the contents of that packet, and possessed himself of the knowledge of the site for future correspondence!

Nothing thwarted him, however; nothing disturbed him in his thief-like occupation; when, having read the letter, he re-folded it, re-adjusted its silken thread, and again deposited it in its resting-place, taking care to leave no visible disturbance of the moss; and having done so, muttering through his compressed lips, " So, so, another spoke in my triumphant wheel!" he crept into the tangled weeds of the morass again, and disappeared from view.

About the usual hour of day, when Willie used to expect to find Marguerite in the wood, he came there attended by his faithful dog, but the expectant delight that used to beam from his handsome features, and the proud buoyancy of his step, were gone.　A feeling fearfully desolate and disconsolate—which many of my readers no doubt have felt, when returning to castle, hall, or bower, amid the scenes or sites of which, in happiness and love, *had* lately fled the golden hours— blanked upon his soul.　Each twig, each root, each leaf and blade of grass, each wild flower, chirp of insect, and song of bird, on that love-fraught spot, was touched by Marguerite's sweet-

ness in the remembrance of his heart, and made
a part of her; and in his mind's eye he beheld
the impress of her little foot upon the moss on
the brink of the cliff over which he now stood.
Overcome, for a moment, by emotion, and by a
nervous anxiety as to whether the secret post-
office he had carved contained anything for him
or not, he leaned against a tree, as if wanting the
resolution to lift the moss and set all doubt at
rest. It was then that the dear old faithful dog
" Luther," whose broad black brow had so often
been kissed by Marguerite's pretty lips, as she
caressed him, and called him by the pet name of
" Cumpey," saw that his master was unhappy,
and came to share his sorrow, and to sit by him.
They were thus close together on the edge of
the chalk-pit, when " Cumpey" sought a leaf, or
little stick, to pick up, and, by presenting it to
his master, so to obtain his notice. However, on
stooping his nose to the ground, he growled and
" winded" in the air with somewhat of an angry
glance to the morass; but ceasing in this demon-
stration, he again essayed to pick up something in
compliment to his master; and curiously occupying himself in the moss above the pit, and
descending into it, Willie saw, that whatsoever it
was that he had got was white, and projecting

from the corner of his mouth, as he walked in little circles proudly round his master. With a thrill of joy and gladdened expectation, Willie stretched out his hand. " Luther," however, was not yet to be caught, nor would he cease from the desire to please, and exercise his master's patience for yet a little while. At last he suffered himself to be caught, and then, tenderly and without injury, he resigned the billet to his master's hand. It is needless to describe how often Willie read and re-read the contents of Marguerite's letter, or how often he kissed the words which told him he *could* " comfort her." Still it perplexed him much to comprehend why she should be locked up on his account, or in what new way he had been wronged. The admissions in Marguerite's letter were little calculated to repress hope on Willie's part; on the contrary, they opened to his loving eyes even a probability of winning Marguerite from all the difficulties by which she was surrounded; and returning home he wrote at once to her as follows, trusting to reach her through the hand of the faithful cottage girl:—

" Oh, Marguerite, thou hast told me not to love; that thou canst not listen to me, nor see me more, lest thou shouldst learn to love me in return. Then it is not im-

possible that we should love, and in our hearts and souls
in friendship sweet make this land our heaven. Oh, if
'tis possible, then, why not let it be ? Thou dost not hate
me now ; and I worship thee—so truly, so forcibly, so
fondly, and so well—that with thee I am blessed; without
thee, lost in an unfathomable deep despair. Thou seest
that thou art mistress of each act and deed ; thou knowest
that the air I breathe seems sent me scented from thy
lips. My eyes reveal untaught the secret worship of my
soul. Then, wherefore dost thou pause? Oh, Marguerite,
come to me when thou canst—come again to the sweet
glades of our own dear wood, and I will find thee secret
bowers that no other eyes shall see, for none but thy
favourite robins know them. Thy little bird has been
peering with its coal-black diamond eyes into my face,
and seems to sing of thee ; for he warbles in a tone suppressed, as if of thee and me alone. Oh, Marguerite, in
thy 'No,' that word for ever on thy lips, I yet can find
enough to feel some future hope, and keep my heart from
breaking ! Tell me, tell me that thou wilt one day grant
my prayer ; that if we sever now, it shall be but till
happier times ; and I will bear delay, and in all its
pangs content myself in suffering them for thee. One
wild hope still is busy at my heart. Oh, let us meet *once
more* when you can, Marguerite : but see me once ; trust
to thine own self-possession, and what you deem a duty,
and for a time we then will bid adieu.

    " Awaiting thy reply, thy most devoted

" WILLIE."

    Having written this letter, he had to wait till
the following day to get it delivered to Mary.

When Willie had concluded the letter, the next thing he had to do was to convey it to the hands of his faithful little messenger Mary, for he was yet uncertain whether Marguerite would send for it or not, if entrusted to the chalk cliff. As it is not my intention to be too minute in the scenes pertaining to this legend, or to continue it to too great a length, we must pass over a few days. During their progress things continued at the Grove much as they were; Marguerite's frame of mind at the continued blind heartlessness of her angry father, militated considerably against her speedy recovery. In the wider world without, and far beyond the little circle of the Grove, there were wild and distracting scenes going on, not only through the constant intrigues which were for ever rife in the Court of Charles the Second, but on account of the Dutch war—an epoch in England's history that was creating a vast stir in the minds of all people, and in the chivalrous ranks of the young nobility, among whom, or with many of whom, the Duke of York was very popular. As if treading on the skirts of the robe of a weak and ill-conditioned king, the intriguing men of every class and description in England were at work, either for their own party, for their Church, or more particularly for themselves. Prince and peer, prelate and priest, politician, libertine, and illegal designer, all had views of their own, and despite the Reformation and the overwhelming flood of infuriated opinion which had not long before deluged, and in places defaced religious observances even to the very walls, the Jesuit, who, like winter, "never dies," had looked up again from the dreary depths that had essayed to crush him, with views secret, subtle, and, though shrinking from the light of day, daring to incline to the very conversion of the Crown. Bad, however, as were the scenes around the Court, they were not so bad as Mrs. Jameson's popular biographies of Charles's beauties painted them. " Popular," perhaps, because abuse of the higher orders is apt to find worshippers in the more numerous classes. The sale of a work having to be considered by author and authoress as one of the first objects, in this instance I fear that the clouds on the surface of the Court society were painted by Mrs. Jameson far over and above their presence on the clear blue sky. As to the real truth respecting intrigue, it may be very safely asserted that there were more intrigues talked of than ever really existed, and that many of those that did exist were never known to the blabbing lips of the envious, the jealous, and the disappointed. A book lauding the virtues of crown, court, and courtier, even in our days, would not make a profit by a single sixpence; but if the contrary were the theme, and failing dimmed the pages with detracting ink, the world would rush to be a purchaser.

One lovely morning the sun sent his eastern beams into an open bedroom-window of the Grove, and they seemed, as usual, to dwell therein with heavenly warmth and pleasure. There was Marguerite's little bed, as pure, as spotless, and as smooth as newly-fallen snow, for she was up and sitting at the window. The toilet-table, decorated

> " With all things sweet,
> To keep her beautiful, or leave her neat,"

bore also a bouquet of cowslips and other flowers; while the creeping plants, ascending to and around the window, gave to the sacred chamber of her maiden rest the delicate aroma induced by dews, wild honey, and the summer air; as has since been sung, " a rose," perhaps, " looked into her window." A slight cough beneath it awakened Marguerite's attention; she looked down, and then Mary tossed the letter from Willie tied up in a little parcel into the room, for with quick perception she had well assured herself that every servant was below.

Marguerite picked up and opened and read the letter, and not desiring to commit herself to any rash promises, but at the same time kindly disinclined to hurt her lover's feelings, she for a few moments, and in deep thought, continued gazing at the document with those sweetly sensible but self-possessed bright eyes for which her countenance was so remarkable. A slight cough again beneath the window recalled her to action, and, taking her pen, she wrote:—

"Willie, we cannot meet, nor must *you* again send Mary with anything for me here. Rest for a time contented; and if I should require your presence or your aid, Mary at the chalk cliff shall be *my* means of communication. Kiss dear old 'Luther' for me, and adieu."

Hastily folding up these few lines, she tossed them to Mary, and then sought to divert her mind from the contemplation of immediate things by her books and work, and even by her guitar, which about that time had been introduced into England by Francisco, and was greedily and gracefully adopted at Court. Up to the period at which this true tale has arrived, since the infraction of her fair chamber by the Jesuit priest, she had never seen her father, who also had been ill. As if vigilant over the schism he had created between father and daughter, and true to the terrible " oath and secret instruction " of the Jesuits, Father Crawl never left, when he could avoid it, the vicinity of his victim, standing between the father and his daughter, and severing them as vigilantly and according to order as he would " prevent a widow from again marrying, who had wealth which could be won from her widowhood for the priests or for their Church."* To deter a widow, who has anything to leave, from marriage, " constantly to lay before her the inconvenience of wedlock," and to prevent her or any girl with money from entering a convent or nunnery, are parts of " the oath," " in order that the widow may dispose of her income in favour of the Society of Jesuits." Father Crawl was, therefore, constantly on the watch. He knew that Mary was the medium of communication between the lovers, but he had views regarding her and Willie which prevented any immediate interference, and he was too well taught by the terrible oath he had taken, and which he seemed so sedulously and so naturally to take to, to do anything in haste, or which in the slightest degree might thwart his nefarious plans. · The summer's day, the morn of which we have thus touched

* See the translation of this oath, published by Seeley, Burnside, and Seeley, Fleet Street, London.

upon, was soon over. The beautiful, but blood-red sunset, and the surrounding piles on piles of purple and blackening and portentous clouds, blended into the sultry night; and in the extreme distance, murmuring mournfully up against the timid airs, was the suppressed roll of far-off thunder. Night wore on. The priest, as if the darkness and the coming storm were congenial to his calling and his nature, had absented himself, at least from immediate attendance on the Justice. The house was locked to all but his latch-key. Marguerite had retired to rest, and every servant was in bed. The Justice still sat up in his study, though it was nearly midnight, listening nervously to the increased thunder: he had, however, latterly fallen into a reverie in his arm-chair, and from wearying thought had nearly gone to sleep, or at least into that sort of doze which sometimes surprises a man who has been ill, and affords him the little rest that had been denied him by his pillow. Either his eyes and ears had not served him as to the opening of the door, or the form of a man had risen from the floor; for there stood in front of him a dark figure in its full height, dressed as a priest; the pale, placid, yet dignified face, fixed full upon him, its keen, searching eyes riveted on his, yet the lips beneath them dumb.

Weak and disordered as the Justice was in mind and body, under unaccountable depression, he rose from his seat at this strange apparition of a man he had never seen before, and asked him who he was, and why he came?

" I come," replied a calm and mournfully intoned voice, the eyes still fixed on those of Justice Wellrode, " by command of Him who sent me, and for your good."

" How came you to gain access to my house, and how did you pass Father Crawl, whom I know to be in the habit of sitting up at his devotions in the entrance-hall?" demanded the Justice.

" I need not a key, nor has any one seen me," replied the same measured and melancholy voice. " He who sent me has given me the means to come; let yours be the ears and the gift to obey. Hear me.   Thou hast a disobedient daughter, who rebels against the ' dictates of her confessor in temporal as well as spiritual matters.' She refuses to listen to ' him allotted for her by Divine appointment,' and ' she frustrates the expectations of our Church in wealth which she has or might have at her command. I am sent to tell thee this, and that it is the will of *Him* who sent me that thou shouldst be firm, and let no weak sentiment of nature interpose between the conduct thus through me so awfully assigned thee. To him, allotted by Heaven as her teacher —to Father Crawl—be assigned the government of thy child, and let her wed Sir Caldwell Hunter."

The theme thus so strangely brought before him, was the one of all that preyed on the shattered and failing energies of the weak and misguided man, and in an agony of feeling and uncertainty he clasped his hand upon his forehead for but an instant, and when he again looked up his visitor was gone. With tottering steps he, as he supposed, followed to the door down the passage to the hall, when there knelt, at his apparent devotions, the placid and undisturbed Father Crawl. " Who came in?" exclaimed the Justice; " and who but this instant has gone forth?"

Father Crawl raised himself from his knees with a look of surprise, and calmly answered,— " None have come in and none gone out; the door is fast, as you see it."

" But the priest, the tall, pale, and stately father, who has this instant spoken to me, and whose steps I followed, where is he?" demanded the Justice.

" I know not," replied Father Crawl; " no living soul has passed this way, for I have never left the hall."

Wellrode stood staring on the priest as if petrified with astonishment, when Father Crawl again broke the silence, saying, "Tall, stately, pale, and a priest, did you say? Strange! but I surely know the man. Look, sir! look here!" he continued, drawing from his bosom a miniature portrait. "Did he seem like unto this?"

"It is the man! the very image of the man!" replied the Justice.

"Then, sir, that blessed father is dead: he was my preceptor—my bosom friend—and now is in the odour of sanctity."

As he said this, the priest crossed himself, and returned the picture to his bosom.* Had not Father Crawl hastened to his assistance, his victim would have fallen to the floor, such power had this visitation had on his shattered nerves; but with this aid he tottered to his chamber, and, in a succeeding conversation that very night with

---

* When Ferdinand II., or "Bomba," as he was familiarly called, was supposed to be inclined to yield to the demands of his people, and to pause in the bloodshed and cruelty by which he governed his unhappy country, a similar scene to the one I have here described was enacted in his palace, and upon that supposed visitation from heaven he continued, as directed by the priests, his atrocities. A copy of this alleged divine interposition between heaven and the tyrant king is to this day handed about among the Jesuits in England, more particularly

his insidious confessor, he pledged himself to assign to Father Crawl not only the direction of the spiritual welfare of his child, but to resign to him, for the future, every worldly interest that she then had or might become possessed of. In that fatal resolution we must for the present leave them.

On the day succeeding the night on which Justice Wellrode had been so strangely visited by the unknown priest, Willie received the short reply of Marguerite from the hands of Mary, and with its contents he was forced to be satisfied. His communication with the Grove was thus, for the time, at an end ; and having no reason to employ Mary any further, though still looking to her as his vigilant friend, he contented himself with wandering around the chalk cliff in the loved wood, and hoping for an event of any sort

among those of the female class, by way of proving to those not yet sufficiently plunged into the blindness of bigotry and the belief of the infallibility of a man, that the days of miracles are not yet over, and that to *the Jesuits alone* is confined *a direct and personal communication with heaven.* The copy of the tale, *as it was first told in Spain,* is in my possession, and in the handwriting of a Jesuit lady, highly regarded by the professors of that faith, so that I adhere throughout this legend *to a system of narration not one atom overdrawn.*

that would again bring him into immediate communication with the idol of his soul. At the Grove, to which we must now return, Marguerite was left in undisturbed possession of her room, and therefore in an uninterrupted and hourly return to health and strength; but at last an eventful day arrived. Father Crawl desired to see her, sending her word to that effect on the authority of her father. Still hoping for some symptom of returning kindness in the Justice, and catching at any straw that appeared to bring her to his side, Marguerite at once, though under feelings of great disgust as far as the priest was concerned, signified her consent to the interview, when to her presence Father Crawl was at once introduced. Still pale, but self-possessed and very beautiful, Marguerite received the man who had been her confessor, and, motioning him to be seated, awaited in silence what he had to say. The priest, cool, calculating, and with features if not feelings strictly under command, took a chair; but nevertheless he was ill at ease, and diffident if not despairing of success, on account of the calm, but resolved bearing of Marguerite. He gathered tact, however, from his oath, and remembering "that care must be taken not to exercise too much rigour in confession, for fear of annoying sisters from whom money could be got," he resolved to be cautious in his approaches as to Sir Caldwell Hunter, for it was his cause that he came to plead: so, to break the ice, the vulgar, and in this particular the clumsy man, according to the 4th clause of the 7th chapter in his oath, attempted "agreeably to entertain her with pleasantries and religious stories," and failed as signally as a pig might be supposed to do when attempting to squeak an accompaniment to the soft-flowing song of Philomel. Marguerite bore with his overtures for a little time, and then requested that he would state the real reason that brought him, by the desire of her father, to her room.

Driven thus suddenly into a corner, Father Crawl told her that her father had seriously explained to him his will and pleasure; but that he himself, though empowered to act as he pleased in the matter, had no desire to annoy her: all he wished was, that, without making any promise, or giving any pledge, she would consent to receive Sir Caldwell Hunter, who was expected every moment at the Grove. If she would do this, the wily priest added, she would at once be freed from her confinement, and allowed *to take her walks as usual where she pleased.* As Crawl said this, his cunning little eyeballs peeped forth from beneath their lids in rays that he hoped would probe her inmost thought. He was deceived; Marguerite disclosed no emotion, and simply replied to the effect that, as her father's *guest*, she was bound to receive anybody. "Then," exclaimed the priest, hastily rising from his chair as the clatter of horses' feet were heard in the precincts of the Grove, "here he is; I will hasten to your father, who is better to-day than I have seen him for a long while—indeed, I may say he is quite well —and tell him of your acquiescence, and that you will come down." He then hastened from the room, and Marguerite, fully acting up to what she had said, hastened to make some slight addition to her toilet.

As the priest descended the stairs he glanced through a little window, which gave him a view of the back entrance; when, to his utter astonishment, he beheld three or four mounted men, or constables, armed, who held their leader's horse: and in another instant he was startled by so loud and authoritative a knock at the front door, as made him nearly precipitate himself down several steps; and which expressed, instead of a wish for

an invitation to "come in," a most decided resolution to enforce an entrance, and that without
much delay. The priest still kept his wits about
him; when, having descended, he stayed the servant, who was hastening to the door, till he had
regarded the intruder through a large keyhole.
The glance was quite enough; for, taking to his
shuffling heels, much to the astonishment of the
servant, and with most unusual, and, in a priest,
unbecoming haste, he ran through the little hall
to a window, which was uncommanded by the apparently, to him, hostile intruders; and, letting
himself down from it by his hands, ran off the
premises, as fast as Jesuitical legs could by any
possibility go.

By this time the door had been opened, and a
tall, pompous man, bearing the appearance of an
officer of the Parliament then sitting, demanded if
Master Justice Wellrode was within. He did not
seem to deem it necessary to wait for any answer,
but told the maid-servant to show him at once to
her master, wheresoever he might chance to be.
On hearing the knock at the door, however, Justice Wellrode had hastened to meet his expected
guest, Sir Caldwell; and, so to speak, between his
study and the entrance-hall he fell, as it were,
into the arms of quite another man.

“ Master Justice Wellrode, I believe?” said the intruder, drawing a parchment from his pocket.

“ The same,” replied the Justice.

“ Then, sir, I arrest you, in virtue of this warrant, as one suspected of evil purposes towards his blessed Majesty, Charles II., to the interests of the Reformed Church, and to the High Court of Parliament, now assembled. Topham, sir, is my name; and you are now my prisoner, to be conveyed forthwith to the Tower. Your horse, sir, I have ordered to be prepared; it now only remains with you to arrange any little things for your immediate journey : but you must touch neither trunks, drawers, nor papers, save in my presence.”

Master Topham, or “ Take-him-Topham,” as he was more familiarly called—by reason of his innumerable arrests—then produced and blew a loud whistle, which soon brought two of his assistants to his aid.

“ Let some of my men surround the house, and see that no one leaves it ; and you, Robert Lentill, do you at once take charge of this house and its effects, and see that nothing is removed.”

While this was going on Justice Wellrode stood amazed, and asked, “ Where is the father confessor?”

" That," said Topham, " is what I very much wish to know.   Lentill, search the house."

While all these strange events were taking place, poor Marguerite was still clinging to her own apartment, in painful apprehension of being summoned to descend and entertain Sir Caldwell Hunter; but she was soon disagreeably startled by approaching footsteps, and without ceremony a strange man, in company with Mistress Abigail, opened the door; and, with some show of civility, requested—as it was the only place where a man could hide — "leave to look under the bed." Having satisfied himself that Marguerite was alone in that chamber, and beckoning the housekeeper to follow him, he retired; locking the room, and taking the key away with him.

The Justice and the officer being thus left for a little while together, the former demanded if the orders were imperative for his immediate removal; or if he might not remain until he had seen his Father Confessor?

" Oh, yes," replied Topham, " you shall see your priest, if he is in the house; I should like to see him, too: but there is as much chance of our finding him, as there would be of finding a bird's nest in the muzzle of a gun.   We know one—a remarkable one—of that feather, who has been here; but he tarried not, whatever his mission was; and we are following hard on his traces elsewhere : good, if you could put me face to face with the Spaniard 'Moya;' his head is worth its weight in gold."*

The Grove, however, was searched in vain; none but its usual inmates were there, with the exception of one, Father Crawl, and he had that instant, with ready presence of mind, escaped, as we have shown, by an unguarded window.

It was never known why the Justice, in such a strait as he was thus unexpectedly put, did not at least ask for an interview with his daughter. He might have done so, and the application might have been refused, as Master Topham was not the mildest-tempered functionary in the world; but

---

* Marais, a Roman Catholic priest, declared before the University in Paris, in 1604, that Matthew Moya, a Spanish Jesuit, had written the " defence of their (the Jesuits') moral opinions," *published by permission of the superiors of the Order*, in order to revive the errors and impurities of the *Apology of the Casuists* (another work of theirs), and to surpass it in impurity and pernicious subtleties. In 1643 the University of Paris declared themselves " ready to prove that there was no article in religion which the Society of the Jesuits had *not corrupted by erroneous novelties ;*" the University terming the Jesuitical teaching as a " doctrine of devils," "to disseminate and feign the character of intimate friends, in order to destroy with the greater impunity."

whatever happened, as a true historian, I am bound to state, that very shortly the Justice was forced to mount his horse, a few necessaries having been placed upon another, and, a prisoner in the custody of Master Topham, he was conducted from the door of the Grove on his way to London and to the Tower, without having taken leave of Marguerite, or even giving any directions in regard to her or to his household affairs.

Master Lentill, one of Topham's men, thus left in charge, became at once a personage of very great interest to those left in the Grove, and they one and all resolved to get what news they could out of him, either by their wits or by their personal attractions, for he was not a bad-looking fellow. Now, with this especial purpose in their view, Lentill soon found himself the centre of a bevy of girls, and in consequence he gave himself considerable airs. Leaving him to cast the handkerchief, or to throw the apple to her who charmed him most, we must for a short space follow the retreating steps of Father Crawl. That worthy, as soon as he saw who it was that was knocking at the door of the Grove, fled with the greatest precipitation to the woods, when, having reached their shelter, he sat down to consider what he should do. It seemed that, in his desire to circumvent Justice Wellrode, he had invited down to the Grove, to impose on his patron and enact a ghost, a man whose presence at that time was calculated to endanger even the most powerful in the land, and one whom Buckingham himself dared not tamper with. Moya, however, was known to Crawl, and was a stranger to the Justice, and in looks, as well as in the fact of his having a miniature portrait, was the man at all hazards to be employed. Any means to an end in view being, in the Jesuit creed, justifiable, Father Crawl, thinking to give Moya shelter for a night, as he then was endeavouring to hide from a warrant issued for his capture, could not bring danger, though it might serve a purpose, invited him to the Grove, and thus by his unscrupulous designs brought upon Justice Wellrode danger even to the life: for in those days the authority of the law was but slightly cared for; lands were confiscated and men beheaded with very little reason, and with less remorse. In the midst of all this confusion and dismay, one ray of comfort only fell on poor Marguerite's unhappy lot, and that was, that with an officer of Topham's left at the Grove, Father Crawl did not deem it safe to darken that door with his hateful presence. What Marguerite did under the circumstances must be told in another chapter.

CHAPTER XV.

LEFT to my own resources, and with very little money to lay out in the way of experiments, I confess I was puzzled in my present shooting-lodge, as it was called, though there was really little or nothing to shoot at, to find out some way of amusing myself other than with the mere gun. It has ever been an opinion of mine, that no man can be utterly alone or bored for the where-withal to do, if he has a certain amount of the face of nature placed at his command, wherein to study natural history in all its branches—the instincts and peculiarly nice beauties of vege-tation, and the curious definitions afforded in the economy of insect and reptile life. The country I have selected, as the Americans would

say, for a "location," is, around my residence,
lonely and barren enough for anything, and covered to an immense extent with a short ground-
furze, so severe and short that dogs will not hunt
over it; and it is so thick, that though there are
millions of mice beneath this defensive cover, even
the white owl forsakes the fir-trees and flies the
country, unable to pounce on a mouse for his sub-
sistence. No nightingales come to it, game cannot get into it, and if a pheasant makes her nest
in it, ten yards from a nide or road, she flies out
of it to the open space, and then calls on her callow brood to follow. If the furze is wet, they
chill and become motionless before they have progressed three yards; one or two may by chance
reach their mother, when, finding that the rest
do not follow, and cease to cry, the old bird goes
away with just the one or two that have been
able to find her, and the nide is spoiled. With
partridges and black game it is the same; and
though I have cut large and frequent spaces here
and there (selling the stuff cut to the lime-kilns),
to enable the feathered game to get about, I
never in my life had to do with a spot so dia-
metrically opposed to the getting up anything like
a considerable head of game. Hares do not like
it; and I am happy to say, as there are no fox-

hounds very near me, foxes do not like the short, sharp furze, to their feet, any more than dogs do : so the foxes do not come to do me any harm among the few nests of game I can contrive to rear. If they did they would be safe, as I could not even thus be an enemy to a creature in the chase of which I have taken so much pleasure. Pinaster woods and short impassable furze; a large extent of bogs, without game, or fowl, or snipe, save an occasional head here and there, and rills of water, excellent of its kind, without so much as a minnow; a few rabbits; a few partridges; three cock pheasants, and two or three hares, with a few persecuted black game, were all I found when I first took to the almost barren wilds in question.

Add to this extreme paucity of game the mud-hutted, squatting population, who for the most part lived a lawless life, and absolutely grazed the whole estate with their stray cattle; each hut having a horse or a cow, or horses, cows, and donkeys, attached to them, *without* a quarter of an acre of land to maintain the owners and their beasts.

The entire situation of affairs afforded *the best possible contradiction to the very vulgar and mistaken idea*, that large preserves of game foster crime and create the rogue and vagabond. In the first twelve months it became the duty of my people to capture and convict ten men in pursuit of three cock pheasants that had been leased to me. As to the repeated times that cows, horses, and donkeys, were pounded, the number of them was marvellous; for their owners tried it on in every sort of trespass — for game, fodder for cattle, and fire-wood — in the hopes of intimidating me or wearing out my resolution.

I do not wish to dwell on the foolish errors of the squatters, for they all behave very well now, and I have forgotten and forgiven incivilities, attempted depredations and ruffianism; and I think they too have discovered, that if I am forced to be, as I can be, a determined foe, I am always ready to be an infinitely more agreeable friend, and thus we have at last come to a thorough understanding. I like to have an offering of the first strawberries from little gardens brought to me, and to have my game eggs and my young fowl taken care of when accidentally met with by labourers and cottagers, who used to swear at me until I suggested the possibility, *if they went on*, of my fining them for all illicit oaths, besides doing all they could covertly to annoy me. Their good conduct, though, inflames my list for Christmas fare, and costs me too some money in other ways : but though it has been, and is, in my power to box, if necessary, I ever felt more pleasure in doing a kind act than a harsh one. So the present state of things suits us all, and I can now grant several little indulgences as to cattle, of very great service to the village; and purchase from owners, whose cows used to be pounded, the cream they make. It pleases me to do so, and to think that I have taught to my neighbours, of whatever class, that which I take to be the graceful duties of a country gentleman, namely, that while I amuse myself, my amusements become a benefit to all.

Well, then, I love on a hot day to hear the murmur of a stream and to look on the bubbling water in the moss-covered swamps around me. I soon discovered that where there was a bog there was sure to be a spring, so set about to make the water free. My hydraulic experiments, of course, could only be maintained or made permanently available below the drainage of cultivation, and luckily there was a very great fall in the lands towards the sea; that fall terminating in white and hungry sand and gravel, or shingle, in black sand, in bad peat, and submerged and rotten birch and ·pinaster: in short, in a humid conglomeration of all that was useless for agricultural interests, and not available to corn or grass.

On this useless surface I set to work with my own spade, with the spades of my game-keepers, when they could be spared from other duties, and with the spades of occasional la-bourers, when good ones were to be had at ·fifteen shillings a-week. In Dorsetshire a really good labourer cannot be procured at a less amount, and that, too, in the face of all the stuff that has been said or written as to the amount given by their masters. My object was, and is, to turn these useless bogs into streams and ponds for fish and fowl, and to make the stuff dug out, by admixture, capable of bearing one sort of willow or the other—the basket-willow where it will grow, and the copse-willow in any place, for I find with the latter you cannot well go wrong. " Well, then, but how will you get rid of the great cost of wheeling or carting away the stuff from the ponds you dig, which creates the chief expense?" was the question mooted. The reply was,—" I will have no carting nor wheeling away, but I will get rid of the stuff in deepening for ponds, by throwing it up into small islands as I go, and carrying the water still on and around them, in continuation of my design." The experiment is made, though still in its infancy, for my landlords have only contributed fifteen pounds in aid of my work, all the rest has been done by me, and I have the first season's shoot of the basket-willow in some places over three feet long—in a few instances four feet long—while the copse-willow flourishes everywhere. And here let me caution my readers on no account whatever to use as manure that rank poison called the gas-lime, from gas-works. I was asked to try it on some of this "sour" land, and assured that it would make it "friable." It was not a bad word that; for though I first exposed the gas-lime to the weather, and then used it moderately and in a pulverized state, well mixing it with soil, it *fried* some of my willows, *fried* my potatoes, and *fried* my buck-wheat, wherever I.did use it, burning everything up to destruction. It is one of those great mistakes, its general recommendation, which the feverish minds of philosophers of the present day are so apt to fall into. I would not recommend it for use in any way. It will poison water-fowl and fish, if used too strongly, and to vegetation it is *death without benefit of grubs.*

Well then, reader, it is a beautiful day in the beginning of summer. Come with me—sit on this grassy bank above my little ponds and streams, or down among the heather; listen to the chorus of wild bees, the cooing of the cushat dove: and then, if you sit quite still, and do not confess your strange presence too much, you shall see a Midsummer Night's Dream enacted, but by day. This is about the time when I am expected; and do not think me mad, but I am going to call in an unknown tongue—at least it is an unknown tongue still to my fellow-man, but not to the birds of all kinds that surround me. In a whistling sort of voice I then pronounce, as shrilly as possible " Pip de viddle e, viddle e ve." On the instant a much more pleasing sound ascends to the air, syllabled like the one I utter, but far more sweet in its tone. It arises from the ponds, and is the reply from a beautiful little goose from Pernambuco—I believe, the smallest of its tribe in the world; and the moment the gander—for he is of the male sex—has answered, numerous cries from various water-fowl arise: for they have learned the language that always proclaims the presence of food; and in a short time strange and beautiful things come down the little rills of water, or up the successive ponds, and sit by me on the bank. The—at that time of year—

gorgeous cock pheasant, with his crimson gills and upright horns, comes crowing to sit at my foot. The splendid American wood-drake—the handsomest-plumaged bird, perhaps, in existence, with his brilliantly-plumed head—comes to me; and, if she is not sitting, guiding his duck from contact with any other aquatic bird; conversing with her after his fashion, and picking up for her and carrying it off, to give her in a more sequestered spot—calling to her all the time—the bit of bread of which he has possessed himself. There, too, is that little *bijou*, the Bahama drake, with his lovely pencilled, cinnamon plumage, his white cheeks, and bright vermilion ring round the base of his bill. The gadwall, the shoveller, and the graceful pintail, are there, with the pochard and tufted duck, and the great, clumsy eider duck, as well as the common wild duck, and some curious hybrids: they all come and sit with me, and have no fears of me, nor of my new young retriever, "Diver," whose "hide I do not drum on" to keep him quiet: because the fowl see no difference between him and my late poor dear old friend "Brutus," whom they had long known.

Well, and is this not pleasant to watch the habits of these beautiful things, and to teach the most timid to be bold and to love me? To sit or lie down among them in the sweet honey-scented wild, far from the reach of any human voice, or the sound of any bell ; to hear nothing but the sweet voice of Nature through her feathered choir, or the music of her murmuring rills; and to know that in the sight of Heaven, in *that* scene, there was nothing wrong; to me it is very beautiful: and one of the things that I am most thankful for is the power to appreciate it.

Well, and where the useless tadpole cut off his entail and became a veritable frog, or succeeding heir to his full estate of reptilism—there where, in mossy slime and stagnation, he used to dwell with his cousin the water-newt, there swims the graceful little trout or delicate gudgeon; in other places the richly-hued perch and silver eel : so that, in a short space, I have around me a little useful and ornamental world of my own, created by me, and by me intensely enjoyed; and I envy no man his wider possession.

And now as to the carriage of live fish. Those men at the Zoological Gardens in London would do well to leave off much of the absurd nonsense they talk about porpoises, sturgeons, and salmon, and serpents sitting like hens on their own eggs, and salmon-fry in the tank in the fish-house kept to feed the kingfishers, but which alleged salmon-fry, in truth, are only common minnows; and get, for the transportation of fish alive, the bag I use to carry trout in. Trout are nearly, or quite, the most difficult fish to transport alive and well: yet, by the plan I have adopted, they may be carried for a great many miles, and kept alive certainly for twelve hours; and restored to, or again put into, the water designed for them, without an injury to a single fish.

Have a good strong bag of waterproof cloth, or canvas, made—say, a yard deep, and more than a yard long. In short, when filled with water, it should be a yard square on its four sides. Externally, to strengthen and to steady it, it should be bound with a network of leather—say, of an eight-inch mesh, or more. When sufficiently filled with water, the water, of course, will keep it stretched to its full extent; and then, with straps to the four corners, it can be fixed in a spring-cart, or spring-carriage; its bottom slightly poised upon the floor, and no hard substance pressing on either of its four sides. In this bag, occasionally supplied with fresh water, live trout can be carried almost any distance; and that, too, with very little change, or addition of fresh water. The swaying of the pliant bag does not in any way bruise them, while the undulating motion keeps the water charged with air.

The bag, when not in the cart, and waiting for the fish as they are caught, must never be still. It should always be made to undulate, and the man charged with its custody should be vigilant in this part of his duty. I have seen questions asked as to the transportation of live fish, in the pretended, but useless, sporting publications of the day, and would long ago have described this method of carriage to the querists; but not approving of the channel through which my communications must appear, I have kept them for my own book: and I shall do so by many others, until some sporting paper is established—and there is at present a good opening for one—which may be sought and referred to by sportsmen and naturalists of every grade.

For a long time at Lord Malmesbury's almost adjoining manors of Heron Court we have observed that the black game never increase, and now they have become almost extinct. Here — though I have taken immense pains with the few there are—here, also, they every year become less and less. I could guard against the evil of the grey-hens never laying until their second year; but I cannot guard against distant pot-hunters, in distant places unpreserved, killing them, as they perpetually do. Though I may teach the black game to fly to my manor as a place of safety, and to breed there, I cannot prevent their roaming flights; nor the grey-hens, which are much tamer than the black-cocks, getting killed by greedy people.

There are still two other things more difficult to obviate than all; and one is, when deep drains are cut through the moors to drain the higher level, made with high and upright banks, down which the young black game cannot go to drink good water without being drowned. The consequence of this is, that in very dry seasons they drink from the " soaks," or stagnant water left on the moss by rains, and which becomes so impregnated with iron, or rotten vegetation, that it amounts, in regard to young birds, to poison. A little iron is good, but too much will be fatal to young things as well as to fish. This, then, is one of the things that I cannot altogether remedy; the other is, the growth of the blackberry, and the greediness of the young black game to feed upon it. I have no doubt but there is some species of food wanting on the Dorsetshire moors, unattainable to the black game, and that that food consists of some kind of berry other than the bilberry or blueberry, for those I have planted in great quantities, though not yet sufficiently, and they take very well. This opinion of mine is suggested by the way the black game die of a sort of cholera, produced by eating too many blackberries. Among the broods I have known and kept my eye on, I have found, when the blackberry fruit is ripe, the young birds, and what is most wonderful, always the young cocks of plumage well defined and fit to kill, become so weak that I have taken them up in my hand and examined them. I felt sure their weakness arose from the fact I describe; and having two young black game in a large aviary—the birds sent to me from Scotland—I caused a very few blackberries to be given them, just to see the effect. The berries having been greedily devoured, the birds were at once seized with a species of cholera, black in proportion as the berries themselves, oats and other dry food in no way acting as an alterative. No more blackberries being given, the birds resumed their usual health and vigour.

I have much to say on this subject; but, not to tire my readers, I will vary my discourse with a short reference to our American cousins over the water—to their birds, their beasts, and aptitude for repartée.

They say there, that there is a plant called the snake-plant on the plains, because the Indians eat it when bitten by a rattlesnake. The plant pointed out to me had a blue flower, and at that time of the season (September) that and the wild sunflower were the only things that bloomed among the everlasting grass of the undulating *peraries*, as the bearded inhabitants of those regions call their lands, laying stress on the first syllable. I was shown also a shrub bearing a blackish, or dark purple berry, which they affirmed was a cure for snake poison; but the only certain cure that came under my observation was an unlimited amount of whisky. The feeding of the prairie grouse puzzled me much, because, when they could get it, they showed such a desire to feed on the maize, or Indian corn, that they flocked at daybreak to it, isolated as the squatters' fields were; and in their flight to the food, and while they were on the spot getting it, they were attended by immense numbers of every sort of hawk known in the Far West, who came to prey on them.

The prairie grouse killed by me out of all reach of corn, were just in as good condition as those killed on the verge of considerable cultivation; and throughout my travels I never could discover what was a substitute for the artificial or cultivated, and apparently better, kind of food.

The settlers in the plains, of course, are very fond of the *perarie* chickens, as they call them, and in some situations the grouse of the plain is the only meat they get. One of my waggons broke down close to a blacksmith's shop, who, by good chance, was settled in the bush, and it was of immense importance to me to get it immediately mended, that I might gain a safe place to encamp before dark.

"I say, my good friend, can you mend my waggon for me?"

"I'll look at it first, stranger, and then I'll tell you."

"Come on then, my excellent man, as we have no time to lose."

"Guess I can't just now, I'm that tarnation busy."

"Busy!" I exclaimed; "why just now you were sitting half-asleep in the sun!"

"Guess I was, like a rattle-tailed riggler, with one eye open, and *ready to bite.*"

"Bite! bite what? you don't want to bite me, do you?"

"No, guess I don't: I'm up to bite a better thing than you!"

"Well, but why won't you come and look at my waggon, and then gnaw the whole universe if you like it, and bite it all to your heart's content? Looking at my waggon can't hurt your holders."

"No, knows it can't; but I jest knows this . . . Wall, then, I've got two *perarie* chickens for my dinner to-day. Them're afore the fire; and though they say fire is a good servant, I knows him to be an out-and-out tyrant if he gets to be president, and I'm not going to trust my chicks to his tender marcies. Arter dinner I'm yer man, but not an inch afore."

So thus we parted till he had dined.

Though on their railways and in their public vehicles the Yankees are slow in motion, the only time they go a-head on wheels is when they hang on by the mouths of their trotting horses, in carriages really made to carry nothing but one man; in all other things they are fast enough and sly enough for any fun or repartée they may at the moment please to follow.

Of course they wish us in the old country to believe, that in every phase of existence they are the go-a-head winners as compared with our quickness, and they never lose a chance to keep up that delusion.

I illustrate this by the following fact, which happened on an English rail:—" Tickets, gents!"—

(how I detest that vulgar abbreviation !)—exclaimed a porter to two Americans seated in a second-class carriage. I don't believe the well-conducted official would have used the word " gent " at the window of a first-class caariage. " Tickets, gents !"

" I reckon here you are," said the American, from beneath a regular down-eastern hat, and above a long, bushy, goat-like appendage beneath his mouth. " Here you are, look sharp! you're mighty slow in these old places: hand 'em back slick out of hand. Now then !"

" You 're in a hurry," replied the porter, ere he had had time to look at or snip the tickets.

" Guess I an't, or should have got out and walked long ago," was the reply.

" Halloo !" cried the porter, cutting the American short in his turn; " this is a ticket and a half: that 's no half along with you !"

" Guess that *is* true," rejoined the Yankee. " It 's your fault, not ours; was a half when he took his ticket, but he 's growed since then."

There is a vast deal of fun in a genuine Yankee, and an immense amount of bluster — bluster which would be bombastic bullying if submitted to by those on whom it was tried, but if not submitted to, to be backed out of when the Yankee finds, even at the last moment, that he is trying to put the wrong saddle on the right horse. There is, however, a high generosity in a true American as to money. Dollar-seeking men as they are truly said to be, if a Yankee knows that he has to deal with a man undoubtedly belonging to the English aristocracy, or "Upper Ten Thousand," there is no sum that he will not readily advance to him without so much as a bond, or receipt, or note of hand of any kind. I met with the Captain of an American trader at Paris, who, seeing that I was at a temporary loss for funds, and that I should be obliged inconveniently to stay in Paris for another day in order to get them, and thus not be able to keep to the hour a morning engagement at the Château Sauvages, he at once placed before me a bag of gold, and told me to take "as much money as I needed," saying, "You can return it at your convenience." On a second occasion, when at St. Louis, in America, a very kind and dear friend of mine, Mr. Campbell, who at that time only knew me by report, on finding that I was not sufficiently provided with funds for a start into the desert, at once advanced to me all the money I needed, and gave me letters of credit on the bankers, to the very farthest limit of civilization, for any amount I might require.

After all the democracy and levelling of distinctions we hear of, it is as curious as it is gratifying to find that a member of the English aristocracy, known by repute, is good in America for any amount of gold throughout the extent of civilization, and that his character and position in life without any note of hand, or even promise, insure the implicit belief in his high honour and his honesty in pecuniary transactions.

If ever any man thus connected with "the Upper Ten Thousand" should belie our nature, and tarnish our name and fame, may the Americans catch him in the unworthy act, and tar and feather him; or, better still, let them show him up to us, and, his delinquency proved, trust to us to find out some way of marking our horror at the falling off, and of meting out to the low villain the punishment he would richly deserve: but I trust in Heaven that not one of "the Upper Ten Thousand" will so miserably misconduct himself.

CHAPTER XVI.

Part V.

On the second day after the occurrences we have narrated, the glorious month of June, green, golden-hued, and lovely, sweet and songful as June is before she begins to fall into the arms of her torrid lover, fierce July, was in all her effulgence; even the winds were hushed to gentler sighs, as if Æolus himself contemplated her as yet untouched beauty. Though the nightingale had ceased, still the thrush sat on the topmost bough, in the hours of twilight, in which he mostly loves to sing, and gave joy to his last fond listening nest; while in deeper and more lowly thicket sang the mellow blackbird, joined in his rich deep note in furze-brake, brier, and blackthorn, by warbler and by yellowhammer, the last bird that sings in summer. The turtle-dove and cushat, too, were cooing; and amidst such soothing sounds as these,

when Heaven seems in nature's softest sympathy
to whisper consolation to the crushed and broken-
hearted, Willie wandered round the lonely woods,
and haunted still Our Lady's Well. Accompanied, as usual, by his faithful dog "Luther," he
had visited the little chalk cliff as a matter of
course, without ever expecting to find anything
there, and had thence wandered among the many
paths in that extensive wood. "Luther" had
strayed away from him, to amuse himself after
rabbits, as he would occasionally take on himself
to do when he saw that his master, wrapped in
thought, continued to walk in one vicinity. As
a whistle would at once recall him, this slight
deviation from duty was seldom visited with displeasure. After some time, however, on this occasion, Willie's reverie was suddenly disturbed by
the rushing to him of "Luther" through the midst
of the cover afar off, the haste and vigour of the
dog's approach not relaxing till he had found and
fallen in ecstasies upon his master, leaping upon
him and testifying his intense delight in the
wildest manner possible. That some remarkable
event had happened Willie knew, and in his heart
he wildly dared to hope that "Luther" had met
with Marguerite. His suspicions were to some
extent confirmed; for in the line amidst the

brambles over which "Luther" had bounded, at intervals he caught a glimpse of a little black face struggling with the difficulties of the cover, and soon recognised the spaniel "Jip." What, then, was all the delight expressed by "Luther?" and were all his master's re-awakened hopes to be dashed at once to the ground by this explanation, by this solution, of the dog's joy? As with the ever ready tenacity of belief in that we long for he suddenly sprang to the one conclusion, so, with a similarly quick · divergence, hope seemingly doomed to disappointment, again came the desolation of despair, and Willie only thought that "Jip" had escaped from home. Taking her up in his arms, however, and covering her with kisses for her mistress's sake, he went with her by a path which he knew would lead · him to the Well; but, looking round to call the attention of "Luther," that faithful friend was no more to be seen, for he had bounded off while Willie was occupied with "Jip."

How often do we find our hearts hoping against hope, and resolved to dwell on anticipations that at the moment seem unlikely to be realised! Willie tried not to hope, yet still his heart overruled his eyes; and instead of letting them be cast down, the eyes went looking, longing on, and on turning into a narrow path, that path, at the end of a hundred yards, was full! "Luther" was leading Marguerite towards him by her gown! Ask me not what the lover feels when thus his cup runs over, nor expect me to prate of sensations in which words can take no part, and whose throne rests on an unsullied silence fanned alone by sighs. Willie knew no more; he was conscious of nothing save that he clasped Marguerite to his heart, and fixing his lips on hers deemed that in that one sweet moment died the misery of time.

"Marguerite!" at length Willie said, "sweet Marguerite, come with me! The priest has taught us that we must not trust to open paths that are pervious to other eyes."

Thus saying, with his arm around her waist, Willie led his willing captive to more secret bowers, and spreading his cloak, which he had brought with him, they sat down beneath the thickest foliage, to be attended, as of old, by their favourite robins. "Willie," she said, "it never would have been thus but for the distrust of my father. While he trusted me his wish was as a law, but when he reviled me in the presence of the author of all evil—that conspiring priest— alas! the bonds so far were broken, and by doubt and ill-usage my father set me free! Free, Willie, to see you; but at the same time, in all duty and affection, bound to watch over my father's interests, and to tend him in his hour of trial. Willie, tell me, what is the cause of his arrest? for arrested he has been; and who is this Topham who has taken him?"

We need not follow Willie in his surprise at the news, nor in his description of the state of the times, when the Puritan, the Cavalier, the moderate Reformer, the Roman Catholic, and the Jesuit,* were outbidding and circumventing each other in rumours and charges as vague as they were insane.

Willie explained to Marguerite as much as he himself knew of the trickery and unsettled state of the times, and congratulated himself on being of the Reformed religion, and therefore free of any suspicion in regard to King or Parliament. As to the vile use that had been made of the picture he had given to his friends in the cottage, and of which Marguerite now told him, on that his indig-

* Many people suppose that the Roman Catholic and the Jesuit are of one and the same faith; whereas the Jesuit is in fact as much desirous of upsetting the Roman Catholic as he is the Established religion. The Jesuits, at a recent date, took every covert opportunity of showing their contempt of Cardinal Wiseman.

nation knew no bounds, even to the saying that, were he to meet the " Snake," he would cudgel him to death. Time flew on, as fast as time always flies when lovers are together, and the hour of parting came. " Luther," who had kept strict watch on the surrounding wood, rose and shook his long wavy black coat, and seemed to think, too, that it was time to move. They parted at the Well, Willie undertaking to learn all he could as to the arrest of her father, and again they agreed to meet on the following day. On the following day they met, and again and again! Willie had ascertained that her father had been taken to the Tower; news also had reached Marguerite in a roundabout way, through the superioress of a small conclave of nuns at the neighbouring abbey of Medenham, that her father was well, and that his interests were looked after; and thus awaiting, perhaps, or thinking that she only tarried for more direct orders from him, she gave herself up to the sweet transgressions of the summer hour—if transgressions they can be called when the misled harshness of a father drives a daughter from her filial duty to seek a better solace in the company of her lover. During the passage of these happy interviews— for happy and uninterrupted they were, the time flying but too quickly—the priest had never been seen; so that, save the presence at the Grove of Master Topham's sub-officer, which kept Willie as well as the priest away, there was scarce an alloy to the lovers' enjoyment.

As the course of true love is said never to run smooth—it does though, sometimes!—this state of things was even now not to last; and we must approach, however reluctantly, the sadder events in the phase of the present scene, and in that phase just preceding these occurrences we find our lovers side-by-side beneath the thickest foliage of Whittenden Park Wood. The moment they were seated,—

" Willie," exclaimed Marguerite, " I have had letters from my father. He writes kindly now, and advises me to take counsel with the priest Crawl, who will provide for me a suitable place of reception while my father's difficulties last. He tells me I shall have to leave home; but I will not, cannot, put myself at the disposal of that vile man. Then, Willie, what shall I do?"

" Oh, Marguerite! my own sweet Marguerite! fly with me. Who can love you as I do, and will for ever love you? and where, where can you be so safe as under my protection? Give me but your hand, give me a right in the face of all the world to call you mine, and then, a willing slave to your father's interests for his daughter's sake, I will watch over all. At this moment I am poor, and have little more to offer you than my heart and hand; still my father's roof can be your shelter until better times. You know that some day I may be rich, though never richer, as far as my ideas are concerned, than when I possess you. Oh, Marguerite! dearest Marguerite! fly at once with me!"

"Willie," she replied, her lovely forehead leaning on his shoulder, "it cannot, at least it must not, be *now*. What would people say of me, if, taking advantage of my father's misfortunes and his absence from home, I fled with one whose society he had forbidden me; and at a time, too, when he most needed the dutiful attention of a daughter! Willie, Willie, do not tempt me, but aid me the rather to work the will of Heaven, and to bear my wrongs. I will, indeed I will, love you all the better, for being in my affliction thus my firmest and my truest friend."

Willie, thus addressed, felt in his heart the delicacy of Marguerite's position, and the one high-toned, generous, self-denying, and chivalric line he ought to follow, and for a few moments, his eyes bent upon the ground, he remained silent.

Not liking thus to see his mournful brow, Marguerite said,—

"Speak to me, Willie; though you usually seem so happy when I am at your side, you have to-day been downcast. Is there anything more on your mind than you have told me?"

"Oh, Marguerite," he said, "it is enough to make me sad, in being again forced to put off that which we might do to-day until a long to-morrow. The to-morrow, alas! may never come; a thousand difficulties surround us to-day, which may grow stronger by delay, but which, cut across and crushed at this moment, we have it surely in our power to overcome. You ask me, then, why I am dull. Have you never observed the blithe bird of the summer-day, when sunny sweets surround him, on the approach of some yet unseen and far-off thunder-storm grow sad, and even be hushed from all songs of love? Have you not seen the dewdrop hang pendent from the bloom or spray in the sultry air, as if afraid to fall, or make itself the glittering herald of the breeze which was about to break the parent bough? As that bird then, and as that spray, am I. In thee, my essence and my bloom of life are concentrated; our hours together seem by decree to be but few; if we part, we may never meet again; and in that doubt, it seems to me, a tempest comes to crush me. Few as my hours have been with thee, thy once withholding mind, sweet love, no longer doubts the devotion of my soul, or all that soul confesses; then blame me not, if in this fleeting hour some saddened monitor within my heart hath whispered that in unfettered moments, by thy will restrained, a world of love is lost to us for ever. Oh, Marguerite, I have been beneath thy window, though not beneath thy roof, in the silent night, shut from thee by bolt and bar. *What* kept me from thy side? Thy window was not high! No door, no bar, no wall, no bolt, no distance, and no difficulty, stayed my lip from thine. The stay of these I owned not, and free as Heaven's curbless winds, I scorned all human fetter *but thy will*. Oh, Marguerite! there was upon me then that which rules me now—the deep, the firm resolve to think of thee before myself, and never, by act or deed, to bring thee into blame or danger."

"I know, dear Willie," replied Marguerite, "that I can trust you implicitly: had it not been so, we had not been here. You once before told me you were sure some fell mischance was about to happen that would part us, and yet we are not severed. Cheer up, then, dearest Willie; nothing depresses me so much as seeing despair in you. I must away now to the Grove, where my poor father's interests yet command my presence. Good-bye, dear old Cumpey," said the even now smiling girl, as she caressed the faithful black dog's head in all freedom from any suspicion of immediate evil; " come with your master to our bower to-morrow. And here, you dear little things," she continued, to the two little robins who always attended her in the wood, " *take the last crumbs I have for you*, and sing to each other till I come back."

Willie, with a heavy heart, then assisted her to rise, when she called on " Jip " to follow her, and they all went as far as the Well. It was there, as usual, that Willie took his leave; and having watched the last wave of her dress that the path in the wood left visible, he turned towards West Wycombe, vainly endeavouring to rouse himself from that mysterious sense of approaching evil which has more than once, and to many of us, proved a truthful monitor, albeit we for ever essay to set such sensations at defiance. With a sense of impending misfortune poor Willie sought his pillow, with very little chance of rest.

On the next morn Willie rose from his bed with an indefinable sensation of dread still upon

him; and when the usual time came he set off to
Whittenden Wood, if with a heavy heart, still
with that alluring fondness predominant in his
mind that leads an anxious lover across precipices
and chasms, and nerves him to brave and buffet
waves in the frailest boat, or with the lusty arm
of the strong swimmer. On arriving at the usual
spot in the wood he examined the edge of the
chalk cliff, as was his custom, and, to his even
painful surprise, found a note from Marguerite. It simply informed him that letters had
arrived from her father, telling her that, though
he hoped to clear himself of any charges as to his
loyalty and peaceful intentions, nevertheless he
might be detained some time on account of
another arrest being lodged against him for debt;
for that, to his astonishment, Sir Caldwell Hunter,
who had lent him money, was resolved to be paid
forthwith. She told him, with many kind expressions, that she could not come to the wood
that day, but on the following day he might expect her at the usual time. " You may leave
a line for me, Willie," she concluded; "and if
our faithful little Mary comes here she shall fetch
it, and deliver it to my hands." This intelligence
added fresh gloom to Willie's still desponding
heart; so, sitting down, he wrote a few lines,

telling her so, and beseeching her to come to him earlier than usual, to make up for the extent of the separation; adding, that he trusted the detestable Jesuit had not dared to approach her. These few lines he deposited in the usual secret hiding-place. While writing this "Luther" had left his side, and, deeming that his master as usual would remain in the wood some hours, had gone off to amuse himself in the chase of a rabbit. Giving a low whistle to his dog to come away, Willie then turned his steps homeward, and did not notice that the signal to "Luther" had been in vain. Some time after Willie had left the wood "Luther" returned to the Swilley Hole, from the chase of the rabbit, to look for his master, when, on hearing the approach of some one, he lay down, thinking that he was returning. It was not Willie, but Father Crawl. On came the priest, stepping stealthily, turning his head from time to time in the most cautious manner, as if to ascertain that the coast was clear. "Luther," when he saw him, crouched more closely among the grass and brambles, as a dog may be seen to lie down, sphinx-like, on the approach of another, or of some object that he hates. The priest paused over the sylvan letter-box, descended a few steps, knelt down, raised the covering of the moss, and took the letter in his hand, when, ere he could possess himself of its contents, with the spring and force of a lion "Luther" flew upon him, making his teeth meet in his arm above the elbow, and pulling him forcibly to the swampy ground below. The priest writhed and wriggled under the fangs of his assailant, who shook him as a hound may be seen to shake a fox; but, fox-like, though the priest was injured and hurt beyond measure, he never uttered a cry, nor opened his sullenly compressed lips, save to bite the moss and lichen, or whatever was shaken within reach of his teeth. At length the sagacious dog, letting go the arm of the priest, seized triumphantly the letter which had fallen from his hand, and, enveloping it completely in his mouth, trotted off with every symptom of successful anger to overtake his master. Willie had left the wood, and was taking a short cut home through the fields, and had nearly attained a wooded valley, known in these days as Hell Bottom—an appellation probably obtained through the orgies of the " Hell-fire Club"—when, on hearing the hurried and galloping approach of his dog behind him, he turned to chide him for his unusually long absence; but a glance at those faithfully bright-brown eyes showed him that something of an unwonted nature had occurred. The point was soon illustrated, for, with a formal whine approaching to a growl, "Luther" made a little circuit round his master, indicating that he carried something for him. Willie's surprise was great when he took from his dog the letter he had just written, and which, though unharmed, was still wet from the panting haste at which "Luther" had brought it. Some people, unused to dogs like this, would simply have supposed that the dog, finding a letter that had been left by his master, had picked it up, and followed with it in his mouth; but Willie knew well that more than met his own eye or knowledge had taken place: so, at once turning round and retracing his steps to the spot, he beheld on the ground the deeply-indented claws of his dog, the torn-up moss, and broken twigs, all testifying to a violent struggle; and among the leaves a portion of a rent, and even bloody, black sleeve, of similar texture to the frock that he had seen upon the back of the crafty Jesuit. Suspecting at once with whom the struggle had been, Willie caressed and encouraged his faithful, four-footed friend; and deeming that, as it was getting too late for Mary to be sent for the note as Marguerite had signified, he refrained from again putting it in the cliff beneath the moss, resolving that Mary should once more have the sole charge of it. Together, then, master and dog proceeded home. Alas! had he waited a little longer he might have met the very girl who was to have been sent for the note, and averted the calamity which followed.

How slight a circumstance will often lead to serious things! a trifle altogether omitted, or a trifle pressed too much, will frequently mar or make a fortune. Had Willie replaced the note in the little cliff, Mary would have found it; and had Mary possessed herself of the letter, and delivered it to Marguerite, Marguerite would have escaped a visitor at home, and have met Willie too early for him to have been drawn into a snare.

On the following day, and earlier than usual, Mary, with her basket on her head, was proceeding from Lane End towards the Grove, when suddenly, from the wild lawns leading up to Whittenden Park, there emerged the man of all others she most disliked and dreaded, the Jesuit priest, his right arm in a sling. He had been almost a stranger to the neighbourhood since the removal of Justice Wellrode from his house, and the continued vigil there of Topham's officer; and as his presence had been so scarce of late, his appearance at the present moment was the more unwelcome. Coming straight up to Mary, who received him with a low curtsey,

he took her with his left hand by the arm, and
said, "Come hither, girl; I would speak to
thee." Poor little Mary could have screamed
had she dared to do so, when she felt his cold
clammy grasp upon her arm ; but as the snake
is said to have a power to fascinate the nervous
and timid bird, so had this vile priest a power
to overawe an ignorant mind, and lead Mary
whithersoever he chose. They left the road, and
ascended to a thick furze-brake, into the midst
of which they entered, when he suddenly seated
himself beneath some old high gorse, and commanded the trembling and fear-stricken girl to
seat herself at his side. As in her terror she
came to the earth with some emphasis, her dress
made a corresponding jump, and disclosed a good
deal of a very neatly-rounded ankle, which she
instantly endeavoured to hide, but was at once
enjoined by her dreaded captor to "let it be."

"Thy leg is pretty, Mary," said the wily
man, "and if thou dost my bidding discreetly,
I'll call thee some day my niece, and instal thee
as my housekeeper."

"Oh, Lord, sir, no !" burst from Mary's lips,
in accents of hearty truth that needed no
backing.

"Hush !" said the priest. "How ! Takest

thou the Name in vain? Thou shalt do penance for the same in a white sheet."

Satisfied with the fear he had inspired in the heart of the cottage girl, he thus continued :—

" I want thee to be the bearer of a letter to one whom thou knowest very well, and whom— do you hear me, damsel?—common report says thou dost love."

" To Master Willie, sir?" exclaimed the art-less girl.

" Oh, yes, of course, to Master Willie; thou wert quite ready with his name. Thou dost love him, then?"

" Aye, sir, dearly, and so I ought to do," said Mary, beginning to whimper; "for he saved my life, and father's too."

" Well, then, if thou lovest him I wish thee to carry this letter—it is for him—and put it in the spot well known to thee at the cliff above the Swilley Hole. How! dost thou hesitate?"

" Oh, yes, sir; please don't make me put it there; indeed, I'd rather not, unless I read it, and knew it couldn't do him any harm: but I can't read" (that the priest very well knew); "so please don't, your reverence, let me have it."

" Mary," said her tormentor with startling sternness, seizing her roughly by the arm at the same time, "thou *must* be the bearer of it: the concealed spot is only known to thee and me; and for very good reasons, which I will explain at some other time, I have a dislike to putting my hand into its vicinity."

This announcement was accompanied by a lively twitching of his wounded arm, bringing back acute remembrances of Luther's teeth.

" Take it thou must and shalt, or thou shalt undergo due penance for the Name thou hast lately taken in vain."

While speaking thus, the sharp eyes of the Jesuit fixed themselves intently for a moment on a thick bush of gorse, and then he continued :

" But what if I show thee not only that thou canst warn thy petted Master Willie of impending danger, but also that thou art specially designed by Heaven to do so? Dost thou know a little bird called the wren?"

" Oh yes, sir! a little brown bird, that the boys call a ' titty fudge.' It builds every summer in the porch of our cottage, and is quite tame !"

" Right, thou knowest the colour of the little brown bird; and what if Heaven has changed it, and shown a miracle to make thee believe and obey. Holy Mother!" cried the priest, excitedly, and devoutly crossing himself, while he pointed to the thick bush of furze, into the depths of which he had been previously gazing: "*Mary, thou art the chosen of Heaven!* and I the humble instrument to explain the Divine will. Lo, the white bird comes!* Look there!" Mary, in an agony of wonder and fear, turned her eyes as directed by his finger; and, to her astonishment, beheld, hopping from thorn to thorn, a snow-white wren. The priest bowed his head, and then suddenly raising his arm, the action of which caused the startled bird to disappear, and pointing to heaven, gave Mary his blessing, and put the small packet into her hands. "Go," he said, "thou chosen of Heaven; go, do as the servant of our Holy Mother hath bidden thee: go, place the packet in the little hiding-place known to thee. But stay," as Mary had risen to depart with it in her hand, "after thou hast done so, tarry not a moment, but hasten back to this spot to me, to acquaint me with the fulfilment of thy holy mission."

Overwhelmed with awe, and frightened and

---

* In the winter of 1862 Colonel Fane, M.P., while shooting at West Wycombe Park, killed a white wren, which was stuffed by Mr. W. Hart of Christchurch, and is now in the possession of Lady Dashwood.

bewildered, Mary departed; and as she left the priest muttered to himself, " May the white wren of Whittenden Park save thy pretty arm, Mary, from the rough usage mine met with from the teeth of the great, black, ruthless dog !"

Poor Mary hastened to execute her mission in a state of collapse, that very nearly made her lose her way as she neared the Swilley Hole. Oh! how she hoped to have seen Willy's tall form still haunting that loved spot : but in that hope she was deceived. The place was lonely and still; the moss above the crevice in the chalk rock had settled again to an undisturbed state; and with an undefined and peculiar sensation of dread, or as if she was committing a deed dictated by the devil, instead of being—as the Jesuit priest assured her it was—a most holy behest from Heaven, she deposited the letter as desired, and without let or hindrance went back to the furze-brake on the lawn, to report to the Jesuit that she had obeyed him. On the execution of her mission being reported, Mary stooped to repossess herself of the basket, which she had, in the first instance, set down beside Father Crawl, when, to her terror and astonishment, he laid his hand upon her shoulder, with the startling words: " Not so fast, damsel: I have reasons yet a little longer to desire thy stay. We will tarry here awhile, and then thou must accompany me to thy father's cottage; for I have business with you all."

Leaving them thus occupied, we must now return to our hero and our heroine.

Willie had failed both that afternoon and on the following morning to find Mary, as she had left her cottage on each occasion before he called there; so, with all the restless anxiety of an ex-pectant lover, he at once sought the sylvan trysting-place in hopes of the interview he desired. He was thus in Whittenden Park Wood about the usually-appointed time; and, as usual, he loitered by the Swilley Hole, and laid down to rest from the heat of the day beneath the beech-trees. He had not lain thus long, when "Luther" sniffed the air and growled, arose from his recumbent posi-tion, and approached the edge of the chalk-pit; his attention to the signs he seemed to snuff in the air being apparently divided between the tainted gale, which rustled through the alders in the swamp, and the exhalation which arose from the concealed cleft, which had so often contained the letters. It had been evident to any expe-rienced eye, that the first impulse of the dog was for an angry rush into the thick cover of the alders; but in his first ideas of this he had been arrested by something nearer still, inviting the attention of his tender and sagacious nose.

Willie remarked only the last of these proceedings; and his notice thus directed to the ground, he sprang to his feet, and took the priest's letter from its hiding-place. He had not time to open it, however, nor even scarce to see the direction, ere a violent rush through the tangled swamp placed two stout fellows on either side of him, their hands on his collar, and their pistols at his head, met as they were by a spring at them from his faithful dog, whose gripe on one of their throats Willie had only just time to intercept.

"Down, 'Luther!' Hold your pistols! How is this?" demanded Willie.

"How is this?" cried a pompous voice, the owner of it adopting a less hurried advance from the alders than had been made by his men. "How is this? Why, I am Master Topham, the officer of the House of Commons, and you are one Master William Barnwell, whom we want, named in this my warrant," holding out a dirty piece of parchment. "I arrest you, sir, as one in secret correspondence with the damnable Popish conspirators in immediate communication with the proscribed Spaniard Moya, now conspiring to dethrone the King, and tread under foot the glorious structure of the Reformed religion.　No resistance, sir, and follow me."

The caution as to no resistance was uttered while the myrmidons of Master Topham were binding Willie's arms behind him, having taken from him the letter, which they handed to their superior, and which letter the man in office very leisurely opened and read.. "Why, what damnable heresies are these?" exclaimed the puzzled officer, reading aloud,—"'To our dear brothers in religion, by the blessings, &c. &c. &c., the time draweth nigh; let the loins be girded and the weapons bared ; when eleven rockets ascend the fiery night, let the city blaze and the country make in, to the seat of all evil. We know we can trust thee, Master Willie ; draw thy men around thee.

> ' A crown, a crown, a monk his hood,
> Give me a cup of strong ale, for that's good ;
> But the crown we want is the crown of all :
> Then up with the lamb, for the wolf must fall.'"

Poor Willie, who had simply prepared himself to hear a coarse lip pronounce the written words of Marguerite's small white hand, now stared in utter astonishment at Master Topham, exclaiming, in some pettishness, "Why, what egregious mockery is this?"

"Not much mocking in it, fair sir," replied the

officer, holding up the document to Willie's eyes.
" Here you are, taken by me, Master Topham, in
secret correspondence with the priests and papists.
If this paper," he said, rapping it with his coarse
heavy hand, " be not food for the enlarging maw
of Dr. Oates, I know not what is.   Here is a
covert allusion to the subversion of all, even to the
murder of the King.   Away with him, lads, to the
Tower!"

"I know no more of that paper," exclaimed
Willie, " than you do.   I can't know much less, for
it is impossible to understand it."

" Oh no," exclaimed the officer, " of course not!
you did not know it was there, nor look for it, did
you?   Come, come, my young sir, that tale won't
wash.   Just be good enough to teach the duty of
your own captivity to this sly-looking, big, black
dog.   His nose is always at the calf of my leg, and
I 'll send a bullet through his brains as soon as
look at him."

" ' Luther,' be quiet!" in a commanding tone,
poor Willie cried.   "No, no!" and Luther
then walked to his master's heels, the latter
well knowing which way the fight would go
against pistols while his arms were tied.   "Go on,
sir," he continued, addressing Master Topham.
" Take me where you like; if you don't tread on

my dog he won't touch you; and the only kindness I ask at your hands is, not to hurt my four-
footed friend—he never plotted nor signed the
cross—spare him then for my sake, and there
shall be no resistance—resistance of any kind—
to an officer of the Crown."

" Spoken like an honest man, young gentleman.
Jack, see that the cords don't hurt his arms: we'll
not bind them when we get out of this gloomy
wood. Now then, sir, here are our horses; get up
behind my man, and away for High Wycombe,
where a horse for yourself shall be provided."

On reaching the town, a horse was at once
pressed into the King's service, and the party,
closely attended by " Luther," proceeded direct for
London. It was a dark and gloomy evening when
they reached the city; and Willie found himself a
moving and uncared-for unit, save as to the vigi-
lance of his captors, among the myriads of people
who yet thronged the streets and thoroughfares.
Master Topham, though he kept his word as to
loosening the cords on his prisoner's arms, did not
entirely remove the fetters; and bound, and closely
guarded, he reached the desired quay on the river
Thames, situated and known as Hungerford Stairs.

The Thames in London even then was not the
sweet, fresh, brilliant stream that it was in its run

through the rural districts; but, as if beginning to
be vexed with the overhanging houses, and soured
by the impurities of civilization, it put on a dark,
a sombre, and a ruffled hue, affording no relief to
the blackened walls that lowered on its inky tide,
and seemed to look down in vain for any reflection.
A boat being soon in readiness, and an order given
" To the Tower !" Willie was put into it, Master
Topham resigning command to one of his men.
" Luther " attempted to leap on board, but was
rudely repelled by the new commander. Persisting
in his effort to accompany his master, he sprang
again as the boat was pushed from the shore, and
succeeded in clinging to the stern with his paws.
Here again one of the men endeavoured to repulse
him, and in the attempt to remove those tenacious
feet from their purchase the officer got severely
bitten; to requite which the ruffian seized his pistol,
and with all his force broke the stock of it over the
poor old dog's head. Stunned, and for a moment
senseless, the boat being now in the middle of the
river, the dog fell into the dark and troubled
tide, but after a giddy circle or two on the surface
the cold bath seemed to revive him. Strong
swimmer as he was, he followed in their wake for
some time, Willie imploring them to stop and take
him in, and longing for the freedom of even one

arm to requite the ruffian for the felon blow. His entreaties were unattended to—a hoarse laugh from the crew was the only reply. The tide, which at first was fair for boat and dog, then turned, and while the strong arms of the rowers drove the boat a-head, the rippling waves flashed in the affectionate, longing, bright-brown eyes of "Luther," and blinded them, choked up his nose, and drove him back from his vain, his perilous pursuit. The round, black, bluff bows of a barge, impelled by one large sail, then came with a surge on the struggling, faithful dog, and whelmed him in the hissing waters. That, then, was the last of the loved companion of his leisure hours that the straining and tearful eyes of Willie saw. He was soon after delivered, at the Felons' Gate, to the custody of a warder of the Tower.

From the fact that Master Topham took his prisoner straight to High Wycombe, instead of by the western village, the news of Willie's arrest did not spread as soon, or as widely, as it otherwise would have done. Marguerite on the morning of the arrest had been detained at home by an unexpected visit from the superioress of the small conclave of nuns that yet clung to a portion of the habitable part of Medenham Abbey. Later in the day, however, she found time at her disposal, and at once repaired to the wood; but she neither found her lover by Our Lady's Well, nor was he at the cliff above the Swilley Hole. The still somewhat disturbed state of the ground, however, and the bloody remnant of a black sleeve, filled her with the greatest alarm, and almost prostrated every energy she possessed. Resolved on finding Mary, she at once proceeded to her cottage, but Mary had gone to the streams at West Wycombe for her cresses; so, in a state of the deepest anxiety, Marguerite returned home, having left word in Mary's cottage, that when she returned from West Wycombe she was at once to repair to the Grove. Mary did so that same afternoon; but, though without intelligence of any moment as to the whereabouts of Willie, she informed Marguerite of her interview with the priest, and of the fulfilment of the mission upon which the wily Jesuit had sent her.

" Oh, then, Mary," passionately exclaimed the weeping girl, " that letter has led my Willie into some fiendish snare! Oh, why did you not bring it to me to read, as you could not read it yourself? You might have known it concerned us both, and you knew of what the priest was capable." Mary could only reply to Marguerite sob for sob; and, wringing her hands, asked what there was she could do to serve her young mistress. " Mary," replied Marguerite, " there is nothing you can do now for me unless you can obtain tidings of Willie. Go to West Wycombe: learn what you can; and in the meantime I will watch the Swilley in the wood: depend upon it, if Willie can find the means of conferring with me he will do so. May Heaven grant he has not come to personal harm !"

Three days passed without direct intelligence of her lost lover, further than that Willie's father had suddenly shut up his house—that house to be seen at the present day with its old clock thrust out over the street, volunteering the time of day to all the village. So sudden had been the old man's departure, no one knew precisely whither he was gone. It was then that Marguerite, in her turn, felt the force of much that Willie had so passionately urged. Had she fled with him when he advised it, and not have done, as so many thousands of us for ever do, put that off for the doubtful morrow which could well have been done to-day, they might now have been together, and united for their lives. As Willie prophesied, not only a life of love, as it were, had now been lost, but, perhaps, years of misery were about to supervene, in all probability giving ample cause to Marguerite sorrowfully, deeply, and vainly to regret that she had not complied with the request of her lover.

Presence of mind is a gift to the few; without it, men and women are often lost in difficulties; with it, they rise superior even to adverse chance, and by sudden action thwart the frown that fate had cast around them. Left entirely as she was to her own guidance, and with scarce a soul to speak to, it cannot be wondered at that Marguerite's whole thoughts became engrossed with the probable fate of Willie. Though deeply imbued with filial affection for her father, she, nevertheless, found that her reflections on him were tempered with the remembrance of his harshness, and expressed mistrust of her in regard to his commands; while towards the wily priest, whose character for duplicity had now been thoroughly brought before her, she felt the most supreme loathing and contempt, regarding the officer who had been left in charge of her father's premises even as a boon, because it relieved her from the detestable presence of the Jesuit. As poor Willie used to haunt the wood where Marguerite had treated him with apparent coldness, in obedience to her father's wishes, so now did she continually hover round the same place, a prey to the deepest regrets. On a spot on one of the

soft patches, near the sedges of the swamp, impressed on the earth, she saw a single fresh
impress of Willie's foot, the last that he had
made, and beside it that of his faithful dog;
and on those traces of a happier hour she
stood to weep as if she had lost a world. If
successful love makes time to fly, distress as decidedly clips his wings, and with its leaden weight
depresses him to a pace like that of the snail: 'so
that, take an eventful life through, smiles and
tears make the clock keep time, and mark the
space as Heaven wills it to be passed.

Though at morn the night seemed very far
off, and Marguerite thought the day would never
end, still on and on for ever went the fleeting hours,
till the loud trampling of horses' feet once more
awakened the retired Grove from its scene of listening rest. The summons given at the door was
replied to, when on the threshold stood a little,
mean-looking man, habited somewhat in the fashion
of a Puritan; a steeple-crowned hat, and a black
patch over one eye, completing his ungainly appearance. Having entered the house, leaving
three or four of his attendants in the yard, in
a voice that did not seem natural to the figure,
he asked for Marguerite, and desired the Abigail
to deliver to her a sealed letter; while at the same
time he himself placed one in the hands of Master

Topham's man. The officer having read it, made a sign of intelligence and obedience, and at once set about taking his departure.

The moment Marguerite saw the superscription of her letter she recognised her father's hand, and the contents of it ordered her to prepare to leave the house under the guidance of the honoured Master Winkenhorn, who would conduct her to a place of safety, as "*he had lent the Grove to Sir Caldwell Hunter.*" Astonished and bewildered as Marguerite was, and in terror and disgust even at the very name of her rich suitor, she scarcely knew how to act; but as Master Winkenhorn was peremptory in the directions he gave the servants, to be quick in packing up and putting the things into a close and lumbering sort of conveyance he had at the door, Marguerite found herself on the eve of departure almost before she was aware of it. In addition to the brief command the letter contained, was a rather gentle assurance that she need be under no alarm, for that she was going to the care of a neighbouring lady, who would watch over not only her privacy, but her comfort and happiness.

Resistance being useless, Marguerite descended to the entrance-door; and a place beside her in the carriage having been refused to her maid, among the tears and lamentations of the household she was driven from the door. After a very rough hour and a half's travel, the windows of the vehicle preventing her from seeing much of the country, the sounds of the wheels changed from their dull, monotonous jolting over bad roads, and rattled on the stones beneath an archway, where the carriage stopped. The door was opened, and she was kindly received by the superioress of Medenham Abbey. The Abbey, prettily situated on the margin of the Thames, about three miles south-west of Marlow, was then in one wing of it just inhabitable, and in the wing still were kept together a sisterhood of nuns. In later years, during the " Age of Reason," the members of the " Hellfire Club" (Sir Francis Dashwood being among them) held some of their orgies there; and it was at Medenham Abbey—so the tale is told— that a large monkey, well blacked with soot, and let down the chimney into the apartment where they were carousing, put them all to flight.*

* The " Hellfire Club," of which Sir Francis Dashwood was a member, as well as several others, including Lords Luttrell and Henry Lord Santry, Colonels Clements, Ponsonby, and St. George, was established, as it seemed, simply to outrage all the refined usages of society, as well as to manifest contempt for religion and the attributes of Divine worship. Not only did the members of this dissolute association drink to excess, but they also sought to carry their obscene orgies into consecrated sites, and to hold their debaucheries within the walls once dedicated to Heaven, as-

Consigned to the care of the superioress, as we have described, we must for the present leave our heroine, and return to the fortunes of others.

A day or two after the arrival of Willie at the Tower he was permitted to have an interview with his father, who had followed him to London; and when his father returned to West Wycombe he entrusted to his care a small slip of stout parchment, the only writing material he could get, which his father was to deliver to Mary, charging her at once to put it for Marguerite in the usual place. Poor Mary obeyed the command, although by that time she had learned the departure of her young mistress—indeed, she knew not what else to do with it.

suming to themselves for the time the semblance of a brotherhood of monks. To such an extent did Sir Francis Dashwood carry out this spirit of indecency, that he caused to be cut out on his estate at West Wycombe the imaginary likeness of the female form divine, tracing the lower limbs by cuttings leading into the lake, through which the streams from the springs at the foot of the hill flowed, and planting in a particular method, in order to convey a better impression of the obscenity of his own intention—obvious to the present hour. It was this desire to defile all things that are usually held sacred that led the Club to select the ruins of Medenham Abbey as a place fitted for their coarse and detestable debaucheries. There is a picture in the possession of Sir C. C. W. Domvile illustrative of the facts to which I allude.

CHAPTER XVII.

PART I.

THE legend which I have now to narrate is one
as far back in its origin as 1657, and concerns
the ancient family of the Percevals: many of the
incidents may be found in the genealogical history
of the " House of Ivery," of which house the
Earl of Egmont is the present representative.
Robert Perceval was born at Kinsale on the 8th
of February, 1657, and was the second son of the
baronet of that name. Gifted with all the graceful attributes that could adorn the human mould—
I wish I could have said, the mind—added to a
figure of the most elastic and muscular proportions,
young Robert Perceval was perhaps the best-
looking youth of his day. Of the middle size
in height, his long, fair hair, fell on either side

a well-formed, good-humoured face, in ample profusion, lit up as the brow of that face was by large,
quick, grey eyes; and, take him for all in all, a
more muscular, but at the same time light and
graceful figure, of the middle height, could not
be seen. At the commencement of his life, his
aptness to learn was proved by his proficiency
in the Latin and Greek languages, and to perfect
his studies he was sent to Christ's College, Cam-
bridge, where he became as great a proficient in
foot and hand, in fencing, running, leaping, and
drinking, as he was, or had been, in learning the
dead languages.

A College life in those days, and I question
if it be much better even now, was no good school
for sobriety and morality: so, to wean him from
the " wine party," and continual rows of " Town
and Gown," rapier and bâton, Robert Perceval,
or " Master Robin," as he was often called by
those who knew him intimately, was soon after
entered at Lincoln's Inn, and desired to make
himself master of that, if lucrative, still not very
amusing craft, the study of the law.

He was also put under the care of the Bishop
of Llandaff, to render himself perfectly conversable
in the abstruse sciences of philosophy and mathe-
matics, and other branches of erudite investi-

gation, as if with a desire to drive from his mind all those thoughts that have their root in youth, and their luxuriant and luscious growth in the passions and desires of nature and of the human heart. The Bishop, however, soon found that the gayer poisons instilled into the mind of this young man, through the bad and licentious example set him by companions older than himself at the University, was infinitely too strong to **be** eradicated by " wise saws," and for that day, " modern instances:" so, by way of a forlorn hope, he was sent back to Lincoln's Inn; and at his chambers there his own master, and with companions of his own selection, to choose between his pains, as dry and uninteresting studies were to him, and his seductive pleasures. Thus, at the early age of nineteen, he became a noted and successful duellist, a hard drinker, a professed libertine, and an inveterate gambler.

Young and eminently handsome as Master Robin was, a graceful dancer and an immense admirer of the fair sex, no wonder that he found at his first start in life many fair women, in the best society, who were willing to take him by the hand, and bring him forward as an admired beau; yet still, for all this, though he might both night and day have mingled with the fairest and the best, still nothing could restrain his wish to quarrel, his desire to be looked on as the best duellist of his time, and his love for "flash" society, the tavern and the gaming-table. In no less than twenty *rencontres* with the sword, ere he was nineteen, he had come off with honour, and almost always with the best success; and if his brain in learning had only kept pace with his hand in "lunging," he would have bid fair to have been "the Admirable Crichton" of his day.

By degrees Master Robin put in fewer appearances at assemblies and balls in the best circles, and more often went to the tavern and gambling-house; when as liquor, which inflames and debases the inclinations of man, had its usual effects on the system it was sure in the long run to destroy, the victim to a pernicious self-abandonment to evil courses too ready at his hand, he became the wildest as well as the youngest *roué* that frequented the taverns in the Strand. He became the pet of the patched and painted female furies, who, like the fabled serpent, brought him the apple to hurl him down from all better affection, and to drive him forth from those scenes in which he might, or ought, to have sought the heaven of refined and exalted love.

Short as the run of Robert Perceval was in

the best sphere of fashion, it must not be deemed that he had not been looked on and admired by the gentle eyes of some who felt his many attractions, and would not have shunned his love; and among them there was a beautiful girl, transcendant in every good quality, who, though in almost the extreme of youth, felt all the high-toned affection of woman for the youth she fancied; and loving him with a love that no word or intention of his had implanted or called forth, she felt that, even in absence and neglect, she could think of him, dream of him, live for him, and watch over him with a guardian angel's care, utterly unselfish, that never thought of requital, nor other guerdon than to feel assured that he was happy, in safety, and alive.

I am aware that some of my readers who have never known the fact will cavil at this, but it is nevertheless true that the heart of woman is sometimes moved to love a man she has never spoken to, and never seen: to love him for his deeds, his character, and his reputation in the world, and for no visible or outward captivation arising in feature, form, or fashion. Such unsought love, when it exists, free as it is from any outward sign, and therefore pure of any approach to passion, is worth from a gallant soldier and gentleman a world of gratitude in return, and, while binding heart to heart, it should exalt the man, and lay him in beautiful fetters at the feet of the trusting girl.

She loved not on account of features nor of limb, for no outward grace or fashion. That which moved her was from a source infinitely more refined, and an hour of an affection such as this might fairly counterbalance years of a slower, creeping intimacy, that had not warmth enough at once to kindle into flame, nor strength sufficient to make the lip confess the priceless fact.

Robert Perceval turned his back on all these things that ought to have rendered life a heaven upon earth, or he never thought of them, or never cared for them; and still under the force of bad example set him by his seniors, he went on in evil courses—deserted the palace, the great houses, the higher or superior fashion and society of his day, and cast himself loose on the deadly sin and the low vices so apt to seize on an impulsive, on a strong, but an ill-regulated mind.

Robert Perceval had that peculiar and very delightful accomplishment which pertains to some gifted men, the power of making himself agreeable to all—that is to say, to all women, of whatever sort or class he came across, and to all men with whom he did not come into more personal contact, either by winning from them their money, their character for prowess, or their loves.

As I have already said, he was immensely admired by the lower and the lowest class of women, with whom the taverns, the streets, and the bagnios, made him acquainted; when, as there were creatures called gentlemen, who seemed to take as much pride in their " flash " successes with barmaids, tapsteresses, and other females of a still more ignoble kind, of course young Robert Perceval had his foes, who loathed him with all the revengeful feelings that disappointment, envy, hatred, and malice, could engender in minds dead to chivalric sentiment or fair consideration for an open and more successful rival.

In addition to this, the twenty combats with the sword, in all of which Robert Perceval had been, more or less, successful, left him at least twenty or more disappointed and discomfited foes, supposing none of them to have been killed, ready at any time to thwart, discomfit, or stab, even to the death, the almost beardless youth, who had cropped their laurels, or cut them out in some low phase of gallantry.

While this state of things existed, I must now

more particularly introduce the reader to the hero of the scenes I am about to record, and to the action of the piece in which he was to play so conspicuous a part.

It was past eleven at night, the hour at which all sorts of revels in those days were kept up in taverns in the Strand, when Robert Perceval and Colonel Lustre were in close conversation in a corner of one of the private rooms of the tavern most resorted to. Though Colonel Lustre was considerably senior to Perceval, yet their intimacy was of the most friendly description; for the Colonel immensely admired the high courage of his young friend, as well as his extraordinary proficiency in the use of the sword.

" My dear Colonel," said Robert Perceval, pulling from his pocket a letter, " now tell me, what do *you* think of this? I betray no confidence in showing it to you, because not only is the letter free from all signature, but I do not know, nor have I ever seen to my knowledge, the writer of it. I will not even show you the hand, lest the character of it should be known to my greatest friend. I will read it to you with this one additional remark, that it is in the prettiest handwriting I ever saw, and the position and character of each line so graceful, that none but the fairest of the fair could so have put her gentle thoughts together.

" It runs thus :—

" ' Before you rush into further peril, and risk that life which these few words will prove to you is dear to the writer above every other earthly consideration, will you give me an interview ?

" ' By this strange request I *may* seem to lay aside the usual timidity and delicacy of my sex, but if I err in your eyes, remember the error arises from a feeling *you* ought to honour, because it shows that zeal for your welfare makes me poor indeed in that self-respect which ought to be my first consideration.

" ' If I come to your rooms in Lincoln's Inn at noon to-morrow, will you pledge me your honour that as I freely and confidingly come, I may be similarly free to leave you untouched, unharmed, and unmolested in every way ?—that while with you I may be in all honour under your protection, and safe from the intrusion of others ? There is no other place at which we can meet, or I had not made this request. Your life is at stake, and I would see and speak to you, and warn you of your danger.

" ' *If you promise me faithfully* to be guided by *my* desire, let your serving-man stand in the right-hand corner of the field on the northern side nearest to Lincoln's Inn; and if a female messenger from me comes and stops for a moment by his side, let him have written on a slip of paper the word 'Yes,' and I will believe in and trust you, and at noon come to the suggested interview.'

"Now tell me," continued Robert Perceval, when he had finished reading the letter, " is it a hoax? is it a trick of any kind? or what do you think of it?"

"Think of it, my dear Robin!" replied his friend; " why, I think it is from one of your fair and numerous admirers — of the better sort, *perhaps* — and may mean very little or a good deal.   Try the adventure by all means; but remember, if you say, as she requires, 'Yes' to this, you *must respect her as your life,* protect and care for her, and let her rule her own actions, and be as free to leave you as she likes.   See her, but in all honour, by all means.   That matter settled, now let's into the table and have a throw.   Hark! what a row they are making!"

As Colonel Lustre said this, shouts, laughter, execrations, and the shuffling as of many feet, were heard, and even the clash, or sliding, scraping noise of rapiers engaged, for a moment and amidst all the din met their ears; when, as they proceeded to an inner apartment, they met a crowd of young men and tavern people rushing to the door, struggling and hustling each other, but more particularly one man in the midst of them, whom they were, for some reason or other, roughly turning into the street.

This row, soon over, did not seem in the least to interrupt the harmony of the generality of the guests, who soon reseated themselves at the gaming-table; when after a few throws, in which young Perceval lost all the money he had in his pocket, he rose from his chair and went into the Strand, unaccompanied by any friend, and proceeded towards Lincoln's Inn, to think of the extraordinary letter he had received, and to write the monosyllable and mysteriously-demanded "Yes," to confirm the expected adventure of the following day.

Ere he had gone fifty yards from the door of the tavern, keeping his eyes about him, as it was necessary to do at that hour of midnight, and in that place, he was aware of a man following him; and being thus aware, he more than once turned his head to see if he knew who it was that thus seemed to be going his way. The form of the man, however, was strange to him, and it evidently was not one in the same class of society as himself, though attired in all respects as a gentleman, wearing a sword.

Resolved to get rid of this figure at his heels, he purposely turned in another direction, and then again altered his course; but still as he changed his line of proceeding the figure did the same, and that so much so, that young Perceval thought himself entitled suddenly to stop and accost his persecutor.

"Why do you follow me?" said Perceval, laying his hand on his sword.

"Follow you!" replied the man. "May I not have business in the same direction as yourself? The streets are open to both of us, and I walk where I please."

So saying the man passed very slowly on, and so slowly that Perceval repassed him again, his footsteps to be again dogged by this suspicious-looking follower. Nothing came of it, however; Perceval gained Lincoln's Inn, sought his chambers, and retired for the night. He wrote the word "Yes" on a slip of paper and gave it to his servant, with directions as to what he was to do with it on the following day.

Robert Perceval sat himself down at his table, simply for the purpose of writing the one word that he had given to his servant; but thus being seated and the man dismissed for the night, he sat thinking over the letter and the adventure that it promised, and guessing in his own mind who the writer could be. Was she young and beautiful, or old and ugly? did she mean in reality what she wrote, or was it only the prelude to a love adventure? While weighing the assignation and many an imaginary circumstance in his mind, he fell into a sort of drowsy trance. He was not actually asleep; he was awake, but moodily out of spirits, and an inexplicable weight seemed to be on his mind—a sensation of the dread of some impending evil, he knew not what, and that he could not account for, hung heavily upon him, and his face was resting on his hands, his eyes closed, and the silence of the night around him. All at once a slight rustle, as of something close to him, made him look up; when opposite to him, and at one end of the table, he saw a spectral likeness of himself, but ghastly pale in face, the arms folded across the bosom, the sheath of the rapier at his side empty, and the clothes soiled as from contact with the ground. Starting to his feet, yet chilled to the soul with this spiritual sight of himself, and for an instant thinking of some deception, he drew his sword, when the figure, calmly but fixedly regarding him, slowly opened his arms and showed a rapier wound on the left breast, open and pouring with blood.

As Robert Perceval, statue-like, and almost turned to stone with dread, yet gazed on this fearful apparition, the form moved towards the door, and seemed to vanish from the room. Brave and reckless as he was, his sensibility and his nerves were shocked at the vision he had seen; when, though he tried to reason himself into doubts as to its being anything but an optical delusion, still a most unaccountable weight seemed to crush his mind, and to deny him the power to shake it off. After some time spent in a vain endeavour to reassure himself, and to drive all thoughts of the spectre away, he went to bed; but sleep had been scared from his pillow, and he could obtain no rest.

Daylight had not long broken on the following morning, when he resolved to seek some comfort by the narration of the circumstance to his uncle and guardian, Sir Robert Southwell; when, early as the hour was, he repaired to his house, aroused the servants, and hastened to his bedside. At first Sir Robert ridiculed the idea, and was cross and annoyed at the untimely disturbance of his slumbers, laying the whole thing to the effects of too much wine, and looking on it as the proceeds of an evil course of life, excitement on gambling and other debaucheries: but when he saw that his nephew really suffered, the very great affection he had for him changed his tone, and he took occasion to try at least to make the state of his nephew's mind subservient to some very good advice.

"Robert," he said, "let this thing, whatever it is, be a timely warning to you. I had hoped that the position you have been placed in, by having had assigned to you the reversion of the office of Clerk of the Crown, Prothonotary, and Chief Clerk of the Common Pleas and Custos Brevium in Ireland, with the additional income these gifts will bring you, would have raised you above a good deal of the penniless company you keep, and made you a better gentleman. *Be* a better gentleman now, if this that you have seen *is* a warning of some impending misfortune, which may or may not happen; take it in time, and profit thus by a lesson from Heaven. Avoid all those 'draw-can-sirs,' and the cut-throat rascals who haunt the gaming-houses and brothels; keep from those scoundrels who win what *they* call 'debts of honour,' but which they themselves really never regard as binding, simply because if they lose they have not got the wherewithal to pay. They do, indeed, wager to win, because they never mean to book up; and this kind of betting really amounts to downright robbery. Come then, my dear Master Robin, promise me to obey the warning you have had; keep your own sword in its sheath, and tempt not others to draw theirs. Make a good beginning; stay at home to-night, or come and pass a quiet evening with me, and let the evil go by?"

" Uncle, dear uncle," replied the nephew, " I have an engagement to-night, to meet a party of friends at the tavern, and to win a bet—not a bet made by me with anybody else, but made by a friend of mine with a man who owes me a grudge on account of some words we had at the play—with Beau Fielding. He has wagered that I will not keep my engagement to meet my friends to-night, because I fear to come. I want to meet the Beau, just to hear what he has to say in regard to my being afraid of anything. At the play he seemed to be in no humour to let his blade see the light; I may, perhaps, give him an opportunity."

" My dear nephew, then what use is there in your coming to me ?" rejoined his uncle. " You will not believe a warning if it comes from

Heaven itself. Go, then; do what you will; I have nothing more to say. Your first warning may not be the last; but a wilful young man will have his way, and all argument is useless. May God be with you, and have you in His keeping! Adieu!"

Young Perceval then left the apartment of his uncle and guardian, and retired to his chambers, to be ready for the interview asked for in so mysterious yet graceful a way. By the time he had reached home, exercise and the cheering rays of a cloudless sky in the blooming, sweet, and glorious month of June, had so refreshed him and cheered despondency away, that he felt a new life throbbing in his veins, and longed for fresh adventure. So pleasing was the approaching appointment to his mind, that he repaired to his toilette, to render himself as smart as possible; and then, some time before the given hour of noon, his anxiety saw him seated in a chair, to listen and impatiently to wait for the romantic advent of the female visitor. The noise of a sparrow at his window made him start; and not a thing could stir but in it he seemed to hear the timid fall of a little foot, or the faint rustle of approaching female attire. At last a foot *was* on the stair; the door was thrown open by a serving woman of the Inn, who reclosed it, and left a female form certainly confessed, but so disguised that it might have been old or young, handsome or ugly, for all the information its closely-wrapped habiliments afforded.

To rise and offer his guest a seat, with the graceful courtesy of which he was so complete a master, was but the work of a moment: his visitor sat down, and for a space they regarded each other in silence. As I have previously said, nothing could be discovered in regard to her figure; her head was partly concealed in a hood attached to her cloak, and what little could be seen of her face beneath it was disguised in a black mask.

" Well," at last said Robert Perceval, "highly honoured as I feel myself by this most flattering and gentle confidence, will you not *now* tell me to what, or to whom, I am indebted for this interview ?"

" Yes," replied a very sweet voice; at least so it seemed, in spite of the masked lips. "I come, sir, as—as—as a friend, to put you on your guard and to dissuade you from running into danger— danger which I feel assured awaits you, if you go forth to the tavern haunts to-night."

" Danger !" replied Perceval. " And would *you* counsel *a man* who wears a sword to shun a danger, even before he knows what that danger is ? No, no, lady ! the female soul ever spurns a coward, and you and all your sex would think the better of me for seeing all danger to an end."

" Do not deceive yourself," replied his visitor, " with any of those high-flown notions of chivalric daring : in *this* instance, at least, it is better to shun than to meet the danger, and the sin that woos you on to ruin and to death. Think not that I have undertaken to warn you in time lightly, and without good cause, or that I have thus so far forgotten my maiden delicacy as to present myself to you in these chambers, which teem with a profligate repute, unless the motive which urged me to do so were of a nature so blameless that, were all the circumstances known, an angel might forgive the deed and pardon my present rashness. Will you—will you bestow a favour *upon me?* Will you promise me not to leave your chamber to-night, or, at all events, to remain away from the Strand or its purlieus for the next eight-and-forty hours ?"

" Lady, it is well for *you* to ask me to do this, but not so easy for me to comply. I am pledged to meet my friends at a certain tavern in the Strand to-night: the word of a gentleman cannot be broken; nor must a heavy wager be lost because *I* flinch from doing that which was expected of me when the bet was made. But ere we go further, will you not extend your confidence to me by showing me your face, and telling me who you are who so kindly take an interest in one whom I fear must be called ' a wild young rake?' Persuasion strengthens doubly when the source is known, and words attain a sweeter and more powerful import when beauty adds its grace to their delivery. Tell me, then, tell me who my kind monitress is; and let me gaze, if but for instant, on your face."

As he said this, seated by her side as he was, he let his hand fall till it touched and then clasped on hers. She permitted it for a moment; and then, freeing her hand and rising suddenly from her chair to her full height, she said, in a still sweet but more concentrated tone of voice:—

" Ought I to let that hand *touch* mine which this very night contemplates an unworthy clasp on others unfit to receive it—others who, if beautiful, are as common and varied in their fitful passions and pressures as the sands upon the sea-shore? Do *you* think that *I* would hold a hand in mine with any loving tenderness, when I knew that the next moment the warmth of mine would be obliterated? No! I seek you now to save you, if I could: for that is a Christian duty in the face of God, of woman, and of man. And, once for all, I beseech you pledge your honour to me, here on the spot, that for the next forty-eight hours—say, if you like, in gratitude for the force and danger I have put on, or risked upon myself, by coming to see you—you will *not* leave your chambers, unless for the society of your guardian?"

" Lady! dear lady!" replied Robert Perceval, " you know not what you ask; you know not how much bound we feel ourselves by our words, or on points of honour: still this, in gratitude to you, I will promise. For the two next days and nights —if you will it so—I will go into no other society than that of my uncle: but to-night my honour is at stake, and I must obey its dictates. I cannot let an unknown lady — a lady whom I have, perhaps, never seen, and may never see again—rule me in a matter of vital importance."

" Here, then, Robert Perceval," exclaimed his visitor, still standing erect and proudly before him, " there shall be no disguise *now* in a last, and, I trust, blameless, or holy effort—no shadow

shall be left that *may* have influence on you.
There, then, lies at least a portion of my disguise"
(cloak, and hood, and other things, in which she
had concealed her richer dress and beautiful
figure, falling to the floor). Her hand was then
about to untie her mask; but she suddenly with-
held it, and paused, as it seemed by the heaving
of her breast, in violent emotion. Struck with all
the loveliness he saw, and moved, too, by her
earnest manner, yet bold in having succeeded so
far, Robert Perceval raised his hand to take off
her mask, when he saw that tears, not evident at
first, because they did not come through the eyelet-
holes of the black mask, were falling from the
bottom of it, fast as summer-rain, and clinging,
like drops of sweet and brilliant dew, to the lovely
contour of the rich, dark vest, that concealed the
snowy whiteness, but not the shape, of her bosom.
His hand refused to free the mask, and he knelt
and took her hand, carrying it, with almost
worship, to his lips.

"Lady!" he said, "dearest, sweetest lady! forgive, I entreat, my apparent obstinacy. Ask what
you will, command what you will, *after to-night;*
but, *for this once,* permit me to redeem my
word, face all foes, and win the wager for my
friend, who laid it on the knowledge of my

bravery; and then your slave will be for ever bound to obey you."

"No!" replied his visitor; now, with an impatient action, tearing off her mask, and in the effort causing her long, fair, wavy hair, to fall wildly, but in beautiful luxuriance, over her neck and shoulders, and almost to the floor. "No, Robert Perceval! I have for a time overstepped the bounds prescribed for *my honour*, state, and station. I have risked *all for your sake, and to give you timely warning.* I came not to trifle, nor to be content with only a portion of the duty from you which I desire. I know your life is in danger: Heaven, in its inscrutable goodness, has shown me that it is so. I believe that, if you could be saved, you are yet born to better things and to a noble and virtuous life. So *once more*, Robert Perceval, for your own sake—for mine, if you will —and for the sake of Heaven, *be warned in time,* and go not to the appointed rendezvous."

As she said this, the angelic beauty in her bright, but tearful eyes, and in the lineaments of her sweet face, were enough to have moved the heart of any man, not wedded to wild courses and to a so-called sense of honour; she was so urgent, so graceful, and yet so terribly prophetic. In fact, she looked like the Goddess of Truth come to chase away false notions from the world. Two steps she made towards the door, haughtily motioning Robert Perceval not to follow.

" Once, then, and for the last time," she said, "I entreat, I implore you — promise me, on your honour, not to keep this appointment to-night? I stay a brief second only for reply. Refuse, *and warning then is vain ;* and you will learn too late, while I speak, that you stand on the brink of the grave."

" Dear lady, I must not break my word, fail my friend, nor live to be called a coward!"

Those words had scarcely passed the lips of Robert Perceval, when, taking up her disguise, and hastily casting it around her, his beautiful visitor left the room, and descending the stairs with the speed and lightness of a doe, she was lost in the fields around the Inn, or received into a chair that had been waiting for her at a little distance, leaving Perceval to digest " the two warnings," and to abide by that course by which he had selected to be bound.

CHAPTER XVIII.

HAVING been at considerable trouble in collect-
ing legends of this description, of course there
are a great many of one kind or another at my
disposal; but as many have been imparted to
me in confidence, and as I know that, in the
minds of some owners of mansions in England
and Scotland, there is not only an inclination
to stifle such tales, but a direct desire that
their names and houses should not be shown
up in their terrors to scare away their guests, of
course I consult the wishes of my friends more
than the interests of my work, and keep both
their names and the names of their mansions
from the reader's eye. I am sorry to be constrained to do this, because, fixing the spot of
their peculiar transactions, and laying myself

open to contradiction should my tales not be true, would fix on the unearthly legends a greater degree of weight than the mere telling of such tales could do.

Though desiring to treat so solemn a subject with all the gravity it demands, I cannot help giving my wayward spirit permission to smile at the immense preponderance of female ghosts that prevail over the numbers of the other sex, and the very restless state in which the souls of housekeepers *par excellence* seem to be, over those of various women whose callings lie in other capacities than in presiding over store-rooms, linen-presses, preserves, and potted meats. Why the old " stuff gowns," " chintz gowns," and other dresses of homely and ancient material, should so much prevail in spiritual attire, I cannot, as a ghost-seer in every meaning of the word, by any means at my disposal discover ; nor can I understand why the phalanx of restless forms—for they amount to it—should ever be old and withered. I know of no *young* house-keeper who has ever appeared, nor any ghost of that class in modern attire, save the female ghost which was seen by myself and the present Earl of Berkeley in the old kitchen at Cranford. She certainly was dressed in the style of the day, as some sort of female domestic, and her figure gave the appearance certainly not of an old person: but to this undoubted fact I refer my readers to tales already written.

In one of the first game counties in the kingdom, though the house shall be nameless now, I have all my life heard of a ghost in the shape of an old housekeeper, who haunted a landing-place on the stairs, on the extraordinary and prevailing mission of this description of ghost, viz. to warn the family of some approaching death in the members who composed it. This apparition was said to have been repeatedly seen, and I select the last tidings told me of it, as the most extraordinary and authentic of all. Mrs. ———, a good, kind-hearted, jolly soul, and a member of the family, was staying in the mansion, and had been there for some time alone. In writing to her friend, a gentleman of my acquaintance, in one of her letters she said, " Only fancy, I have been here for a length of time, and up that said-to-be-haunted-staircase, at nearly all hours of the night, but I have never been lucky enough to see the mysterious visitant in the old brocaded gown!" Or words of similar effect.

A period of some little time then elapsed,

and she wrote again to her friend in her usual good spirits, her letter exclaiming, as far as written words could exclaim, " Only fancy, last night I saw the ghost!"

Again a short period elapsed, and the next letter, from a mutual friend, was to announce the death of the lady with whom he had so recently been in correspondence.

In all the multitude of legends of this kind it is very seldom that a ghost becomes tangible, or palpable to the touch. Generally they content themselves with putting in appearances, sometimes prophetic and sometimes not : opening or shutting doors, or seeming audibly to do so, that are fast locked up, and knocking against walls and under floors, as though disturbance and little else was their mission from the other world. As to their noises, my friend, Lady Shelley of Boscombe, near Bournemouth, can speak in the most emphatic manner, as she heard them, as well as other friends of hers who had done the same : but I must here tell those readers who have the happiness of being the guests of Sir Percy B. Shelley and his lady, that these extraordinary noises were not within their peaceful and most agreeable mansion on the sea, but were in another house, to which it is not my purpose more particularly to allude.

Not very long ago—perhaps not more than two years previously to the publication of these volumes—a lady, a very sincere friend of mine, for whom I have the highest respect and regard, told me, that about that period the following curious circumstance occurred ; and *this* tale, as the *ghost certainly in this instance did*, should carry some weight with it, the appearance put in being tangible as well as ocularly demonstrated, and felt as well as seen.

Well, then, about two years ago—dating back from this time, November 1866—a lady, a little beyond the heyday of youth, clever, sensible, and nice, and what some people, perhaps, might term "strong-minded," went on a visit to a mansion in Scotland, belonging to a host and hostess whose "names shall be nameless" now; and who, with their accustomed and most agreeable hospitality, were at the time entertaining a large party. The first evening of Miss C.'s stay passed off pleasantly enough—as all the evenings were accustomed to do there; but having travelled, she went early to bed, seeking her chamber at about ten o'clock.

The chamber itself was a large and handsome one, of the old-fashioned kind; its chief feature being a huge antique bed—an out-and-out massive four-poster, or four-pillared domicile for sleep, in which an occupant could ever find a cool corner or a fresh place if inclined to restlessness, or a change of recumbent position. Of course its legs and feet—I mean those of the bed, not the lady —were of the most stalwart description, and as black as the old blackest oak could be. Over these steady understandings, as well as over the living treasures the bed contained, there stood up, reaching high, gloomily but haughtily to the ceiling, a canopy, that in its lugubrious stillness mocked at motion, and nodded not to the fair weight above which it so loftily presided, even when the bed beneath felt the pressure of no inconsiderable form.

Miss C. had been in bed but a short time — and had not yet succumbed to the drowsy god, when she was suddenly aroused by a sense of pressure, as of some weight on her feet; and on gazing in that direction, there, confessed and standing up —upright on the bed—considerably indenting it and oppressing her legs, was the figure of a woman, but without the semblance of a head.

Miss C. confesses that the horrible terror she then felt was beyond description, for there was nothing to screen her steadfast view, nothing to mystify the outline of what she saw; but above her, on the foot of the bed, fully confessed in the light of a still blazing fire, there for an instant paused this terrible spectre. While awestruck, terrified, and motionless she thus gazed, the figure deliberately *walked*—no gliding, no nonsense ; heavily, visibly, and tangibly stepping, indenting the clothes and making her feel—three times, backwards and forwards across the bed; and then, instead of vanishing promiscuously, or fading away, the ghost slowly *got down* from the foot of the bed—using its legs to do so—and in the action rustled the curtains of the bed considerably. No sooner off the bed than out of sight; because, of course, the tall pillars that supported the bed and the ample curtains screened all further view. Nothing daunted, though, of course, considerably shocked and affected, Miss C. rose and looked round the foot of the bed, and then all over the room, but not a glimpse of the ghostly visitant remained : so, feeling no inclination to sleep, nor desire to disturb the house, she lit her candles till the dawn of day, and awaited the advent—to call her—of her maid.

Then, feeling it to be impossible to face another night in that haunted chamber, on the next morning she pleaded the excuse of sudden and important business, and left the house.

In narrating this extraordinary occurrence to my friend, with a shudder she said, " I seem still to hear the rustle of those curtains even now, as the thing let itself down upon the floor."

Sometime after this occurrence, Miss C. heard from a friend — to whom she had not at the time narrated it — that she, too, had been a guest in the house, which was thereafter put in repair; and that while some repairs were being done to the bedroom of the host and hostess, they changed to the room in which she had been put to sleep: but that on the following morning, in evident haste, they left the room and returned to their own room, although in a state of considerable discomfort. " I really think," said her friend, at the same time laughing at the conceit, " *that that house is haunted.*"

In these times of spiritual insanity, when the souls of supposed-to-be-departed people knock their heads against boards and turn the tables, perhaps on even the sensible and well-informed, guiding pencils and pens held in mortal hands to things, to words, and signs, that if they mean anything mean immortality, and therefore, to my mind, impious detraction,—I repeat, in these times of pretended spiritualism, when the sly silurian self-seekers, who profess to deal with spirits as the wretched gambler deals with loaded dice or thumb-indented cards, to cheat their dupes and win themselves a living by the prostitution of the libelled dead; now is the time for some old woman clothed in chintz, brocade, and even without a head, to haunt, if she can haunt anything, those disciples of a self-invented, despicable art, out of their false clothing, and send them to wander restless through the disgusted world. If disembodied spirits are to appear, in Heaven's name then let them effect some good, and cease from doing, as they do now — slurring morals and adorning tales.

Here, then, let me give another ghost-story, one of the best-authenticated that I can give, known to a good many of my friends as " The Chintz Lady." Some say that she was the ancestress of the family; others, only a domestic, and if so, a thousand to one but she was a housekeeper.

In passing, perhaps, my readers will help me to solve the doubt as to the why and wherefore that all these unpleasant appearances are old women, or women chiefly of one particular class; and never young, never pretty, and seldom of any

other calling but that of a housekeeper or store-
keeper, whose occupation offers a wide margin for
peculation and dishonesty.

Is it that age alone is bad enough to be sent
back to earth to do mean and unholy things—sinners so old that there is no excuse for their not
knowing better, and therefore not possessed of the
same plea for pardon as the young and comely?
The old figure of a housekeeper is said to haunt
one of the old-fashioned bedrooms at Belhus, (or
Bellhouse, as it was formerly spelled,) the mansion of my friend Sir Thomas Lennard; she has
been seen seated by the dying embers of the
fire in that room by my friend Lady Wood, the
mother of Lady Lennard, whose eyes, in passing
through the room, by the steady glare of the red-
hot embers, encountered the outline of a lap seated
in an arm-chair, with two arms with withered
hands resting upon it. Lady Wood stayed nor
tarried an instant to see more, and dared not lift
her eyes in search of a face, but hurried on to the
apartments of her daughter. I have slept in that
room, and in the night I awoke and found myself
gazing, by the red glare of dying embers as well
as the light of a night-lamp, on the very chair
said to have been so occupied, my mind at the
moment full of the scaring legend; but I saw no-

thing but the chair, fell asleep again, and forgot all about it.

But to return to " The Chintz Lady."

The embodiment of the apparition in question is commonly supposed to have been a domestic, who, for some unexplained cause or other, committed suicide. Of the frequent appearance of this ghost I have heard much, but my kind and valued friend, to whom I have previously alluded,. has given me the still more authentic information which follows:— Sir —— —— was on a visit at the mansion with his daughter, who has since married, when on one evening the young lady attended the dining-table with a severe headache, in the hope that the pain would cease. The hope was vain: during dinner it became worse, and she was forced to leave the table and seek the retirement and quiet of her own room. In ascending the stairs, the usual waiting-place of these old, unpleasant spirits, she suddenly perceived — on a landing-place, of course — what she supposed to be an old domestic of the family, dressed in a chintz gown, and standing by a table on which was placed a lamp. Under this very plausible impression, and having no sort of superstitious dread about her, Miss —— accosted the old housemaid, as she thought, and wished her to go down and

" send up her maid directly to her room." To this the apparition returned no sort of reply, and the young lady went on, but suddenly recollecting that she had not said whose maid-servant it was that was wanted, she returned to the figure, still standing by the table, and addressed to it the necessary explanation. On this again the chintz dress made no sort of verbal reply, but turning on its heel, it pointed with a shrivelled hand to *a* door at the end of a passage.

Supposing the old woman to be either deaf or quite imbecile, Miss B. then hurried off, reached her own room, and directly rang her bell. Her maid having answered the summons, the young lady at once told her of what she had seen, with a view to elicit some information as to the poor creature whom she had accosted by the table and lamp on the landing-place. The answer to her quiet interrogatory was a burst into tears and hysterics by the maid, between whose sobs her young mistress made out the words, " Oh, Miss, you have seen *the thing* that haunts this house!" By this time, the rest of the ladies having retired, the hostess came up to the bedroom of the invalid, to inquire as to the state of her health, which it is needless to assure my readers was not benefited by the adventure in question. The maid having been dismissed, the hostess on being told the facts admitted that this apparition had frequently been seen by her visitors, as well as her servants, but never on any occasion by any of the members of the family. At the close of her remarks and explanations she added, "*I hope she didn't point to any door?*"

To this hope her guest replied, that the ghost had pointed to *a* door, and leading her friend into the passage she pointed out the very portal the withered hand had indicated. To this indication the hostess replied, "It's the chamber now occupied by our friends the —— and their baby; but don't speak of the affair, nor mention to any soul that you have seen 'The Chintz Lady;' for when that fatal sign is made to any door, those then occupying are about to die a violent and untimely death within the next twelve months."

It is a fact, and an extraordinary fact, that *six months after this occurrence* those who occupied the doomed chamber thus signalized by that mysterious hand *were among the first victims slaughtered in the Indian Mutiny!*

Now there is no gainsaying evidence such as this; there are those alive now who know the truth of my narrative even better than I do: but why or wherefore such things are permitted by what is believed to be an Omnipotent Power, for no beneficial nor perceivable purpose, and to answer no end of religion or worldly good, in the present nor in the future, it is impossible for man in his imperfect state to imagine. Such things are, such things have been, and such things may be again; they are beyond all explanation, and, as far as mortal and unbiased judgment goes, above all doubt—a mystery to be solved when all truths are known, and the Disposer of events deigns to lift the superhuman veil that for the time severs the mortal from immortality.

CHAPTER XIX.

THE LEGEND OF WEST WYCOMBE PARK, BUCKS.

Part VI.

During all these occurrences the summer had nearly passed, the harvest had almost sped, and autumn — rich, golden autumn — began to redden on the woods. It was on a very dark night about this time, when a labouring man, a resident in the village of West Wycombe, rather the worse perhaps — certainly none the better — for too much beer, was descending into the little hamlet from Church Down by the lane in which stood, and still stands, Willie Barnwell's house, always to be recognised by its projecting clock. The hour was dark, and all was still, for the night was well-nigh done; however, dark as the surrounding air was, the chalky dust on the road was not so dim but Hobbs could distinguish right in the middle of it, and under the projecting clock, a large upright thing, much blacker than the night, and which seemed resolutely to confront him on his way.

"Helloah!" cried the labourer, halting in his approach, and staring as steadily as he could amidst the rather giddy swayings of his figure to and fro; "Helloah!—dwon't think to frit me; ye's got but one other to scaren if y' do. I say—come out of that! Helloah-ah!"

The violence of this exclamation, excess of fear, as well as beer, sent the blood into Hobbs's head so suddenly that for a moment he lost his sight, and nearly tumbled down; when he looked again, the object of his terror had disappeared. Catching the humour to fly from the supposed apparition, the valiant clod turned about and took to his heels, skirting the foot of the Down, and entered the village by another way. On the following morning the tale was told and re-told, and, losing nothing by repetition, it got wind that at the dead of night the fiend, in his own shape, was seen sitting beneath the village clock, his eyes of fire fixed upon the dial. "No doubt"—so some of the old cronies in the village said—"come on some of his jobs, as he used to do, when every night he carried the stones with which the monks were building the church at the bottom of the Down up to the top of it, till the good fathers were fain to erect it in the highest as well as the right service, though bidden to do so by one in the wrong, who ought not to have meddled in the matter."

During this time Mary was inconsolable for the loss of her young mistress; and one day, as she passed through the wood, she thought she would just look if the little slip of parchment she had deposited in the cliff was safe; but, to her astonishment, it was gone. With the greatest industry she examined the ground to see if there was a footmark other than her own; but the ground there, though always moist, gave no traces of intrusion, and she could in no way account for the abstraction of that which the poor girl regarded as a treasure entrusted to her care. How to account for it, or what to think, she knew not. Had the priest been there? But, no, she could have tracked him, and he seemed to have left the neighbourhood. Had her young mistress got it? Perhaps she was not far off, though she had left the Grove; and in that hope the girl resought her cottage.

The days had now become visibly shorter, the foliage of the woods put on those beautiful hues which in their brightness presage death, and the white frosts at break of day made rustics as they sought the fields whistle through their fingers to give them warmth. At night, when the mists rose from the swamp in Whittenden Wood, the great lamp was lighted to guide the cottagers to their homes. One evening a conclave of rustics assembled at Lane End, and sat drinking in the little taproom of the Monkey's Hood—the sign so corrupted from the ancient one of the Monk and Hood, which had in former times decorated the doorway when steeple-crowned hats shaded the brows of most thirsty travellers of condition. As is usual in the meeting of boors in a public room, where every man feels or thinks himself as good as his neighbour, every soul, mug in hand, was speaking at the same time, and every mouth was blowing clouds of very bad tobacco. This state of things had continued for some time, when suddenly a thin old man, in a shrill key, almost shrieked the words,—" I telly 'twas see'd a week ago last Wednesday."

" What was see'd?" cried another.

" I heard of nothin seen, 'cept the score of sheep as was worried to death one night in Farmer Drillham's shipfold; blessy, half-a-dozen of their insides was pulled out, and only a bit of kidney eaten here and there: all the rest was killed wanton like, and no mistake."

" It warn't nothin about a ship as I was a-saying had been seen. I was a-talking of the ghost at Whittenden Park Wood. Neighbour Stoul—you all knows neighbour Stoul—him it was as sin it, and here he is to speak for hisself."

Stoul at that moment entered the room. All eyes were turned on him, and all voices asked him what he had seen; the younger members of the company were inclined to laugh, although they edged their seats nearer to each other, and one or two were heard to say, "Gently, mate, it's I's turn now," the mate addressed having gone out of his turn at the tankard.

"Well, neighbour Stoul, what was it as ye did see?"

The old man, very far from having any levity in his manner, took a seat, ran the butt of a pipe through his lips, stuffed the bowl of it full of tobacco with the end of a thumb, the skin of which might have made a boot for a cart-horse to wear in a garden, lit his pipe, stretched out his thin legs, called for some beer, and thus began:—" A week ago last Wednesday—leastways I thinks, as I said to my neighbour there, it was a week ago last Wednesday—I had to come through Whittenden Park Wood. You knows as none of us likes to be there much after dark, on account of the strange noises about the Swilley Holes, and them corpse lights; and you know as old Joe—that's me—if anything frights him, whoever does it has got but one more to frighten, and that's so. Well, as I was saying, just as I got through the wood, there I see the ghost, the White Lady of Whittenden Park Wood, the same as sits on the gate on Dashwood Hill, a waving a scarf to me just a one side of the beams of the Beacon Light.* I stops dead to look at it, and then I see it a getting thinner and thinner, but as white as ever was new milk."

"That's a lie!" said a husky voice, seated by a little table in the corner; " the ghost of Whittenden Park is no more a white lady nor I am. He's as black as a coal; I must know, for I see'd him this very night, not an hour ago."

On this startling communication, neighbour

---

* The apparition of the "White Lady on Dashwood Hill" was said to haunt a gate at the top of that locality, and down to within the memory of very old people of the present day it was the terror of all postboys on their return home. The strongest confirmation of this ghost is yet remembered in the alleged fact, that one night, on the return of a postboy with a pair, she suddenly transferred herself from the top bar of the accustomed gate to the back of his hand-horse. Boy and horses, in a frenzy of terror, started off at full gallop, and the lad was taken from his saddle beneath the archway of the Black Boy at West Wycombe, and died in a brain fever on the following night. The death of the post-boy is certain, but the oldest inhabitant does not know where the White Lady " got down."

Stoul, who at first struggled to get out of his smockfrock in that peculiar over-head way which rustics even to this hour indulge in, with a view, it was supposed, to drink up the last speaker's beer, and to defy him to personal combat, re-adjusted his toggery, and sat staringly still.

" I say," repeated the last speaker, " the ghost is black, for I see'd him not forty yards from me; and I warn't, blessy, no I warn't a bit afeard—no, not I."

" Well, what was he a like?" murmured all the company; "tell us all about it!"

" Like!" replied the husky, stout old rustic, whose name was Codger; " like! why, look here, he sat bolt upright, black as jet, summut like a big dog, with great shiny eyes and a fiery tongue— might be about six feet high."

" Well, what did you do?"

" Who, I? Look here, I warn't a bit afeard, but, thinks I, I 'll draw my customer more into the light, to have a good look at him, for he sat just one side the rays of the lantern, so I turns about and pretends like to run away."

" Ha, ha, ha!" roared the younger part of the company; "and never stopped till ye got ere! ha, ha, ha!"

Gaffer Codger, thus jeered, paused for a moment in contemptuous silence, when, firing a royal salute from his pipe, he exclaimed with much offended dignity, " Well, gentlefolks, if you knows better nor I do, you may have the rest of the story to yourselves."

A cold blast of wind arising from the opening door then told of a fresh comer. " Is Farmer Tufold's shepherd here ?" said a voice from a head looking in; " there's the bell-wether of the flock a-rattling's bell around and around the field, and I thinks as summut's after the ship." Out bolted the shepherd to look after the flock, and the conversation turned once more on a rumour that a great many sheep had lately been killed, over a wide extent of country. In those days sheep were not so numerous as they are now, although less land was in cultivation, and consequently there was a wider scope for pasturage, albeit a good deal circumscribed by woods. It seemed, from the conversation, that the supposed depredator had been seen in the shape of a large and shaggy wild-looking black dog, but that his inroads on the flock having hitherto been confined to the hours of the night, and never under the light of the moon, he had not been visibly detected in the onslaught. He had certainly been met about the woods and the fields, and suddenly disturbed from his slumbers beneath lonely ricks, and from under hedges on the sheltered side of banks he had been observed to scamper off, it being the commonly entertained opinion that the real holt of the marauder was in the thickets of Whittenden Park Wood. All sorts of stories were then told by all the company at once, of the doings of this black dog, and of the narrow escapes he had had from balls and charges of shot. So thoroughly illustrated was the old adage of " giving a dog a bad name," that anywhere in the vicinity of Wycombe at this time it would not have been safe for a black dog to have been seen off his master's premises, or he would at once have raised the cry of " Sheepkiller!" and, right or wrong, been killed. The rustics sat up late that night, and might have sat up later, had not neighbour Stoul slowly but resolutely risen from his seat, and without saying one word, a combative thirst still on him, seized and drained to the last drop the private pint of Gaffer Codger. This was too much for any old man to stand. Stoul and Codger clasped each other, and, pummelling away at their respective ribs, fell helter-skelter over the benches upon the floor, where they were soon smothered out of all power for blows by all the legs of the rest of the visitors. A constable, the oldest and most decrepit man in the village, having been called in, in respect more to his office than to any personal prowess he possessed, the Monkey's Hood was then cleared of all comers, and its doors fastened for the night.

On the opposite side of the river to Medenham Abbey, then, as we have shown, the temporary residence of our heroine, there was some grazing ground for sheep, along the level of the Thames, and on that ground a farmer maintained a large fold. It had been a stormy day, the one following the drinking bout at Lane End, and night was again fast closing in, when the shepherd' of that flock, who had remarked that his sheep looked already very much disconcerted, armed with a brass-mounted firelock, which had a hazel-stick for a rammer, having enclosed and foddered his sheep for the night, began to look round for the most comfortable spot in which to ensconce himself for his nightly vigil, armed as he was to kill the dog that had now become the terror of the country. The best place, as it seemed to this shepherd, to hide himself in, was to leeward of a heap of pea-straw, that lay along one side of the fold. He was anxious to conceal himself quickly, for his flock would not settle to their feed, but, huddled together, kept staring at him, or in his direction, while he was hollowing out a cavity in the straw in which he might sit down, not only to be out of sight, but also for the purpose of shelter against the cold driving wind. Having arranged the straw, his great coat, and an old blanket, to his satisfaction, he sat himself down with some impetus, exclaiming aloud to himself, " That is cumfy!" No sooner were the words uttered than a large, black, dishevelled head, on the top of a long, lean, hairy neck, thrust itself up from some thickly-growing sedge, mingled with the scattered pea-straw, within five yards of the shepherd, the two bright-brown eyes of which fixed on him in sleepy but suddenly-aroused wonder. Up the shepherd snatched his gun, and, scarcely in his haste bringing it to his shoulder, he fired it full at the head he saw. Following up his aim amidst the smoke, which from the shelter of the straw hung to the spot a good deal, the gallant shepherd, clubbing his musket, tumbled into the sedges to close upon the expected carcass of his dead enemy ; but *where* was the big black dog ? Staring in dismay, the man had slain nothing. He found himself, however, standing in a round warm nest, whence some animal had that moment departed, sufficiently proving to him that he had lost the best chance that ever was of winning the reward that had been offered for the sheep-killing dog's death.*

We must now return to our heroine, whom we left in the convent of Medenham Abbey. On the second day of her incarceration among the ascetic-visaged, waspish old nuns, whom she had seen, it was announced to her that the good father would attend her with ghostly consolation; and while expecting this visit the door opened, and, to the dismay and disgust of Marguerite, the hated Jesuit Father Crawl entered. She arose, but so cold and repellent was the expression in her face, form,

---

* A similar instance of such a miss as this came to my knowledge while hunting in the forests of France. When we were out for boar or wolf, though powder and fire-arms were illegal in the hands of the peasantry, a great many of them, to our very great danger, often joined us so armed, in the hope of killing a wolf and getting the Government reward. While I was hunting a boar, several wolves being on foot, a French peasant found in the side of a hill a small pit whence stone had been taken, situated among the high grass of what in England we should call the "young spring" of the cover. Thinking that in this pit he should find good ambush as well as a warm place in which to sit, the Frenchman got into it, and placing his gun beside him, first set about arranging a comfortable resting-place for himself. Having concluded this

and position, that once more the wily Jesuit felt abashed; and, his small grey eyes fallen in their glance to her feet, after they had for an instant sharply regarded her, he found it difficult to begin his errand.

"Mistress Marguerite," at last he said, "I am aware that circumstances, over which I had no control, on their first blush may have set you against me; but I have been acting on a higher behest than one emanating from man, and I have but been the chosen instrument, under our Holy Mother, in endeavouring to avert from the good man, your father, the ruin brought on his grey hairs by a disobedient child." He paused; and Marguerite, without a word, motioned him to pro-

business, his next move was to make a parting in the high grass on the edge of the pit to look through. Taking some grass in either hand, his gun resting against the side of the pit, he thrust his face into the opening, and then as suddenly met the nose of a large wolf, apparently come to look into the very place where he was when he was looking out; with a yell of terror and astonishment the Frenchman seized his gun, but the muzzle went beyond the wolf, and all the Frenchman saw was the vault of the gaunt beast away, between the lock and smoke from the muzzle of the gun. All Billingsgate, joined to the vocabulary of every cab-stand in London, would have been bland in expression to the oaths and execrations the disappointed Frenchman thundered at the chance he had lost.

ceed. "Your father has been accused of treasonable proceedings; the witnesses against him know that their testimony amounts to very little; and that being so, gold well and discreetly applied could make their testimony—none. That is not the only strait your poor father is in. The rich man, Sir Caldwell Hunter, who has advanced your father money to meet the liabilities his extravagance has brought upon him, sees that as other creditors are pressing their claims, and have arrested your poor father, he will lose a chance of obtaining the sums he has advanced, unless he enforces his claim as well. If all these claims are enforced, your father is for ever irredeemably ruined; and you, his only and heartless child, will have to beg, or at least to work for your bread, with the terrible knowledge that you have brought destruction on your house." She made no reply. "You have," continued the tempter, "pledged your love to a wild young man, who, to other bad qualities, adds the fact of being of a different religion—if religion it can be called—to yours; or, at least, to the one you have been brought up in, by the direction of your sainted mother; and in which holy faith it has been my toil and duty to endeavour to keep you." (At the allusion to her mother, poor Marguerite's eyes filled with tears;

but she never spoke.) "I come, now, as that priest appointed by your mother to watch over you—as the priest who has had the care of your conscience, and has rendered a listening and forgiving ear to all your sins (for there are none that have not sin), and who has seen with the deepest grief some signs of your defalcation from the Cross, to call on you at the eleventh hour to save your father, to rescue your house from destruction; to duties, in fact, that are not wholly mundane, but which, if performed, will win you the blessing of our Holy Church, and a life in the time to come."

Poor Marguerite had been so absorbed in listening to the priest, in trying to determine what course she should pursue, that she had not noticed the noiseless entrance of the superioress, who, coming close to her side, affectionately and entreatingly took her hand.

"Hear the good father," whispered the abbess, as she might for the time be called, in a voice peculiarly soft and winning; "listen, my child, to the good man: with tears I entreat you to regard him as a minister from Heaven, and to obey the call."

At that moment a heavy step was heard advancing to the door; the door opened, and Sir

Caldwell Hunter himself stood before them. Scarce a look passed between the superioress and priest, but they glided from the room, and Marguerite and the Knight were left alone. He was a tall, robust, elderly man, whose bloated face and figure denoted every species of excess; but still in bearing there was proof of his having once been used to good society: a fact which will even cling to forms in rags and filth; an impression made, as it were, by the mint on the surface-bearing of the coin that cannot be entirely effaced, however depreciated in currency that coin may have in after years become. He advanced to Marguerite with a semblance at least of respect, and essayed to take her hand: this he did not accomplish, however, for she drew back in scorn.

"Well," he said, "I see, young lady, that with you, at least, my suit has not progressed. I therefore waive entreaty and prayer as useless, and at once appeal to your duty as a child, and to your compassion for your lover." Marguerite started, but listened in silence. He unfolded a paper, and extending his hand showed that to him had been made over, by her father, the entire of the Grove Estate, in acknowledgment of sums of money advanced; while within this deed there was also a smaller official-looking paper, which, rapping it with the back of his fingers, Sir Caldwell said was a warrant for the committal of Willie to imprisonment in the Tower for five years. Silent and still as Marguerite had forced herself to be through these cruel interviews, she would have fallen under her severe restraint, had not a burst of tears come to her relief; and then she sank into a chair. Noiselessly the door again opened, and with a small bottle of some essence in her hand, and with the bland, sweet-toned notes of motherly persuasion, the superioress knelt at her side, and put her arm round her.

" My child! my dearest child! — listen to me, your godmother; for such, in this painful moment, I must remind you that I am: indeed, now I may be supposed to take the place even of your sainted mother, for thou hast none other to befriend thee. Listen to this noble Knight; remember the words of our good father: and if there be anything on earth that thou canst do to save thy poor father from ruin, and thyself from beggary, that is sanctioned by our Holy Mother, I beseech you grant the request of Sir Caldwell; for I know he seeks thy hand, and can redeem the evils that now have fallen upon thy house."

Overcome at last by her emotions, Marguerite's head sank half fainting on the shoulder of the superioress; who, taking from her pocket a small cup, poured a little of the essence from the bottle into it, and applied it to Marguerite's lips. After that, Marguerite had no recollection of what passed; she had vague ideas of a pen and writing materials, of her hand being held, and of signing she knew not what, and then of returning consciousness; and her eyes beheld, or seemed to behold, the knight and the abbess kneeling on either side of her. Then said the superioress, "Thou wilt save thy father and thy house, and give to this noble Knight the right to protect thee in all hours of peril, and cancel those hideous deeds?"

There was a pause. Marguerite's lips opened like an affirmation, and then her head sank down in unconsciousness, and she was carried senseless to her bed.

On the morning following poor Marguerite awoke with that peculiar sensation attendant on stupefaction arising from some narcotic. Scarcely were her eyes opened beneath her aching brow, than with that stealthy, noiseless tread that waited on her guileful manners, the superioress approached and knelt at her bedside. "How hast thou slept, my child? I bear thee the best of news. After thy solemn promise, verbal and in writing, yesterday made in my presence, and that of the good

Father Crawl, to accept the suitor then kneeling at thy feet, he set off to watch over thy father, and to arrange the approaching wedding. Thou hast saved thy father and thy house, and the third day hence sees thee united to Sir Caldwell Hunter."

It was with a shriek, that electrified every one that heard it, that Marguerite received this news: shrill were the accents, and so heart-broken their tone, that even the superioress rose to her feet, and almost repented of the act she had committed.

" Oh, no! no! no!" sobbed the wretched girl in accents of despair. " I cannot, will not, do anything so wicked! Oh, save me, Willie! save me from a fate so horrible, or we are lost!"

It is not our intention to pain our readers by a further description of Marguerite's sufferings. Suffice it to say, that even the superioress feared for her reason, when, having administered such soothing remedies as the convent afforded, the patient, from sheer exhaustion perhaps, as much as from anything else, fell into a deep and death-like slumber.

The next morning found Marguerite more calm; it was not till then that she had brought herself to regard her situation with any degree of resolution, but it seemed as if a weight was still on her mind, that kept it from any healthy action, so depressed and weak was she, that scarcely stamina was left her to resist, and at that moment she might have followed the steps of even her detested suitor to the foot of the altar itself, had he been there to take her hand. Towards the afternoon Marguerite walked feebly forth into the little garden, shielded from the winds on every side, save that which opened on the river, and had seated herself on a stone, cheered by the rays of the unclouded sun. The day was mild and beautiful — one of those days when dying summer clings to life, and begs of winter yet a lingering hour, and the river, looking like a mirror, reflected only there the deeper blue of heaven. All at once the distant shouts and wild cries of men in pursuit of something reached her ears; dropping reports of fire-arms, and then a continuation, and, apparently, a nearer approach of all the noise. Marguerite wondered what it could be, when suddenly, from some thick reeds on the other side the river, she saw something black glide stealthily into the water from the bank, and swim direct for the garden where she sat. It approached, and she saw two bright-brown eyes, that seemed to turn anxiously on every side, expecting the aggressions of surrounding enemies. With a start of breathless astonishment, it seemed that that creature's face was familiar to her. A great, black, wild-looking, gaunt dog, then crept into the garden from the river. The water, alas! that streamed from his close-lying lank coat, stained with blood from a wound in his shoulder, ere he shook himself, told but too sad a tale of his starved and hurt condition, and in a thrill almost of awe she gazed on the dog, still doubting if she knew him. Apparently the dog was for a moment as much bewildered as she was, for he fixed his eyes on her with extraordinary intentness, as if to discover whether she was friend or foe; an instant afterwards his brown eyes brightened with intenseness of joy at recognition, and, assuming a very different gait from that in which the poor fugitive had at first presented himself, he limped once or twice proudly around her, and then pushing his lips against her hand, she felt the corner of something he carried in his mouth. With a look of the deepest gratification poor " Cumpey " placed in her hand the slip of parchment that Mary had long ago deposited in the secret cleft in Whittenden Park Wood. Was it likely, therefore, that the honest thing had carried that treasure, when making those raids on the sheep that had been attributed to him? It is impossible to describe the caresses and tears which

Marguerite lavished on her four-footed friend, or
to portray the re-awakened sensation of hope that
returned to her now healthily acting brain. She
reviewed the scenes of the preceding days, and
came to regard them almost as a delusion—a
delusion, at least, so far, that whatever she had
been induced to say or do, at a time when she
was not a free agent, and able to distinguish right
from wrong, could not be binding; but the extraordinary incidents of the next day, the dreaded
day, had yet to come. Marguerite easily conveyed
poor " Luther " to her room without being seen ;
and, having procured him some food, she made him
up a comfortable bed beneath hers with her cloak,
and signed to him in ways with which she as well
as " Cumpey " were conversant, that he was to lie
in his hiding-place and watch; her only fear being
that, if the priest attempted to approach, a scene
beyond her control might be enacted, to the discovery of her guard. Poor old " Cumpey " licked
the gunshot wound in his shoulder, which was not
severe, and then employed himself in drying his
coat, thoroughly enjoying his comfortable quarters,
and free to seek the sound, safe sleep that had
been unknown to him for weeks. The few words
contained in the slip of parchment comforted Marguerite, and assured her up to a certain time of

Willie's probable safety. The morrow came, and on that eventful day Marguerite went early to the garden, revolving in her mind the course she should pursue; and there for a time we must leave her.

Not very long after Mary had placed the billet she had received in the cleft of the Swilley Hole, and had missed it from its position, which billet at last had safely reached her young mistress in the strange way we have narrated, another sealed billet reached her, which she was to deposit in the same place. Poor Mary took it to the given spot; and on her way thither she met a friend of hers, a girl from a neighbouring cottage, returning from attempting to sell a couple of ducks. She had sold one, but was taking the other home. They sat down by the Swilley Hole, which was on that day carrying off a good deal of surplus water, and for the first time Mary made her friend a confidant in all she knew of the affair between Willie and Marguerite. She did this because hope in her heart by delay had grown sick, and she had come to despair of ever seeing them together again.

"Here, Jennie," she said, "here's another letter I'm to put in this cleft under the moss: but I'm sure it's no use putting it there; it will only be eaten or carried away by the mice."

" Where, Mary, do you think your young mistress is, then?" inquired Jennie.

" I don't know," replied Mary; " I wish I did for certain. Some say she is shut up in Medenham Abbey, but there's no telling."

" The Abbey!" cried her friend; " why, that's there away some miles," pointing with her finger towards the valley of the Thames. " It's no use to leave the letter here, then, if you want her to have it; better throw it into the water down the Swilley Hole."

" And so we will," said Mary, half in play and half in sorrowful earnest; " the water must go somewhere, and as well put the letter into it as leave it here: it will at least be safe from getting into the wrong hands."

" Stop," said Jennie, half laughing, for she was as merry a little soul as ever lived; " I don't want my duck: let's put the note under the duck's wing and tie it there, and then put her down the Swilley Hole; I can get at it: so my bird shall be the messenger of love, and our Holy Mother guide her."

As she said this she crossed herself, for she had been one of the flock of Father Crawl; they then tied the letter firmly beneath the wing of the duck, and, in spite of the great disinclination of the bird to go down the dark abyss, they forced her into the trough of the running water, and she was carried from their sight. They then returned to their homes.

That eventful day on which Sir Caldwell Hunter was to repair to Medenham Abbey, for the purpose of making Marguerite his bride, came; and early that morning Marguerite was in the garden on the verge of the Thames, with "Luther" seated at her side. All at once something attracted his attention in the mid current of the river; it was a bird alive, but rumpled, dirty, and in part denuded of its feathers—it was a duck, and the weakened and distressed thing seemed to be drowning, or not to have strength enough to reach the shore. The recollection of wounded wild-fowl was too much for "Cumpey's" well-practised sensibilities; so, swimming out into the open river, he seized the duck, and as he did so the report of a gun was heard close by, a bullet struck the water close to his head, and skipping thence across the surface of the river buried itself in the Abbey wall. Regardless of this attempt upon his life, or deeming, perhaps, that the shot had been aimed at the duck, "Cumpey" turned his head to look in the direction whence the shot had proceeded, and then swam back to the garden and gave the bird into the hand of his mistress. Her astonishment may be more easily conceived than described when she took from beneath the bird's wing a slip of parchment, addressed to her in the handwriting of Willie. It bore date, as far as she could make it out, but a few days back, and contained these few lines, now nearly defaced,—

"I write, fearing to say too much. Keep up your heart, dear Marguerite; believe nothing that priests or enemies may urge. I know where you are, and it shall not be my fault if *I am not presently at your side.*"

Resolved more than ever to resist to the uttermost, and to repudiate the miserable engagement into which she had been entrapped, Marguerite composed herself for the worst, when a loud clamour at the entrance-door of the convent reached her ears. In another moment, the entrance-door to the garden half opened; but before the intruder could be well seen, "Luther" hurled himself, with a roar, headlong at the apparition, and the door closed just in time to save the villain priest from his furious jaws. The uproar from without still continued, and after Father Crawl had retired for a few minutes, it arose again with renewed fury. "Down with the Papists! Smoke 'em out!" resounded from a dozen or more voices;

and it was evident a riot had commenced. Assembled round the porch was a mob of excited rustics, armed with guns and pitchforks.

"Give us the ship-killing dog!" cried the rabble. "We know he's here, and out we'll have him, alive or dead!"

The priest looked forth from a latticed window; and in his cold, imperturbable, bitter tone, said,—

"My friends, the sheep-killing dog is here, and you have a right to destroy him" (no doubt he remembered "Luther's" rough usage to his arm), "and I will presently admit two gunners to kill him where he lies."

"That's right!" cried the man who had but just now fired a bullet at poor "Cumpey." "I see him a-killing of the convent ducks!"

Some little time then took place while the superioress and the priest were consulting how they could admit two men without the others rushing in; and the mob, impatient of delay, began to throw stones at the grated windows, to batter at the door, to suggest an incendiary fire, and to incite each other to more mischief by loud cries for vengeance on what they now termed the "convent dog." Marguerite was listening to these outcries, in terror of she knew not what, when suddenly the noise was profoundly hushed, and there were murmurs as if some other personages had come on the scene. Considerable commotion was soon heard in the nunnery, as well as outside, and the clank of more than one hasty spurred heel was distinguished by Marguerite's anxious ear in the stone passage. One, however, seemed to come on far more hastily than the other.

"O, Heaven help me!" cried the terrified girl; "it is Sir Caldwell Hunter!"

The door of the garden flew open, and she fell into Willie's arms! As to "Cumpey," he also sprang to greet his master, but finding Willie's caresses occupied in another direction, the joyous old dog picked up a leaf, as he could find nothing else that lay on the neatly-kept turf, and walked around the lovers in gyrations proudly happy. That hasty step, then, that came in so fast before the other was accounted for; the next appeared, and her father stood before her, not as a foe to Willie, but as his approving friend. The rest of the legend is soon told. Willie's rich old aunt had died, and done the reverse of many a rich old lady gone before and since—she had left everything to the handsome nephew who so much needed it; and with the means most amply in his power Willie was just in time to pay off Justice

Wellrode's liabilities, and to free the paternal estate of Marguerite from all incumbrances, and in right of his wife to make it his. Of course this could not be done without the knowledge of Sir Caldwell Hunter, when, having a pretty good idea that his chances with Marguerite were over, and not thinking that the jesuitical proceedings of himself, the superioress, and Father Crawl, would bear investigation, he retired to his estates further north, and gave to his successful rival, Willie, the triumph of his heart.

Leaving the chief personages of this tale, then, for a few minutes together in the Abbey garden, we must return to the now overawed crowd of rustics who had been so angrily pertinacious in their accusations against " Luther." In breathless haste they were joined by a shepherd.

" Here he is!" cried a dozen voices to the new-comer; "we have run the big black sheep-killer here into the Convent garden ; the Justice is in there, and we'll soon have him out and get the reward."

" No 'y won't," said the newly-arrived rustic ; " the dog's neither black nor white, and he an't here. The keeper up yonder," pointing to West Wycombe Park, " has killed the dog, there away," pointing with his hand, in the midst of Farmer

Hillock's flock of sheep; "he had worried three when the keeper kill'd un, and a great, long-legged, *red*, lurcher-like customer he was!"

Thus then poor "Cumpey" had got, like many more innocent dogs, a bad name; but instead of being hanged he was restored to his loving friends.

Matters for instant departure to the Grove were soon arranged; there was a horse and riding apparel for Marguerite, and as she gracefully rode from beneath the Abbey gateway, attended on either side by Willie and her father, the surrounding rustics cheered them heartily, their cheers rendered not the less hearty in that Willie had given them ample money to purchase any amount of beer. On arriving at the Grove, everything had been hastily put in the best order; and as Marguerite turned her horse sideways to dismount at the dismounting-stone, at the door of her now thrice happy home, the smiling and delighted Mary received her as her appointed maid; and little full-eyed "Jip," whose being in the incidents of this tale has almost been forgotten, came out testifying the greatest satisfaction at the sight of Willie, her mistress, and her playmate "Luther."

As to Medenham Abbey, its superioress, her

nuns, and the wily priest, they all in a very short time disappeared, leaving the handsome ruin to be for the future the resting-place of owls.

If any kind reader who has perused this legend wishes to see that beautiful wild old wood, and be led to Our Lady's Well at the Swilley Hole, a visit will fully repay the trouble; for Whittenden Park is one of the highest points of Buckinghamshire, and from it may be commanded the prettiest views imaginable, looking across the high road from Marlow to Stokenchurch, and upon the church that crowns the Down above West Wycombe Park. The wood itself is on so high a level that on a clear day it can be seen from Windsor Castle. At Lane End there are one or two old people who are acquainted with the mysteries of the wood; and one old man who remembers seeing the "great stags," as he calls them, who once haunted the beautiful rides and drives which the then proprietor used to keep up. For years this splendid old remnant of the forest has been utterly neglected by the Dashwoods; and to this moment it stands a gloomy object of magnificent decay, without a gate or trimmed ride to keep it safe, or show its splendid sylvan scenery. The stones that once were by the well have been removed; there are, however, a few of them strongly impregnated with iron yet to be seen, cast into some of the adjacent ruts of the neglected rides, to give support to the wood-cart on its wet and wintry way.

Alas, for the taste of the times!

CHAPTER XX.

THE TWO WARNINGS — THE FIRST LOVE — HONOUR AND SAFETY—THE COMMENCEMENT AND END OF THE TRAGEDY —A BROTHER'S RESOLVE—HIS UNTIMELY DEATH—A SCIENTIFIC CERTIFICATE.

PART II.

It may seem to some of my readers strange that a very young and beautiful girl, of high descent, should so far break through the conventional rules of the age in which she lived as to visit, alone and unprotected, so to speak, a wild young man in so wild a place as his chambers in Lincoln's Inn; where, each set of rooms being in the exclusive command of the occupant, supervision there was none, and thus each introduced to his rooms whomsoever he pleased. It is, for a man, delightful to have a "Liberty Hall" of this description, and a charming incident in his life, when the opportunities it affords are not abused; but I much regret to say there are those who prefer the most questionable female society, as we have seen in our time, to the far superior

one that enhances life, and can " gild refined gold,"
or "throw a perfume on the violet;" and I regret
that, as an author, I must admit the lamentable
truth.

There is no time in woman's life at which she
will do more, or risk more for one she loves, than
at her very earliest stage of spring, when verging
on her nearly approaching summer. There is no
period of her chequered, and, through pain and
sorrow, happiness or contentment, beautiful existence, when her love, her first, real, sweet, romantic affection, is so splendid a gift as it is ere
she reaches twenty years of age.

Her heart may be captivated without even
speech, without a word from the object that has
fixed and engrossed her thoughts, and she may
love her hero with a devotion that all the personal attention in the world could not have
induced. This was not exactly the case with the
beautiful heroine of this legend; she had once met
young Perceval in society, and had danced with
him, though he had forgotten it, and through
good repute and evil repute, and in continual
absence, she had clung to the recollection of the
first impression he had made; and when she heard
him spoken of for his skill, his success, and
extraordinary gallantry in combat, then the wild

fashion of the day, she drank in the praises he received as the sweetest nectar of the gods, and her soul would cling to his more than ever.

To save him then from some apprehended danger, the origin of the dread of which in her had never been explained, she broke through the usages of society and risked all; her only consolation being that she knew, in spite of his wild deeds, that he was a gentleman; and thought, and rightly thought too, that however she might endanger her interests and commit herself, a man of honour, and, therefore, the only type of a true gentleman, would, while under his roof and in his power, protect her just position with his hand, his life, his heart, and soul, and take care that she should leave him as she came; and whatever the circumstances that involved her might be, while she was by his side she should be the supreme mistress of his actions and her own desires.

When his beautiful visitor had left him Robert Perceval threw himself into a chair, and did not restrain some bitter and almost repentant tears that trickled down his handsome face. The horrible vision of the previous night again seemed to occupy the spot where it had appeared to stand —a warning, as his guardian said, to keep him from danger, the gaming-house and tavern; and

now a spot upon the same floor, still more impressed on his mind from the loveliness of the
thing that had stood there, pleading in all its
beauty, not in its hideous terrors, loomed up and
prayed to him to obey "*the second*," and what
might be the last "warning" he *could* receive.
He felt all this; he would have given worlds to
have recalled the pledges made to his jovial companions expected for that night's recreation: but
as his eyes roamed restlessly from place to place
in his chamber, they fell on his invariably successful sword lying on a table, where he had cast
it just previous to the visit of his lovely monitress.

It is strange how small a thing will change
the current of man's thoughts, and pervert his
better resolution. That sword seemed to awaken
him from every soft idea, and to harden his heart
to the temper of its own pointed blade. He took
it up, and even kissed its hilt, muttering as he did
so, " To-night my trust is here, and so is my
safety, too; let this night be got over, then, sweet
girl, my life shall be passed in search of you, and
when you are found, then, indeed, *be* my angel
from heaven."

Dismissing all sad thoughts, light and volatile
as his spirits were, ever too buoyant to be depressed for long, he then set himself about his

usual occupations.   It is not in my power to narrate how he passed the rest of the day, or where he dined, but a still, dark, hot night, early in the month of June, when every flower was closed for rest, and none but the full-blown rose cast its sweetness on the fragrant air, found him proceeding from the direction of Lincoln's Inn towards the appointed tavern in the Strand.   No wonder that, with the two warnings he had received from life and death, he was cautious on his way, his eyes endeavouring to peer into the ill-lit places, and his " beard very frequently on his shoulder," as one who listened for something that *might* be in the rear.   He had proceeded nearly as far as the Strand without hurt or hindrance, when as he came down an alley which led across the Strand to the door of the tavern to which he was directing his steps, he became aware of a man behind him, and there was sufficient light for him to see that it was the same man who had previously dogged his steps, and with whom he had already had a few words in altercation.   At that moment he reached the Strand, and at the same time he thought that the figure behind him increased his speed, and made some gesture with his arm to two men, now also in sight, on the same side, and on either side the door of his tavern, and that they too quickened their steps as if to intercept him. All this happened in far shorter time than it takes me to write it. In less than a second Robert Perceval saw that an assault was intended; his sword flew from his scabbard and he rushed on. One of the figures, who had not drawn, sprang to the door of the tavern, with his back to it, just as Perceval reached it, but too close in conjunction to make the rapier's point available. A blow on the temple from the hilt of Robert's sword, however, knocked him backwards, and falling or slipping down, his back to the door, his extended legs tripped another of the assailants up, just as the one from behind missed a furious lunge and broke his sword against the wall; Perceval's sword at the same time piercing the body of the one who had stumbled over the legs of his companion, and who, sword in hand, had regained his feet and was renewing his assault.

In the midst of this sudden fracas the tavern-boy, hearing the noise, opened the door, and Robert Perceval dashed in: the boy then, who was much attached to Master Robert, closed the door; when from the tavern room there rushed out a multitude of "pretty gentlemen," all to see what they called the "turn up," and among them many of Perceval's friends and boon companions, as well as some of his jealous, envious, and secret enemies.

It took a little time to explain the matter, but as soon as it was known that there had been three swords set upon one, several young men rushed forth, calling to the murky night to raise its veil and let the would-be murderers stand confessed: but the night still frowned an Alsatia for the guilty heads, and, as the ordinations of the universe often do, night screened the guilty and blinded the eyes of vengeful retribution.

When the confusion had subsided, it was then discovered that Robert Perceval had received a slight wound in the leg; so slight, that binding it up with a handkerchief, he joined the company assembled at the tavern in all the boisterous merriment of the day, and would have claimed the wager for the friend in whose behalf he thought himself pledged in honour to attend, but none of those having to do with the wager were there: they had no doubt found more agreeable occupations elsewhere; and the long and the short of it was, that Robert Perceval himself might just as well have been absent, and have profited by the *two warnings* he had received, and that too, without the slightest stain on his bravery or honour.

Disgusted at finding himself at the tavern at

which he supposed his arrival would have been greeted on the part of several friends with much satisfaction, but who had not thought it worth their while to come, after a brief sojourn among the choice spirits of the hour, and rather out of temper with himself and everybody else, he resolved to betake himself home, and on the following morning to discover if he could, and to throw himself at the feet of the beautiful girl from whom he had received the mysterious visit. Scarce lame from the slight wound in his leg, and about the hour of midnight, he left the supper-table and announced his intention of proceeding to Lincoln's Inn, which called forth a wish on the part of several young men of his acquaintance to go with him to see him home, as they thought, and with good reason, that there was a design on his life.

" And what if there was, or is ?" he replied. " I have pricked one rascal and ' done his busi·ness ;' and as for the other two, let 'em draw again if they dare."

It is always very easy to decline or get rid of services, when the services may include wounds and death to those who proffer them ; but there was one present, the little tavern-boy, who pertinaciously implored Master Robert, as he called him, not to go home alone; and from his solicitations Perceval found it very difficult to escape, nothing sufficing to make the honest little fellow hold his tongue but a severe rebuke, and order "to mind his own business and be silent."

With tears in his eyes, that poor boy saw *his* favourite customer at the tavern depart, while some of the best-inclined of the roystering blades came to the door with him, saw that at least, for a short space, the coast was clear, bade him adieu, and leaving Robert Perceval in a very moody frame of mind, almost wishing for some one to assault him on whom he might work his will, they returned to their carousals at the gaming-table, and thought of him no more. One sentence that Robert Perceval had uttered that evening alone dwelt on some of their minds; it was that wherein he had said, " he had done for one of his assailants :" this, as well as his further assurance to the tavern-keeper on leaving the door, that he, the said tavern-keeper, " should recollect that he himself knew that his assailants bore him an old grudge, and that if he should be murdered his friends who took an interest in him *would know and find it out.*" These assertions together made a very deep impression.

Whether, at the time of his leaving the tavern,

there was any prophetic feeling in his mind or not, cannot be known : from something that had fallen from him in the earlier part of that night he seemed to have shaken all gloom away, and to be looking to the following morning as one to bring him a long term of happy life and sunshine, and a better object of pursuit than any that had of late engrossed his thoughts, when he should be able to slight *the first hideous warning*, as the fiction of a dream, and *the second warning* as a beacon dear, the light of which should lead his steps to happiness and love.

The second warning might have done so, had it *not* been neglected : as it was, before day-break a watchman discovered his lifeless body lying beneath the Maypole in the Strand, pierced to the heart by a sword-wound beneath the left breast, his sword in his hand drawn, and also streaked by blood, and a strange hat, with a feather and a bunch of green ribbons in it, lying by his side; by which it was hoped, at the moment, to gain traces of the murderers.

On the morning of the 5th of June, 1677, the watchmen then carried the lifeless limbs, and the pallid face, still in death handsome and resolute in expression, and laid it out in the watchhouse, to be sought for by the relatives and friends.

Sir Robert Southwell, his guardian, was the first to gain these evil tidings and the first to claim the body, deeply grieved to find that even the warning his nephew had told to him had had no effect in thwarting the resolute determination of poor Master Robert to keep an appointment, as to which no one really cared much but himself.

Many suspicions were bruited about as to the cause of his murder, and who his murderers were. It was not unusual in those days for a gentleman to be found killed in the streets, in a brawl at night, and among friends to either party standing by to see fair play; but then it was also tacitly known and understood *how* it happened and *who* the parties were, and the matter was eventually hushed up.*

In this sad case rumour was damaging to Beau Fielding, and also to the wife of Sir Robert Southwell; the evil tongue of scandal saying that she, in some way or other, was mixed up in the affair.

With respect to Beau Fielding, it was well known that one night at the play Robert Perceval

* See " History of the Ancient Family of Avery."

and the Beau had had high words, but what about has never been clearly known.

Poor Robert Perceval, second son of Sir John Perceval, lies buried under one of the pillars in the north-west end of the burying-ground beneath the chapel in Lincoln's Inn, interred there the day after his murder, and above him may still be seen this short inscription :—

"ROBERTUS PERCIVALE, ARM. OBIIT 5 JUNIJ, 1667,
ÆTAT. 19."

Perhaps, in all the legends that have come under my notice, not any can offer to the reader's consideration more extraordinary proofs of some occult power presiding over the destiny of man than does this, the one of "two warnings." The strange evidence of such communications, however, does not rest alone with the personal death of Robert Perceval. Mrs. Brown, a resident at Bristol, dreamed that a Mrs. Sherman, who at that time lived with Sir Robert Southwell, came to her bedside in Bristol, on the night of the murder, and asked her "for a sheet, which she wanted to wind the body of poor Master Robin in, who had been killed." Mrs. Brown asked "how he had been killed, and when;" and the reply she received, or seemed to receive, from the likeness of Mrs. Sherman was,—"Poor Master Robin lies dead in the watchhouse in the Strand." Mrs. Brown then awoke, and subsequently heard of the death alluded to, at or about the hour she dreamed the dream.

Shortly before the tragedy thus recounted, Sir Philip Perceval, the elder brother of Robert, had returned from his travels in foreign countries, and had made the tour of Ireland. The news and manner of his brother's death affected him immensely, and he at once declared "that he would trace the assassins to the death." There can be no doubt in my mind but that, from some secret intelligence he received, he deemed that the assassins or assassin had fled from London to Dublin after the murder had been committed, and therefore he tarried in Dublin instead of coming to England to conduct the search, and, if possible, to fix the crime. He was, like his younger brother, a man prone to violent impulses, brave as a lion, and at all times ready for an appeal to the sword. If he had not received some clue to the whereabout of the murderer, he would not have remained in Dublin instead of coming on immediately to London, nor been subject to an impulse thus described:—"He was walking in the town one day, when he met a man decently dressed and wearing a sword, but who was evidently not one in the first society; and, curiously enough, he completely answered the description, which Sir Philip had not then heard, of the man who had dogged the heels of his brother. Without, then, any assigned cause or reason, the moment his eyes met the figure of this man, his breast became dilated with an uncontrollable sensation of horror, hatred, and rage against the individual, when, calling on him to draw and defend himself, with a furious lunge at his heart he commenced his assault; but, ere the passing of more than one or two lightning-like thrusts and parries, the passers-by made in, the hostile swords were struck up or down, and the combatants seized by their arms and walked out of sight of each other."

Thus, so far, ended *that* hostile meeting; but, strange to say, though it was expected that in some more fitting place the duel would have been fought to an end, nothing more came of it, and the man thus furiously, and on the spur of the moment, assaulted by Sir Philip, *was never afterwards seen in Dublin.* Sir Philip then divided his time and his continuous researches for the means of avenging his brother's death between England and Ireland, and, as far as I can ascertain, came to the conclusion — and the result proved his conclusion to be correct — that *in Ireland* the hands that were stained by the blood of poor Robert were concealed; and in Ireland, with all the relentless pertinacity of a bloodhound, he continued to seek for retribution.

In 1680, no less than thirteen years after the murder of his brother, he was again, or still in Ireland, and was taken suddenly and seriously ill in Munster; at a time, too, when it was supposed that he still held some clue to the man or men he so assiduously searched for. At first it was alleged that his malady arose from " a surfeit," caused by eating " too great a quantity of nuts;" but at an inquest held on his sudden demise, the sworn evidence of his two attendants — Margaret and Richard Conran — attested as follows : —

" His body swelled up strangely immediately after death, so that his neck raised up to his chin-bone. His eyes swelled as if they would burst from his head; his nails grew mighty black; his hair grew red; and his whole body grew very black, and smelled strangely."

To commemorate these depositions, two " *eminent physicians* " signed the following *elaborate* and *astonishingly scientific certificate:* —

" The dreadful alteration which happened in Sir Philip Perceval after his death, induceth us to conjecture of some extraordinary miscarriage in this matter.

" Given under our hands.

"(Signed)   DAN. CONNELL.
THAD. CALLAGAN."

To this conclusion, then, I think the reader will come—that is, like myself the reader may be "induced to conjecture," that the "extraordinary miscarriage in this matter" arose from the secret administration of poison, given at the instance of those who felt that Sir Philip Perceval—an avenger of blood, even at that remote period from the shedding of it—was behind them; and that the same hand that killed the younger brother caused to be given—if it did not actually administer—the deadly drug that reft the elder representative of that ancient family of life.

During my search for legends connected with the Castles, Halls, and Houses of "the Upper Ten Thousand," many very strange tales have come under my notice; not only from very ancient dates, but even down to the present time; so verified by circumstantial as well as personal and living evidence, that it is almost impossible to discredit their narration.

Among the many whose truth is vouched for, and thoroughly believed in to the present day, and to this hour strangely borne out by attendant circumstances and the signs of a prophetic curse, is one where, in times long past, the second son of a high lineage was supposed to have got rid of his elder brother by purposely pushing him into the river, by the side of which they were seen to have been walking; and then returning home, pleading ignorance of where his brother was. Though the body of the brother was discovered in the water, nothing was ever proved as to the manner of his death; but the foregoing tale of the " House of Avery," and the verbatim " certificate" from the hands of two "eminent physicians," as rendered by me, shows how vague were the opinions of scientific practitioners in the bygone time; and how little and how loose the investigation was that followed on the heels of murder. Though in this last instance a motive was evident in regard to why the elder brother's death should be desired, and the fact of the younger one succeeding to the title and estates, and their having been last seen in company on the water's edge, yet no proof was arrived at by the agency of man that a murder had been committed. Though mortal suspicion was, to a certain extent, rife in the matter, Heaven alone was left the awful and the all-seeing Judge in this instance, as in many others; and by all that is in our limited power to descry, *Heaven has visited*, and *is still visiting*, some deed of darkness on that once rich, prosperous, and powerful family. A curse seems to cling to the ancient lineage and to the estates, for nothing prospers; male heirs are wanting; and site after site of the ancient and now divided heritages are sold and selling—passing into strangers' hands: the home, and the once warm .and prosperous hearth, being known no more; decay descending on them all — on name and lineage; and that on account, as men sup-pose, ·of some deed of darkness, suspected on earth, but surely known in heaven.

CHAPTER XXI.

THE PICTURES ON THE WALL.

In one of the best sporting counties, the name of which I leave to the reader's imagination, stood a fine old castellated building, the seat of a noble Lord. High and commanding, and surrounded by its deer-park, it was, perhaps, and is, as aristocratic a residence as can be found within the limits of Great Britain. Its venison, its foxes, its wild-fowl, and its pheasants, could not be surpassed; but within its halls, and beneath its roof, there was one attraction which threw all others into shade, and that consisted in the face and figure of the Lady Grace, the third and youngest daughter of the noble Baron.

It has fallen to my lot of late to describe so many heroines, that to attempt to put the Lady Grace before my readers as she really looked and was, would be a failure, or at best but a repetition of lovely form, lovely hair, lovely eyes, and other admitted attractions: I shall therefore only say that the Lady Grace was beautiful, was dark, full of innocent fun, and very witty.

On a fine bright winter's morning, in the end of November, the Lady Grace had left the Castle with her basket on her arm to feed innumerable feathered pets, when, in turning a corner of one of the drives, she met Tilter, the head-gamekeeper, coming in for orders.

The keeper's hat was off the instant he saw her, with the deference due to her rank, as well as to the way in which she was respected and beloved by the whole household.

" Good morning, my lady," he said ; " it's seasonable weather,"—that was, it was bitingly cold : " but, my lady, please don't 'y get wet in the feet, for it 's dampish-like down among the ducks."

" Good morning," she replied, with a smile that ought to have warmed the coldest winter in the world : " good morning, Tilter : any curious things to tell me to-day, or anything about my pets ? "

" No, my lady; nothing about the pets. 'Cre-noline,' as we calls the duck as can't dress herself 'cause her neck's too short, she's still at work to reach the big tail on her, and can't do so ; but ha, ha, ha, my young lady—begs pardon for laughing so in the presence on 'y—but ho, ho, I'se summat amusing to tell; leastways I don't know as I may tell it to you, but hee, hee, hee, I dies on it!"

"Well, Tilter," replied the laughing girl, much amused at seeing the mirth of the old servant, "if it's anything I should not hear, you do right not to tell me; but if it is about my pets or creatures you may talk to me of, why then you always know I like to hear all about it."

"Well, your ladyship, it ain't about your pets, ho, ho; nor it's not about nothing to be ashamed of, nor as I mayn't speak on afore you: it's about our Passon; and as you goes regular like to hear he, perhaps, my ladyship, you may please to hear tell on him, as I see'd him last night out of his pulpit loik, and a enjoying on himself."

"Indeed!" replied the Lady Grace, very much amused by the manner of her old servant, as well as curious to hear what the Incumbent of the living had been doing. "I am happy to hear Mr. Stiflesin was 'enjoying himself;' the duties of a clergyman in a large parish are often onerous, and sometimes melancholy, and it is but fair they should have occasional recreation. Tell me, Tilter, tell me all about it."

"Well, my lady, then 'twas just this: you

knows Woodcock Spinney, as we calls it, as lays along the side of the ploughed land atween that and the meadows as coasts the river. You always goes there, you know, my lady, for the first primroses; and you'll remember the steep bank or fall there is from the footpath by the end of the Spinney down into the meadow, where I've so often helpt 'y down to pluck the first cowslips?"

" Yes, Tilter, I know it all very well, and the thick hedge there is on the top of the bank between the footpath and the meadow below it — go on."

" Hee, hee, hee, ho! Well, my leddy, in Woodcock Spinney there always is a pheasant or two gets up to roost every night, and it is there that we gets an occasional run-away shot, bang and off again, and I longs to catch the thief. It being a likely night, no moon, but starlight, with a breezy wind, I takes my stick, and I hides myself in the Spinney, close to the path as leads from Squire Mufflum's to our village. Harn't been there long, when I hears a step a-coming about midnight on the frosty ground. Now, thinks I to myself, here they comes, and into some on 'em I'll just about be, or my name's not Tilter. Down I drops my overcoat from my shoulders, and I handles my stick, when roosh summat goes through the thick hedge from off the high path into the medder below, and then it comes down with a squilsh like, and there it stops.

"'Hallo!' says I to myself, 'what's that? can't make it out; it's no blackguard ater our birds.' So I goes out of the bushes and looks down below, and there I sees the dark form of a man like a-sitten on the damp grass. 'Hallo, master,' says I, 'what be doing on down there?'

"'Who's that?' says a voice from below, as I knowed to be our Passon's; so down I goes to see if anything was the matter, and there, sure enough, was Mr. Stiflesin! I gives him my hand, and up he gets.

"'Ish this you, Misher Tilter?'

"'Yes, sir,' says I, 'it's me. But how's ever, sir, did'y get down here?'

"'Shat's jest what I wishes to know, Misher Tilter. You've dug away sh-path after your detestable rabbits' sh-holes; t'ant shafe for your betters out after dark. Shank you to fill them holes in; and now lend us sh-hands to get back upon the path.'

" I gives him my hand, my lady—he, he, he, ho, ho!—and helps his Reverence back on to the high path, when he turns round, and a-drawing himself up to the full stretch on him, and a-looking me full in the face, says he to me, says he, ' Misher Tilter, good night.'

" ' Sir,' says I, ' I think you'd better let I assist ye like on your way home.'

" ' Misher Tilter,' says he, with a deal more dignity like than ever I heard un speak afore in the pulpit, or anywhere else ; ' Misher Tilter, I'se wish to be alone. I shank you, shir, but have no wish, shir, for your company. You've been drinking, Misher Tilter, sir, and I can't stop to take care of you.'

" With that he turns round on his ways home. He warn't scarce out of sight when roosh I hears him go through the hedge again, and squilsh down upon the meadow, a heavier like still. Down I goes, and there he was seated, and a-leaning on his hands.

" ' Hallo, sir,' says I, ' what, be down here again ?'

" ' Yes, Misher Tilter, I am : there's sh-summat wrong in that path o' yourn; it's given me a bad hurting like this time.'

" ' No, sir, you ban't hurt, surely,' says I; ' let me help'y up.' So I takes him by the arm and sets him on his legs. ' There, sir,' I says, ' you be all right now.'

" ' No,' says he, in a melancholy tone of voice;

'Misher Tilter, I fear as it's my head as is hurt I'm blind like, I carn't see.'

" ' No wonder, sir, as you carn't see,' says I a-looking for his face; 'you've druv the hat on'y down over your nose, and into your mouth There,' says I, a-pushing on it up, ' you be al right now; and come, sir, I'll help'y back again.

" ' Misher Tilter,' said he, ' I'sh happy to take your arm.' So, my young lady, with a deal to do we rights ourselves on the footpath, and then says he, stopping and looking at me, 'Misher Tilter, says he, ' it'sh unpossible for me to shank you for your company sh'night in a few words, so you shall take my arm as far as my door, and then I'sh explain my feelings. Come on, andsh keep steady.'

" So, my lady, I gets our Passon home; bu excuse my laughing, my young lady, it wor a rummish job, and one I didn't expect just abou then and there, whatever I might have done nearer home."

" Well, Tilter, I'm very sorry to have heard what you have told me; keep your own counsel and do not mention it to any of the people in the parish. Perhaps something disagreed with the good man, and made him giddy."

" Humph! might be so, my leddy; but I've

seen a good many sitch cases, and never see'd real giddiness interfere afore loik with the gift of the gab."

"Well, good-day, Tilter," rejoined the Lady Grace; "mind what I have said, and forget all about this giddiness; I am going on to my pets;" when she hurried away to conceal her own inclination to laugh at the way in which the old keeper told his tale, and at the curious errors of the English language which he narrated as indulged in by the reverend divine.

It was a most interesting sight to see the Lady Grace among her pets of all descriptions; the wildest creatures tamed at once to her hand, and those that were savage forgot their ferocious propensities in her gentle presence, and abstained from violence. Among the leading young men of the day she was deemed cold, or what in common parlance would be described as "difficult to get on with:" but the real fact was, that she saw through empty protestations and compliments, despised assumptions and conceit, and never having been in love herself, though worshipped by rich and poor, by all who knew her, she walked the world alone, or stood aloof, a lovely flower above the fields of grass that the scythe of Time kept mowing, or the wooing hand of man gathering up to garnish the awaiting homestead and adorn his hearth.

The noble lord her father, the thirteenth baron, was descended from a long line of ancestors, who had invariably been soldiers or sailors for the last four hundred years; and, indeed, one of them had been selected to assist as a chief mourner at the funeral of Henry VIII. Sprung, then, from high lineage, and even from a royal source, no wonder that the gentle nature of this beautiful girl was tempered by a soul of fire, which, if the light within it was not seen, there it nevertheless burned in all its purity and strength, to be touched to life some day, perhaps, by one she had never yet seen.

Days ran on. Time never stays, unless by the side of Sorrow or of Pain. Men of the highest rank and best pretensions came and went from the lordly halls of her father; all paid the Lady Grace attention, yet gallant after gallant failed to make any perceptible impression. She sang to perfection, her soft contralto voice and wonderful talent and feeling giving to all she attempted a brilliancy and grace that ought to have brought kings and princes to her feet; but yet, though all admired and some adored, still not a lip had dared to speak of love, or if love had been alluded

to, a cold but gentle disinclination to listen froze
all warmth from the suitor's mind, and made him
feel the utter hopelessness of his attention.

Things continued in this way; the Lady Grace
still loved her pets alone, and still fled from empty
protestations; and, perhaps, if she changed the
even course of her life in the least degree, it was
in being more attached to her books, though she
always read a good deal, and in confining herself
rather more to her own boudoir.

It was on a fine, early spring morning, that
as she wandered forth to her favourite woods and
streams she again met the gamekeeper, Tilter, who
had been busy in mending an aviary, the repairs
of which he had not quite concluded; when she
sat down on an oaken chair to speak to him.

" Well, Tilter," she said, " have you anything
amusing to tell me to-day ?"

" Why no, my lady, nothing as is directly
amusing ; but I remember once, when I served
his Honour—him, my lady, as I lived with afore
I come to you—a thing as happened as would
make you laugh. You know, my lady, I have
often tell'd ye, that his Honour was one in a
thousand; for he was good-natured, kind to all,
powerful, and brave ; and though he could, and
had taken his part against many a man—some-

times with weapons, sometimes in a boxing way
—there warn't nothing in this world too small for
him to defend in times of danger, to cherish, and
to love. He would always hold his own, and
make people obey him where he had a right to
command. And nothing ever pleased him so much
as coming in between right and wrong: particularly if any female was in the case, and needed
some one to take her part. Lord! there, my lady,
I have seen him thrash a big burly ruffian, who
had struck and ill-treated a poor girl; and not
mind a blow or two in doing so; and then tears
ran down his face when the poor girl and her
mother thanked him for it. Tears, my lady, as no
ruffian nor pain could have got out on him; but
ready enough to fall on a kind word like."

" That is very right, Tilter; and I am glad to
hear you speak so well of your former master.
Well, go on and tell me the amusing part of
what you remember."

" Well, my lady, 'tis about a Passon like,
agin. Somehow or other, them black-coats are
very often betrayed, as is most likely, by Old
Gooseberry—saving your ladyship's presence; for,
in course old G.'s business lies more with them
than with others: the same as my business lies
among them as comes ater the game: only in that

case I'm the good man, and t'other the bad 'un. Well, this here aggrawating Passon sets up a claim to fish a river anywhere he had a mind to; standing to no repairs as to other folks' rights, but going in for what he said was his own, and a-doing what he pleased. Now, this here river was not a complete royalty; if there ever had been one on parts of it about where I was, it had all got into the hands of the Lord of the Manor, and the fishing rights belonged to the land. That is, those proprietors who had land on either side the river could fish half the stream; or, if they had land on both sides, they had an exclusive right to all of it, so far as they abided within the limits of their acres where they abutted the water. This here Passon was a cantancarous little party, always in hot water with some one or other. And if he could not find a stranger to dispute with, he'd kick up what the lawyers call a hamicable Chancery suit at home. He warn't a good paymaster to his servants and labourers; and how I never could tell, but wherever he lived, there man, woman, and child warn't fond of him: 'twas quite the t'other way.

"Well it came round that at last his Honour, my old master, got a right over a part of the fishery, and he sent to the Passon to say he was very sorry to interfere with him, but he was not a-going to stand any sort of trespass; and that a neighbouring proprietor was of the same mind: so he, the Passon, had better confine his net to the limits of the river abutting his own land.

"Well, to this the Passon sends a hangry reply: telling his Honour that he should come and fish wheresoever he liked; and referring his Honour to his lawyer if he wished for further information.

"Directly my old master got this letter he sends back jest a few lines to say 'he would not have anything to say to the Passon's lawyer; his business, if trespassed on, would be with the Passon himself.' Thus matters stood till about the middle of the day.

"Well, the long and the short of it was, that a waggon was seen a-dropping through the lanes with two boats and a large drag-net in it, a big bait-box, poles and oars, attended first and last by the Passon and eight or nine men. Well, they looks first at his Honour's fishings, and then they gets wind of summat as didn't please 'em, and they goes off to the neighbouring proprietor, and on to his manor and fishings; and then they puts their two boats and nets into the water to begin their draw. No sooner was they in than up comes his Honour with five keepers, four from the lord of the manor, his self, and one of his, and says he to the keepers 'Seize that net and all the fishing-gear!' and down he goes with the keepers to see as it was done. 'Pulley-hauley,' then, 's the word, my lady!— one agin t'other; them in the boat a-trying to keep the net in, and them on the shore a-hauling to get it out. The resistance was but weak; the Passon's men soon let go, and I see 'em a-grinning like at his Honour, as if they was glad to be quit of the whole scuffle. The only one as lost his temper was the Passon, and he did just about get pale, and grin, and garbot fearfully, taking up the heavy iron-shod boat-pole, and, under pretence of pushing off his boat, a-prodding with it at the legs of every body, downright spiteful.

" ' Sir,' says his Honour to the Passon, ' you will see that I have not lost my temper; nor could I do so with one of your cloth: but as you seem not to be able to keep yours, and are inciting your men to blows, and assaulting my men yourself, if you continue this unseemly behaviour for a clergyman and justice of peace I shall be constrained to handle you ; so pray be careful.'

" Well, some one snatched the pole out of the
Passon's hands, and his Honour cautioned everybody not to kick up a row, and his own men to
be quiet, saying, if he saw the necessity for
blows he would be the first to strike; but he
hoped there would be none. By this time the
net had been landed, and a good many villagers had come up, some of whom set about
getting a horse and cart ready by his Honour's
orders.

" ' Now,' says his Honour to the Passon, who
still sat in his boat, ' perhaps, sir, you 'll land,
for both them boats are forfeited as fishing-gear
illegally used for salmon, and we are going to
haul them up and carry them to a place of
safety.'

" ' Sharn't muve !' says the Passon. ' And
you, sir,' he says to his Honour, ' I 'll have
you in the lock-up afore night.'

" ' Humph !' laughs his Honour, and every
one as was by, at the hidee of his Honour
at the lock-up.

" ' Humph !' says his Honour; ' the lock-up
would be a good place for a bad Passon; but,
sir,' says he to the Passon, still a-sitting in the
boat, ' there is a *much worse place* than the
lock-up to which a clergyman *might* eventu-

ally be condemned, if regardless of his Christian duty.'

" ' Whoo, whoo, whoo !' roars all the villagers as was by, man, ooman, and babe; for they could not abide his Reverence, and always stuck to his Honour, though they all on 'em knowed his Honour would hold his own, and liked to keep people in order. Well, my lady, down comes a cart-horse and traces: they put him to the boat, and up they hauls the Passon on to the road above, high and dry. After this was done, ' Let's duck him !' I hears among the people, but his Honour let 'em all know as the Passon should not be touched.

" ' Now, sir, please leave the boat,' says his Honour.

" ' Sharn't !' snaps the Passon as afore.

" ' Then, sir, as we must lift the boat into a cart which is in waiting, you will perhaps fall out ; but I can't help it.'

" No, he won't get out ! so up goes the boat, first a-standing on its stern, which brought the back of the Passon to the ground ; still, to it he clings ; then, like a horse a-jumping, down goes the bow into the cart and up comes the stern, the Passon's jacket-tails a-flying as if he were on a horse : but he wouldn't be unshipped ; and there he set again, all the villagers laughing at him. Both boats and the Passon, oars, poles, drags, and bait-box, was all a-huddled together, the Passon as furious as ever, and no doubt a blessing internally the jeers of the villagers, as his Honour was a-doing all he could to keep quiet.

" ' Now, sir,' says his Honour again to the Passon, ' we are about to turn the boat you're a-seated on over on its side, for the convenience of packing and safe carriage. I fear you will tumble out over the wheel of the cart if you try to sit in it, so perhaps you will oblige me by getting down ?"

" ' Yes, sir,' replies the Passon, a-rising up, ' as you have drawn me into the road I *will* get down.'

" ' Thanks,' said his Honour. ' I would sooner have your absence than your presence, sir; so we are so far mutually satisfied.'

" All this time the Passon had been sending to the village where he lived to get up all the blackguards they could make to come and assist him, and the same to the village hard by ; but he was so unpopular, and his Honour so well known, that only a few came, and they would have nothing to do with it as soon as they knowed who was there, and heard a few words from his Honour. 'Now,' says his Honour, 'the Lord of the Manor and the owners of the fishery and land are in possession of the forfeited gear. It is in our safe-keeping now, and if anybody tries to take anything from our keeping I shall resist the robbery, even to blows.' So off went all the gear."

"Thank you, Tilter, for your story. I have read a good deal about your old master, and anything that you tell me of him amuses me. They say, that in his own country where he was bred up they will do anything for him there, and that the cottagers call their cottages his houses, and he has rooms in them whenever he likes, and they won't charge for it."

"Yes, my ladyship," said Tilter, "that's just it: where he's most known he's best liked. And depend on this, my dear young lady, if ever you hears any one say anything to his discredit, ax them where, how, and when, and with whom he did the thing as was wrong, and if they can truthfully reply to these questions my name's not Tilter—they carn't do it!"

After this conversation with her humble dependant the Lady Grace walked on, as gracefully but more slowly than usual and seemed, with eyes bent upon the ground, to be lost in deep consideration. She had long, so to speak, though she was quite young, looked upon the world and on the giddy round of London's fashionable seasons, and what she had seen and learned only sent her more than ever to her books and innocent pursuits—to her birds, to her pets of every description, and to the face of nature. No man had found his way to her heart, though many had done so to her eyes, and as yet she trod earth's bosom the purest and the fairest, and the most free to use the future as she pleased.

It must not be supposed that there are not teazing, vexing, anxious mothers in castles, halls, and mansions, as well as there are in houses and cottages, who are for ever on the watch *to make* their daughters make a good marriage, and to seize on any high-titled man, with riches and rank in hand, or about to come into his possession, whatever may be the defects of person, of habit, and of mind, to whose questionable keeping they would assign the happiness of a lovely girl. Thus, all that is most desirable and best worth the having in the world, the entire care and direction of a beautiful, a refined, and gentle girl, is often bartered for gilded state and station, and set up for a brief span on pillars, the rottenness of whose base is sure to bring the entire construction to the ground.

The sisters of the Lady Grace had all married, and what the world calls married well. And during their courtship, as in after life, her much younger eyes had shrewdly observed the difference in men "before and after marriage;" and that a beau at a ball and a husband at home were as much unlike each other as a stately buck in his sweet, wild, sunlit woods, and a bear in his darkened den.

She had seen the thing that is vulgarly defined "an Exquisite," lounging in perfumed boudoirs, and murdering the Queen's English by a sort of lisp, or panting, feeble way, of indistinctly pronouncing words; and, in the latent exuberance of her really gay and merry heart, she longed to have set him on some of the hunters she had read or heard of in other lands, and to have shaken him out of his too feeble assumptions and conceits, and lifted him up to be a better man. Lounging on rails in Hyde Park and puffing smoke from pipes, however well-rounded the elbow and gracefully held the hand, she detested; nor would she open those beautiful lips of hers to more than "Yes" or "No" to any one—to the highest in the land—if he ventured to come near her with a cigar. "Life" *did* "lie

behind her, as the quarry whence she obtained tiles
and copestones for the masonry of to-day." And
from the scene at the rear of the stage, on which
she now stood, she made a background for herself;
which gave scope to her inner life, and brought
out in full relief the fine points of a better life, so
often the property of woman's gifted soul before
the dissolution of the limbs, and yet so seldom
permitted during life to come to its full perfection.

Time went on, till at last the Lady Grace was
sought by one, the heir of an old earldom, with
everything in his favour—good looks, good manners, wide manors, and winning ways ; at least
they had been supposed to have been so by many
fair girls, who thought him fair game at which to
gild their hair, as " caps" cannot be " set" now:
but he had played a short game at love with them
all, and retired, first from one and then from the
other, without having gone far enough for an
anxious mother to ask him his intentions; though
she might, perhaps, have plainly showed hers, by
accidentally saying, " her daughter never looked
so happy, nor danced so well, as when she and the
noble love-player were together."

At last the fair citadel of the Lady Grace was
surrounded and besieged, and besieged by sap and
storm, by skilful generals and determined troops;

for mamma and her married sisters, and all her worldly relatives and friends, went to work with a will to win Grace — the sweet, the gentle, the refined girl—to the arms of a man who, however great his pretensions, she felt she could not love; for she had never seen the man yet for whom she felt one soft emotion. For, in some way or other — in trifles, perhaps : trifles often do a great deal in this life—no one that she had yet seen came up to her idea of a creature whom she could respect, admire, and love; on whom she could lay the sweet nosegay of her mind's tenderest flowers, and feel at rest that, for ever and ever, they would be treasured and respected, and never disarranged nor wantonly displaced.

It is almost an impossibility that such a heart and disposition as those possessed by the Lady Grace should thus lie fallow from the tenderest touch of nature, and be proof against any approach to love. The heart of woman, by the hand of Heaven, is ordained to be susceptible of impressions—assailable, we are told, even to an apple, when presented to her by the hideous and most loathsome reptile that crawls the earth—a fitting messenger for the fabulous thing depicted with horns and a cloven foot. If, then, the first woman fell under such an unworthy and ungraceful siege, no wonder that many since have yielded to temptations infinitely more bewitching. Still, the Lady Grace stood forth an exception to a rule: she neither seemed to care for one man more than another, and the citadel remained unshaken until the moment we are approaching. What the shock from united efforts did, and what the siege caused her to do, I will lay before my readers in as few words as possible, as my volumes are coming to a close.

An author is omnipotent in regard to characters, feelings, and events; and thus in that capacity I assume to look into the gentlest, sweetest bosom that ever beat, and to discover what led to the consummation of my tale. I have before revealed that the Lady Grace had seen much and heard more of the world, had looked and listened, and learned and put together things thus brought within her sensible observation. She had read much, and made herself acquainted with the general disposition of humanity, and the customs of men and their manners, and the way in which they were apt to value or undervalue the true worth of the sex to which she belonged. No man she had yet seen came up to the mental picture she had drawn of one to love; but there *was one* whom she had *not seen*, but of whom she had heard and read, whose inner life she thought she knew, and whose "inner life" seemed known to hers, as we in this outward world seem suddenly to know places we have never been in before, thoroughly and well when brought before us, but which we never could have previously seen, save in a dream.

Well, the united forces attempting to move the fair citadel of the Lady Grace set to work. High and courtly were the attentions of the lordly bridegroom that wished to be; multitudinous were the solicitations in favour of him from the sisters and their worldly friends; and floods of tears from mamma to " the only daughter unmarried whom she wished to see settled before she died," were shed to strengthen the current of solicitation, and soften the heart of Grace: but all were of no avail. Our heroine still remained coldly, but gracefully civil to her suitor, amiably affectionate to her mother and her sisters, but as firm to the man she thought of as Constancy itself could be. She had selected for herself through her inward life, in her heart and soul, and pictured to herself a hero whom, by the attributes she had heard and read of, she felt she could and did love, and but for the way in which she had been besought to give her hand away, surrounded by the walls of her castle in the air, in that frail but brilliant building she might tacitly have dwelt till time had become eternity: but it was different now, and the besiegers brought it on themselves.

As we sometimes find that secrets do get about by some strange chance or other, but on no apparently sure grounds, a sort of suspicion arose that the Lady Grace must have some secret affection for some one, known perhaps only to herself. The authors whose works she had been known to read were thought of, and among them, for some reason unexplained, one was selected, and so selected purposely to be decried and run down as to make the Lady Grace dislike him if he really was the man that she admired. There is, perhaps, no greater mistake ever made than that of abusing a man behind his back to the ever-inclined-to-be-generous ear of woman. Women detest back-biters as much as they do cowards. Backbiters and cowards really are one and the same thing; therefore let me caution all mammas never to attempt to decry particular people whom they dislike to their daughters, under the impression that it does any good to the thing they aim at, or harm to the man abused: for it only arouses the noble generosity of woman, and makes her angry that her lover, if he be so, is not at her side to defend himself. In this case the mamma happened to hit on the very man most in the gentle thoughts of the Lady Grace—on the man she really loved, though she had never seen him, with a love of the mind, of the heart and soul, of the inner life, a thousand times stronger than can be gained by the outward signs through eye or ear. More pure in its nature, too; for there could not be any personal desire nor dross of any kind in this high-toned love of the inner life: it could have arisen only in some mysterious relations as between life and life, and it had nothing to do with passion.

And what said the mamma against him?—" He was always getting into quarrels, always fighting, and known to be a successful lover, or rather love-maker, with many women. He was poor, and apt to squander money!"

It must not be supposed that the Lady Grace heard and bore this tirade with patience; her high-toned soul was at once up in arms, while at the same time to her mamma and sisters she admitted no more than indignation at the abuse of a soldier and gentleman who was approved of in the world. Under that phase of feeling she asked, " why he quarrelled,—why he fought,—whom he had loved, —whom he had ever injured,—and why he was poor,—and how he squandered money?" It was easy to ask these questions, but perfectly out of the power of her mamma and her sisters to reply with the shadow of truth, in the disparaging way they desired; when, finding them thus at a loss, the Lady Grace rose from her seat, perfectly collected and gentle in her bearing, and said,—

"Hear the reply and explanation to these calumnies on an absent man. He never quarrelled with any one; he simply punished undue aggression, and fought in the cause of an injured girl. He acted as second several times to the highest and most gallant in the land, and ever terminated the quarrels of others in all honour, and without bloodshed. As to squandering money — oppression, usurpation and robbery, dissipated it for him; and he has withstood persecutions to which most men must have succumbed. Who has he ever injured, or on what girl or woman has he ever brought a stain?"

She stood up as she paused on this question, so fair, so graceful, and with so much dignity, that her hushed relations looked at her abashed, and yet still puzzled. She professed no particular or direct interest in the man they had been abusing; she defended, or seemed to defend, what might have been, to her, nothing more than a gallant gentleman: yet the real sincerity that flashed in her beautiful eyes could not but betray a feeling of the deepest origin, the strength of which at no far-off time they were to discover. They were left, then, just as they were; as to moving her in the direction they desired, the united attack certainly shook the fair citadel, but in no way led to a capitulation with the allies: far from it; she resolved to raise the siege, and follow the bent of her own inclinations.

The sentiment for the man, the Master of Beverstone — for we must give him a name — she had mentally imagined, and which she had treasured really as her inward life, at once gained a footing in her mortal heart, and all that was beautiful, all that was feminine, came forth without a fetter; for between her and the hero of her worship in the firmest and most implicit faith she *felt* there could be no wrong; and without the aid of vision, without the adjuncts of the ear in regard to the unseen one's voice, though she had heard and read of him, she was as much or more in love than a girl who had been systematically wooed and won. She worshipped, and had worshipped in her mind, in her soul; she now loved with her whole heart, and in perfect, splendid reliance on her ideal hero, she resolved at once to throw her-

self on the reception he might accord, and to
abide by the honoured estimation, at least, in
which she felt sure she should be held. She
wrote to him as follows:—

" In thus addressing you—addressing one I have never
seen, and to whom I am personally unknown—should you
but see in my letter that which thousands would only see,
namely, what ought to place me very low in your respect
and. esteem, your silence will rebuke me, and you will
hear from me no more. In my inner life at least I know
you so truly, that if you shun my future friendship, or
doubt my reality and truth, I am sure you will never
betray the faith I have shown in you, nor wrong the confidence of woman. So far, therefore, am I at ease, I need
no other assurance than your character through your life
has afforded, an answer that you do not misunderstand
me; or your silence sets my heart at rest, makes me
happy, or turns me away for ever.

" In the position you find yourself I am unknown and
unsought by you : all blame is mine. If you answer me,
therefore, disguise not your true feelings ; write not according to that tenderness and grace that pervade so
much your disposition, and so mislead me from a desire
to spare, but write as you feel, write in that ' wisdom
which is greater than prudence,' the wisdom and instincts
of the heart, in the truth of the inner life, and by that
communication I will advance or retire. Listen: such is
my implicit faith in you, I should not fear at this
moment, were I by your side, to place my hand in yours
and say I loved you. In saying so I am sure there would
be nothing in your eyes as they met mine, before which

mine would fall—nothing to prompt me to forget the barrier which might effectually prevent our friendship from passing into what *the world calls love*. Friendship such as that felt by me, really is love in the highest, best, and purest sense of the term—love without the desire for personal appropriation, but still not without the longing for full and free communion; not without even jealousy, and the ambition to be first with the selected and trusted friend, caressing and caressed, so to speak, without danger or impending disgrace. There are those who would say this was impossible, but 'the world should never know what it cannot understand:' the world would not understand me, nor does there exist a man in countless millions who would take a just, a self-unassuming view of the friendship and fearless confidence I have for and in you. If, then, in your heart, your inner life, you can appreciate, or are in a position to reciprocate a friendship such as mine, tell me so; if not, then burn this letter and think of me no more."

Now the Master of Beverstone had passed a life in the gayest scenes of the world, and had been brought prominently forward, precisely in those phases of existence wherein Byron says,

> " Men are the sport of circumstances, when
> Circumstances seem most the sport of men;"

and it can easily be imagined, therefore, that in more than one instance adventures unsought, and sometimes accepted, met him. Some there were that deserved respect and attention, others that were frivolous or not worth pursuing, and which were allowed to drop without much notice: but in the present instance there was something in the character of the hand, in the shape and method of the letter, and in the tone and grace of the expressions, that riveted his attention, and led him at once to press the signature to his lips.

The reader will easily imagine, that after such a preliminary as this the reply of the Master of Beverstone, or of "his Honour," as the old keeper called him, was full of gratitude for the good opinions expressed, and assurances that a friendship or love such as that alluded to by the Lady Grace was, in his opinion, a thousand times more valuable than any arising from personal admiration or worldly desires for "appropriation;" that he understood her allusions to the inner life, his heart really and faithfully feeling all the high sentiments of affection she described, and with which she so honoured him. He only desired now to see, to make the acquaintance, of one who had shown her trust in him, and breathed a purpose as to his friendship so flattering, so faultless, and sincere.

The reply which the Master of Beverstone received ran as follows, commencing with these lines,—

" ' The sunniest things throw sternest shade,
And there is e'en a happiness that makes the heart afraid.'

" I felt the full force of these beautiful words this morning. You have made me too happy; I am almost frightened by it. Were I with you, I think silence would be my most eloquent speech ! But a 'virgin page,' as Moore says, would but poorly convey to you the deep, delicious sense of happiness which your letter has awakened in my heart. The *restful* feeling of *perfect trust!* It must be trust in love, which casts out fear. I *am* glad now that I wrote as I did; but indeed the certainty of how you would receive my letter was far greater than the uncertainty. Have you not wondered, as I have done, at the never-to-be-explained power which *can* create so deep and pure a feeling between those who have never met? I have been called, and by some who should have known me better, hard, cold, and immovable. I know I am not so; you now know I am not so: but I rarely, if ever, appear as I am, except to you. You have, by hearsay and by deeds, kindled my nature with a magic touch of true sympathy. Space and circumstance divide us now —may divide us for ever; but there is a power that can bridge the great gulf, the mighty power of a pure, strong, and trustful affection, and the basis on which the span rests lies in our own fair keeping.

" Distance does not sever us, but time may.

" Then must I be content with life as it is; and I am glad to be able to say that, God helping me, I cheerfully exist amidst surroundings in which, if there is affection, it does not satisfy me, and never can satisfy the longings of my heart, or, as I may call them, the sentiments of my nature.

"I have then your friendship, your love, call it which you will. In my inner life I sit by your side, sheltered by your strong arm, and sun myself in the light of your love. You see I freely throw aside all reserve: no such barrier need exist between us now. You say you have a reciprocity in the affection I profess. I at once believe you. Can I then say more than that, with all the strength of my heart, and its depths have never before been stirred, I return your affection? Words are too weak to express my thoughts. 'The tenderest, truest secret, must ever linger, e'en in the deepest depths untold.' What makes you like me? I may be plain and ungrateful to your eye, for all you know. I liked you *first*. I liked you for the noble chivalry of your nature; for your knightly qualities; and in that you were 'a selfless man and stainless gentleman,' equally at home 'in the world's broad field of battle as in a lady's bower.' I could not care for a man who was only in his proper element when always in or always out of a drawing-room — a man to whom women were only toys for an idle hour, and who would rate any woman who had the misfortune to belong to him 'a little better than his dog, a little dearer than his horse.' I could only bow before a master, and to submission would be added worship, if that master's rule was not only firm but tender. A silken thread would lead me, if held by a loving hand. Now can you, affectionate as you tell me you are, build my character out of these materials, and make me the mistress of your soul?"

Without filling too many pages of this, the last chapter of my present work, I need scarcely add that the Master of Beverstone replied in terms as affectionate and sincere; and that much correspondence passed between him and the Lady Grace; a something undefinable, a feeling inspired by he knew not what, stealing softly over his inner life, silently and sweetly as a beautiful dream, and waking him at early dawn with the name of Grace upon his lips.

Among the correspondence, which continued thus from time to time, was a letter from the Lady Grace as follows:—

" I was thinking a few evenings ago, when looking at the lovely light that was lingering in the West after the sun had set, and later, when the fair young moon had risen, that you too were inhaling the sweet airs and quiet, peaceful beauty, of the same scene, and I longed with an intense longing to be with you. 'Tenderness *is*, perhaps, the repose of passion.' Tenderness I have, but Heaven knows no wilder wish is in my heart than to be in all grace and rectitude your loving, faithful friend! That night my usually even spirits left me, and there seemed around my pillow some strange boding sense of evil about to happen to you; and something whispered to me that we should never meet, and that I ought to be by your side—the mouse to free the lion from his toils: but the dim, the lonely, fearful sensation left me, and the next day brought me your loved letter, and made me calmly glad as ever. I used to feel alone—alone in the midst of multitudes—at the balls at Buckingham Palace, and at all the best things in town; for, to use the beautiful words of Owen Meredith—of the gifted Lytton's son:—

> ' And all the men and women whom I saw
> Were but as pictures painted on a wall;
> To me they had not either heart or brain,
> Or lips or language—pictures, nothing more!
> Then suddenly athwart those lonely hours
> Which day by day dreamed listlessly away,
> Thy presence passed, and touch'd me with a soul:
> My life did but begin when I had found thee.'

" ' Thy presence passed,' or say, thine ethereal essence; for as we never met, there could have been no more than what is called the ' second sight;' and yet my life —my inner life—lay dormant long, and then began with you. And shall we ever meet? Until we do, my music and my books will claim my best regards. Macaulay says in one of his essays, that books are the best friends in the world; that they never worry you, and never change. ' Plato is never sullen, Cervantes never petulant, and Dante never stays too long.' I used to agree with him; but now a letter, even a little note, from you, gives me more pleasure than all my library holds.

" Your ever-loving and your faithful

" GRACE."

Thus then lived, or still live, two hearts, the orbs of light above which had never seen the limbs, the looks of those that possessed the gifts so mysterious, so soft, so gentle, brave, and beautiful—and yet at times in others so harsh, so stone-like—so treacherous, so cowardly, and so mean. As an Author and Historian, if they ever came, or if they ever come together, then indeed "lightly" ought "to fall the foot of time, that only treads on flowers;" that the feet of my hero and heroine may, when they meet, be firmly set "on rocks and not on sand," is the devout wish of my pen. An Author's heart ought ever to be in his pen, or his discourse will never reach the Bosom's Soul, whatever it may do as to the Wig of Wisdom.

If, then, my readers—why they are always designated as "gentle readers," though I hope they will be so to me, I know not—feel interested in a loving pair, who have never seen each other, and accord to my humble efforts a patronising meed of approbation; why, who knows, but in a new work I may yet once more solicit further attention, and that, to me, encouraging, kind, and forbearing criticism, which my works have hitherto obtained? "To amuse all, and to offend none—unless unfairly attacked"—has been, and ever will be, the motto on my flag.

THE END.

NOTE.

"The Great Governing Families of England."

At the conclusion of what assumes to be a correct account of "the Berkeleys," in a work entitled *The Great Governing Families of England*, by Messrs. Sanford and Townsend, as published by Blackwood and Sons, there is the following *very erroneous paragraph:*—

"The fate of the family is a strange one; but Opinion and the Crown combine to override the decision of the House of Lords, and the owners of the Castle are considered the legitimate as well as the lineal representatives of the great family whose name they bear."

A more wanton or erroneous statement than this was never gratuitously palmed upon the reading public. There is not a syllable of truth in it.

The legitimate branch exists in Thomas Moreton, the present Earl of Berkeley, and in myself as Heir Presumptive. The Crown, as well as the late Lord Palmerston, the then Prime Minister, *refused to permit the present Lord Fitzhardinge to be created Baron Berkeley*, contingent on my Memorial to the Queen and Petition to the Prime Minister, as Heir Presumptive, *not to create to any one of the four Baronies of "Berkeley," "Segrave," "Braos of Gower," and "Mowbray,"* those Baronies being within the Earldom, to which *I was the established Heir Presumptive.*

Lord Fitzhardinge, on the death of the late Lord Fitzhardinge, paid the illegitimate duty on his accession to the property of the old Earldom of Berkeley, and neither the Laws of the country, the Crown, the Peers, nor the People, hold *the very unjust and impossible opinion* attributed to them in the work to which I thus refer.

GRANTLEY F. BERKELEY.

London: Printed by STRANGEWAYS & WALDEN, Castle St. Leicester Sq.